WOLF ALLIANCE

HIGHLAND WOLVES OF OLD
BOOK 2

TERRY SPEAR

PUBLISHED BY:

Wilde Ink Publishing

Wolf Alliance

Copyright © 2024 by Terry Spear

Cover Copyright by Terry Spear

Discover more about Terry Spear at:

http://www.terryspear.com/

Print ISBN: 978-1-63311-107-3

Ebook ISBN: 978-1-63311-106-6

SYNOPSIS

Caught between a rock and a hard place, Accalia has to prove her worth to one prospective mate or wed another who could bring ruin to her clan.

Erik is much more at risk of marrying another woman, but trouble roars to the front as an aggressive wolf takes drastic action to make Accalia his own. Erik requires an alliance with her father to keep the antagonist at bay.

With such high stakes, are the couple fated to mate, or will they be torn apart forever?

If you like hot, Medieval Highlanders with a wolfish appetite, this is the series for you.

Click Wolf Alliance to leap into the past where wolves rule the clans in the Highlands.

This book is dedicated to Cathaline Baugh, whose home country is Holland, and who loves Scotland as much as I do. Her late husband said if you visit Scotland, you leave a piece of your heart there. That is so true. Thanks, Cathaline, for loving my books!

1

————

Dread poured through her veins as Accalia glanced out her bedchamber's arrow-slit of a window of Hillshire Keep in the Highlands, looking for any sign of Lord Erik Norwulf and his men's arrival, and seeing none. She was almost relieved.

"Are you excited about meeting the white wolf chief?" Niamh asked Accalia, helping her dress in one of her nicer burgundy gowns. Accalia's da felt her blond hair made her look washed out and the more colorful gown would make her stand out. In the worst way, her da wanted her to appeal to the white wolf chief.

Frowning, Accalia shook her head. Her stomach had been tied in knots all morning. She kept imagining what it would be like seeing Erick Norwulf, talking to him, learning if they were wolf compatible.

"You barely ate your bread or venison when we broke our fast."

"I wasna hungry." Her da expected her to win Erick Norwulf over from the first moment they met, entice him to mate her over the week he spent with them, and forge an alliance with him. She was sure that wasn't possible.

Her redheaded friend shook her head, freckles dotting the

bridge of her nose, her cheeks, her eyes blue and clear. "You are one of the most positive people I know. This will work out."

That's what Accalia had thought with the last wolf she was supposed to mate. "What if Lord Erik Norwulf does the same thing that the wolf I was supposed to mate pulled?" Seasons had changed from spring to summer, but she still hadn't let go of feeling angry at Uilleam's or Clodagh's betrayal.

"That snake. He didna deserve you. What I canna believe is that he took off with Clodagh."

"You dinna need to remind me." Accalia had been friends with her since they were young. "I've...overheard our people talking about it—saying I didna know how to win a wolf over."

"Uilleam wasna worth having. Dinna listen to rumors and conjectures. You know how it is. Everyone has an opinion about something, even if it's wrong." Niamh sighed.

"'Tis true. Finding the right wolf is the key."

"You have a whole week to visit each other and learn if you're right for one another." Niamh plaited Accalia's hair. "Before I arrived at your chamber, I overheard your da tell your uncle that Erik was the one who asked to meet you. Did you know that?"

Surprised to hear it, Accalia slipped her *sgian dubh* into her boot. "I thought my da had been desperate to seek another ally through my mating Erik once Uilleam betrayed me."

Niamh fastened a belt around Accalia's waist. "Mayhap the white wolf chief will be the one for you."

Accalia attached her sword in its sheath to her belt.

Niamh grabbed up her leather pouch and handed it to her. "Uhm, your da said none of us maids can go with you to meet with the lord."

"Why no'?" Accalia couldn't believe it.

Niamh pushed a loose red curl of hair out of her eyes. "You know."

"Nay. Because da is worried some other lass in our pack will entice Erik more?"

"He didna say so, but I suspect that's the case."

Accalia let out her breath in a huff, thinking it was the most unreasonable thing he'd ever done. "Does he think to keep all the women in our pack away from Erik the whole week he is here?"

"I dinna know, but all the women are dying to see him."

Accalia had heard the younger lasses twittering about his arrival, dressing in their finery, their hair plaited beautifully, eager to see Erik. A pack leader who needed and sought out a mate. A clan chief who owned a castle.

Footfalls headed toward her chamber and a chill went up Accalia's spine. She and Niamh glanced at the door as the footsteps grew closer. Then they stopped at her door and a fist pounded, making her and Niamh jump. "The scouts have reported Lord Erik is nearby. Lord Baldur wants you to join him now," one of her da's men said.

It was Tormod, her da's commander of his forces. She wasn't surprised her da would send him to fetch her, not one of the guards. Tormod wouldn't let her wiggle her way into doing something she wanted to do if her da didn't wish it.

Niamh hugged her, and she hugged her back. "This will all turn out the way it should," Niamh said.

Accalia sure hoped so, but after her previous near miss on a mating, she doubted that anything would come of this arrangement. Niamh opened the chamber door, waiting for Accalia to leave the room, then joined her.

Accalia planned to take Niamh with her despite her da's supposed ruling that no woman would attend her even though she knew Tormod would strictly follow her da's orders.

She took Niamh's hand, but Tormod shook his head. "Just you, my lady."

The notion was absurd to think that her da could keep Erik away from other she-wolves in her pack.

Accalia hugged her friend again. "I will see you soon."

Accalia walked next to the commander, keeping up with his long stride, wishing Niamh could have come with her. Despite concealing her outward nervousness, she couldn't control her rapidly beating heart or her anxious scent.

She caught him glancing at her. "What?" she snapped as they left the keep.

He cast her a smidgeon of a smile, his long, curly black hair caught in the breeze, his blue eyes filled with dark humor. "Ye are no' going to the gallows, lass. Just a possible mating." He looked down at her sword and the *sgian dubh* tucked into her boot. "Why are you so armed?"

"You never know when you might need to defend yourself."

His smile broadened and he nodded.

When they reached their horses in the inner bailey, her chestnut mare whinnied at her in greeting, saddled up and ready for their next adventure. She reached out and stroked Whinny's nose. Tormod helped her up onto the saddle and patted her horse's neck. He climbed onto his horse and led the way.

"Where is my da?"

"Waiting for you, my lady, out in the glen."

Annoyed with her da for not allowing her to bring Niamh with her, she followed Tormod out to the glen.

When she arrived at the glen, her da turned to greet her with a nod. She sat with them, her gaze fixed on the rolling hills and valleys, searching for any sign of Erik and his entourage. Trying to settle her nerves, she breathed in the sweet smell of heather in full bloom among the meadow grasses wavering in the steady warm breeze. But the scent of men, leather, and horses kept her grounded in her current situation.

Erik, accompanied by his brothers Logan and Finlay, led a group of six men on horseback towards Hillshire Keep. Eight of his men wore their wolf coats. As the group approached, they could see the majestic outlines of four eighty-foot towers standing in the distance, dominating the surrounding area.

Logan said, "You've been quiet this whole trip. Philbin said the lass is bonny and would make a beautiful mate."

Philbin had been the one to take the message to Baldur, asking for this meeting with his daughter. But Erik still had concerns that he couldn't shake. "Her da was quite detailed about her talents— that she can take care of the staff and manage the keep while he is battling his enemies. She can travel without complaint on long journeys, is sturdy, and will provide me with more bairns."

"But?" Logan asked.

Erik gave him an irritated glance.

"Your sons, aye. But her da said she was good with children."

Erik shook his head. "Many wolves who have lost a mate never mate again. Some wouldna agree with mating a wolf like that." He couldn't shake off the concern that Accalia would object to that.

Logan sighed. "You are thinking of our brother Leifson."

Erik was. When their parents died after their boat had sunk, their older quadruplet had taken over the clan. Leifson had lost his mate in battle and when he tried to secure another, two different families had turned him down. It didn't matter that he held a position of money and power.

"Well, dinna think of him. He isna half as agreeable as you." Logan smiled.

Leifson's policies forced Erik and the rest of his brothers to take those who agreed with them away from their homeland and abandon Leifson. It had been either that or fight Leifson to the death and they preferred leaving and settling in the Highlands under Erik's rules.

Logan added, "Her da said she was good-natured and that wouldna be an issue."

Finlay chuckled.

Logan and Erik glanced at him.

Finlay shrugged. "Any da hopeful of mating his daughter to a chieftain would say anything."

Erik knew that. Her da had not said one thing that was disparaging about his daughter, which was understandable. But the situation with his late mate hadn't been ideal and he didn't want to repeat that scenario.

"'Tis unnatural for you to mate your daughter to a white wolf from the northern reaches, whom we know so little about," Dunbar Hamilton said to Accalia's da on horseback in the glen, his gray eyes narrowed in irritation.

Accalia's da, Baldur, was the pack leader and chief of the Hamilton gray wolf pack and clan, a two-and-a-half day's ride from Erik's castle and territory. Hillshire Keep loomed in the background, as they waited for Erik to arrive while Accalia listened to her uncle speak his mind. He'd been vocal for a fortnight about her mating Erik.

"Tis no' a done deal, brother. Erik might no' want Accalia for his mate. No one wants to war with his pack," Baldur said, "so dinna do anything to cause discontent between our clans. He has already taken over Crawford's castle. Do you understand?"

Dunbar, her da's advisor, spit on the ground. "Accalia should go to a gray wolf pack, not to this—this abomination. As to Crawford, he was an incompetent human asking to be overrun."

Accalia had heard stories of Erik's noble battles and how he liberated Crawford's people from their oppressive leader. But the reason for Erik and his people's departure from his northern home remained a mystery. She'd been to Crawford's castle before and knew the lecherous old man had wanted her as his bride, even when she was a young lass. She wasn't sad to hear of his demise, but she had liked the members of his staff.

"'Tis said the white wolves descended from the great lights in the sky in the distant north. Mayhap their gods are as impressive as ours. We dinna want to offend them. So you will welcome them to the family while they are here as I am bound to do for the sake of our clan, our pack." Baldur sat taller in his saddle. "It would be wise to ally with them. Neither Erik nor I trust Freigard, and we may need their support if he tries to push our boundaries. And we both know he will."

Then they saw Erik ride forth, six warriors flanking him and eight white wolves running beside them. Some of their wolf coats were like wind-driven snow, others with a goldish tint, and others wearing a little gray on their faces and the saddles on their backs.

Her da and his brother were as tall and broad-shouldered as Erik. They were dark-haired, whereas she was blond, and Erik Norwulf had light brown hair with golden streaks and braids draping over his shoulders.

As much as she didn't want to mate him when she didn't know what he was like and how he would treat others of her clan and his own, she couldn't help but find him physically appealing. Muscled, tall, impressive as a warrior, his jawline strong, his face chiseled, a bow at his back, a sword at his waist, he looked ready to do battle.

"This is a mistake." Dunbar shook his head again.

"God's wounds, brother. We need another alliance. If we dinna have one, Freigard will claim Accalia, and we will have no alliance with him." Baldur gave his brother a condemning look. "You know how much Freigard wants her, but they wouldna make a good match. She is way too headstrong. No' only that, I willna give my daughter up without getting something in return."

Accalia smiled about her da saying she was headstrong, though she hid the smile when her da caught sight of it and frowned at her.

"You believe she will be less stubborn with the white wolf chief?" Dunbar asked, sounding incredulous.

"I can always hope. No one else is suitable to marry her off to unless it's to that young Ian Sutherland."

"Nay," Accalia said. He acted way too young, and he was arrogant and spoiled.

Her da glanced at her. "Then you better behave while you visit with Erik, or I'll have to resort to the offer with Ian's da. But it doesna mean his da will want you to marry his son, or that his son will be agreeable, though his da has said he would like an alliance with me. Erik is our best bet. He was willing to see you sight unseen."

"We will be in battle with Freigard over this. You know we will. You should have conceded and let him have her," Dunbar said.

Baldur stiffened in his saddle. "Enough. You have said enough. I will hear no more on the matter. While I rule the clan, 'tis my decision to make. Besides, Erik's men look as though they can put up a good fight against a foe and win."

Accalia's da glanced back at her to ensure she held her head high, her gaze fixed on the man who would be her husband in a week if she pleased him. Which irked her. What about him pleasing her?

Her da nodded, looking pleased she behaved like a warrior in front of Erik, not fearful or cowering in his presence. She had to admit he was a formidable-looking chieftain, but would he be as arrogant as Freigard?

"Times are dangerous for our kind. Too few of us exist and keeping our secret is tantamount to our survival," Baldur said.

Wild wolves were being hunted down too, which made it even worse for the *lupus garous*.

"With fewer prospects to choose from, those with any power in the region to make the alliance worthwhile must mix their blood with the few packs in the area to provide healthy and thriving offspring." Baldur moved a little on his saddle to get comfortable.

Erik and his wolves and men were close to them now. She knew he would look at her, to size up her appearance, but she had thought his stern gaze would turn to her da. But it didn't. He focused only on her.

Without warning, Erik spurred his horse forward, closing the gap between them. The vibrations of hooves hitting the ground caused Accalia to grip her horse's reins tighter. Her horse's muscles coiled and tensed beneath her. Erik reached her horse, a breeze from his sudden movement and the heat from the animal's body colliding with her.

The scent of horse sweat, leather, and wolf caught her attention. His blue-eyed gaze caught and held hers for a moment suspended in time. Her throat felt parched, her tongue drawing over her suddenly dry lips, his gaze following her innocent action. She swore he almost smiled, but she could have been mistaken. His brow furrowed, and he didn't look pleased to see her.

She expected him to greet her da first and then acknowledge her with a smile. Unless he felt that was unbecoming of a clan chief and a warrior.

Instead, he seized her reins. "We will send word in a week if she suits me, Chief Baldur." The white wolf pack leader galloped off, pulling her horse with him.

Shocked, she gasped. Glancing back at her da, she expected him to force Erik to release her.

"You must stop them!" Dunbar cried out.

Baldur's guards remained where they were, watching Baldur's reaction, prepared to fight Erik's men on his command.

"He is a chief in his own right. He will convince her she wants to be his if we are lucky," Baldur said. "If this is how he feels he must learn if she will be the right woman for him, then so be it."

She couldn't believe Erik would take her away like this. Or that her da would allow it.

Erik's commanding voice was impressive, and powerful, brooking no argument with her da, which meant he had the skills of being a powerful pack leader. No she-wolf would want to mate with a weak leader. Still, she prayed to the gods that her da had not made a mistake in agreeing to unite with Erik's forces by marrying her off to him, should he be as much of an ogre as Freigard.

"Bah, you have lost Accalia and with no alliance in the making," Dunbar said, still within her excellent wolf hearing.

"In a week, we will have an alliance," her da said to his brother, typical of what her da would say when he wanted to will something to happen.

She knew her da had prayed she would prove to Erik that he needed *her*.

Then she could no longer hear their words, though with their excellent wolf hearing she knew the white wolf chief had heard both her uncle and her da's conversation.

They rode hard for a while, their horses snorting, their hooves pounding the green grassy meadows as they headed for a hilltop, her horse straining to keep up with Erik's mount as if her mare was thrilled to run with him. Traitor. He soon released her reins so that she could ride beside him. The wolves ran on either side of the horses, keeping out of their path, panting, tongues lolling out of their mouths, chests heaving, appearing to enjoy the run.

Her heart was beating as hard as the horses' and wolves', her thoughts in turmoil. She always planned out her days, and now she was at the mercy of the white wolf chief?

Angry that she had no say in her life, she was still curious about the rumors she had heard about him. "You are as much a beast as they say," Accalia said to Erik. Aye, he was a chief, and she was but the daughter of one, and that didn't give her much choice. But he *had* agreed to visit with her da and her for a week at her castle and not steal her away to his domain.

Erik was so intense, so focused on leaving the area, she didn't think he heard her. After a couple of hours, he stopped and began giving orders in a strange tongue. It got worse and worse.

They stopped high on a hill covered in rocks and bracken, perfect for watching for anyone approaching from some distance

She glanced at a nearby loch, looking for any signs of danger, but only saw the green leafy trees bordering it, reflecting in it. Light wispy white clouds drifted across blue skies, ground fog rising off the loch to the south of them. Fog could hide trouble, she knew, and she stared at it for some time, trying to see any movement there.

A rainbow of light formed over the fog with the sunlight hitting it just right. The sight captured her, but then she peered around for trouble again. Her skin prickled with unease. She usually loved riding her horse, but she just felt...unsettled.

Erik rode up to her on his black stallion. His blond hair was tousled from the wind and his eyes were full of determination. "We take a short break now." He slid off his horse and came around to her as if he would help her down, but she didn't want his help.

"My da," she said, dismounting on her own, "said you would visit us for a week. No' abscond with me like this." Though she had admired Erik's taking charge as he did, which could prove he could make strategic plans in battle and succeed, she wanted him to know how *she* felt about the whole matter.

She had envisioned riding with him in the glen and forests around her castle. She looked forward to taking walks and watching him spar with his men, trying to outdo each other as warriors. They would talk about their interests and dreams for the future.

But she knew her role would most likely be limited to being a mate and mother, though she also planned to take on the leadership of the wolf pack and manage his staff in his absence during battles. "I will have no interference from your family in this matter," Erik said, his deep voice capturing her attention.

"My da planned a feast to treat you like an honored guest."

"Some would not have it so. His brother, your uncle?" Erik arched a brow as he towered over her. She was tall, but he was much taller.

"I doubt he would have bothered you." She didn't believe Erik would bow to anyone, which, for a pack leader, was important to keep the pack together and for that, he impressed her.

His eyes captured hers, blue like the sea, mesmerizing. He looked at her like a wolf determining her strengths and weaknesses like she was his. "I will have no interference from anyone and that includes from you."

She straightened, hoping to make herself appear more formidable. "If you think to win me over..."

"There's no need."

She arched a brow. Ohmigoddess, he was as arrogant as Freigard!

"This is a matter between your da and me. He needs my help to fight Freigard and any other clan who plans to battle with yours. I wish to know if you are worth the trouble."

She was so angry, that she wanted to strike out at the beast, despite how tall and muscular he was. But she feared she would entertain his men—and him. And she had no intention of entertaining any of them.

"Your da said you have ridden for days without complaint. You will do so for me." He motioned to a man who joined him and Erik spoke in his northern language.

She felt alienated from them at once, wondering what he said, and why he wouldn't speak so she could understand him. "Doesna he speak Gaelic?"

"Aye." But Erik didn't say anything more about it, which concerned her. "He's bringing us food."

Would they keep secrets from her by speaking in their strange tongue while she was at their castle?

The blond-haired man inclined his head and left to get her something to eat while the rest of his men were eating some distance away—all watching for any signs of trouble.

The man Erik had sent to fetch their food returned with brown bread and cheese for Erik and her and she ate some of her bread. Then the man who had brought the food walked off to survey the land below them while they ate. She ate the food after having had very little to eat to break her fast this morn and drank the ale.

Erik continued to eat his food and tossed down some ale. "It's time to go." Then he rose and held his hand out to her, but she ignored it.

She knew she was stubborn, but she didn't want him to believe she was some silly maid who couldn't take care of herself. She rose to her feet and walked to her horse.

She saw him hesitate to help her mount her horse. To her frustration, she couldn't climb onto the saddle because of her long gown. Without a word, Erik stalked over to her and hoisted her onto her saddle. Grateful, she took a deep breath.

Niamh was right. Accalia had a pure drive to succeed at anything she tried to accomplish. And she needed to think more positively while she was in their company. "Thanks be to thee."

"Think naught of it." He climbed onto his horse.

"Why did you agree to this arrangement?" she asked, as they began to ride off again, her mare jostling her with every step. She needed to know what he hoped she would provide for him, just as she had needs in a mate.

"The same as your da wished—an alliance, and to get you with child to expand his legacy and mine."

It was the way of their wolfkind and clan chiefs in general. She'd considered having a child by the chief, but she hadn't considered how tall he would be. Freigard was much shorter in stature and not half as muscled.

"And we couldna do this at my castle?" They were supposed to get to know each other's worth during the weeklong visit.

He raised his brows at her, a small teasing light in his eyes.

Her cheeks burning with embarrassment, she scoffed. "I dinna mean getting me with child. Do no' say it. You wished no interference." She wondered what he thought she would have done to interfere. She would have tried to be on her best behavior under her da's watchful eye as she had always longed to do what he approved of. Not that she hadn't gotten herself into much mischief over the years. But she had attempted to please him.

"Our travel days dinna count toward the week we have to get to know each other. According to your da, we could handfast for a year, and if in that time we didna have any offspring—"

"'Tis no' true unless we were—"

"Human, aye. He was talking about humans. I dinna believe 'tis a bad notion."

"We are wolves," she reminded Erik as if he had forgotten that.

"Aye."

"We...we..." Well, goddess take him. "We dinna attempt to have children unless we are mated...for life." This man was infuriating. She wasn't about to hear anything more from him about making love without agreeing to be mated. "And if we dinna suit?"

"I will send word to have your da come for you."

She scowled at Erik. "You know he is as much a chief as you are."

"Aye, and he is glad for the arrangement."

"Taking me to Ice Haven was not what he agreed upon."

"Whitehaven."

She feared she would accidentally call it that if she didn't watch herself. Everyone in her pack called it Ice Haven, believing the northern men were made of ice and could fight any foe. Which would be a reason to be allied with Erik.

"Has your da followed us to take you back?" Erik asked.

"Nay," she said, reluctant to admit it. She hadn't wanted her da to have to fight on her behalf. But she wished he'd stood up to Erik to let him know he couldn't have his way in all things concerning her.

"Then by leaving matters as they stood, he has agreed."

"My da didna tell me you were a tyrant chief, either."

He cast her a small smile, but then it faded. "'Tis better to be quiet in this area. Danger lurks nearby."

2

_____

E rik was sincere about the danger in this area. They'd already encountered thieves on the way to her da's castle, whom they had dispatched, but he worried about Accalia's safety now that she was with them. Everyone was keeping a lookout for trouble, including the lass.

As they journeyed to his home, he was pleased to see the lass had spirit. He could not abide a woman who was meek and mild-tempered, who would faint at the first sign of danger and could not ride for days without constant complaint. He'd been amused when she'd stood up on her own after having a break, annoyed with him, not wanting his help, but then couldn't mount her horse and he had to help her.

She seemed to have a warrior's fierce determination. She was a pretty woman with a stubborn chin and flashing green eyes. Though it was a plus, he had more important reasons to take her as his mate.

Her golden hair was braided and pinned up, a wool hood covering most of it. He would like to see it down, hanging about her shoulders, to touch its silkiness, to smell her fragrance, her wolf and woman's sweetness and spiciness. The breeze had been blowing in his direction, carrying her scent to him when he first saw her, of lavender and thyme, and he'd wanted to press his nose against her hair and take a deeper, closer whiff.

"Do you know how to use the sword?" He motioned to the sword belted at her waist.

"Aye, of course. We have many barbarians roaming the land."

"But only one tyrant chief?"

She cast him a hint of a smile.

He chuckled, glad she seemed to have a sense of humor, but then got quiet. They needed to be silent through this area. Brigands looking for whatever treasure they could take would attack an unsuspecting party. One such as his, maybe not so much. Except for the prize they escorted through the land.

He wanted to know if Accalia was the right one for him who would carry on if anything bad should befall him. And who would bear his children to increase their clan numbers and be the mother to his three young sons.

They'd traveled for a couple of miles, surprised they hadn't discovered anyone. Maybe they had cleared out all brigands in the area the first time through here.

Then a scout came riding back to them. "We have seen movement in the woods ahead," his scout warned. He spoke in her language so that she would understand the threat.

"Are they wolves?" she asked.

"Humans, thieves," the scout said.

That's when they saw them watching from the woods. Seven brigands who looked to be thieves, dressed in motley garments, and judging from their ages, around twenty to thirty years old, but they must have thought Erik's party wasn't as large or armed as it was at first.

Erik's wolves growled at the men hiding in the woods.

"That's Norwulf," they heard one of the thieves say. "And his vicious wolves."

Erik had never hidden the fact that wolves were part of his chiefdom. People would think what they would. Most believed that instead of having trained hounds, he had wolves.

He drew his sword. Logan and Erik readied their bows.

ACCALIA UNSHEATHED HER SWORD, ready for a fight.

"He killed Olson and the others," a thief said. Then the thieves slipped back into the woods like mist and vanished.

Erik glanced at her sword in hand. "These thieves learned of us killing the ones who attacked us on the way to your castle."

She was glad that they hadn't had to fight. On the other hand, if they had eliminated the threat, they could have safeguarded other travelers coming into this area who were not as well-armed. "I guess they willna follow us and try to attack anyone isolated from the others."

"They would have a pack of wolves on them in an instant. They wouldna be successful in any case."

The damp chilly air made Accalia shiver as they stopped to set up camp. And she realized her wool brat to wrap herself in was all she had to withstand the cold night air. At her da's insistence, she'd worn a gown more for showing her off than wearing something for riding long distances and through the night. Now she had no other clothes to wear for the week she was at Whitehaven.

She shivered, unable to control the tremors running through her body. If she'd had a tent, she could transform into her wolf in private. She was usually comfortable doing so in front of her people, but in front of Erik and his men, she hated to admit she felt bashful and hesitant. Typically, she would retreat to her chamber to undress and shift in private.

Erik and his men were conversing quietly with his brothers.

Erik looked back at her. He motioned to one of his men, spoke with him, and said, "Take my fur blanket to the lass."

"Aye, my lord." The man grabbed a fur blanket from Erik's saddle and brought it to her, then inclined his head to her.

"Thank you." Grateful for the warmth, she smelled Erik's male wolf scent on it, of horse and the piney woods where the fur had rested on the ground at some point. She laid it out and then wrapped herself in it on a cushion of pine needles.

The air was brisk and chilled her. She was glad that the fur cloak helped to warm her considerably. She closed her eyes to try and sleep, but she couldn't stop her mind from conjuring up all kinds of concerns—his people wouldn't like her, he wouldn't either, and she'd be faced with mating some other wolf who could be much worse than this one.

She touched the sword at her waist and unsheathed it, prepared to fight any brigand who might come in the night to attack them.

"Do you think she is sturdy enough?" Erik's quadruplet brother Logan asked, drinking ale from his flask.

Erik studied her, knowing she wasn't asleep, drifting off, mayhap, but listening to the conversation most likely.

He hadn't thought of how she would need something warmer to wear on the journey, mostly because he had decided at the last minute to take her with him—a slight mistake on his part. Though he was certain his men would believe he was testing her in this. But he was not. He didn't want her to fall ill.

Then again, one thing about being a wolf, if she wasn't averse to stripping naked in camp, she could have called on her wolf. Then she would have been warm.

"We will see." Erik hoped she would be and could bear his children without difficulty. He wouldn't want to lose her at any rate. His concern was to ally with a wolf pack that could expand their numbers. But his wee lads needed a woman's motherly touch, and he hoped she would manage them fine. Better than his late mate who hadn't cared anything about them.

He realized he would have to have some of his dressmakers make Accalia some gowns for the time she would be with them. Maybe he should have told her da that he was taking her with him to prepare her for the journey and then stay with his people.

Erik pulled another fur blanket off his horse and laid it gently next to her so as not to wake her. She appeared to be asleep.

"You could warm her, brother," Logan said.

"I am. As a wolf." Erik pulled off his fur cloak, shirt, and tartan. Then he shifted.

"If it were me, she would be mine, sturdy or no'." Logan stalked off.

Erik was sure that if Logan were the chief, he would do the same as him. Logan was as honorable as he and their brother Finlay were. Their brother, Leifson, who had remained behind to rule the rest of their people, was a different story.

As a wolf, Erik curled up next to the lass's feet. She shivered slightly, and he snuggled closer to share his body heat with her as a wolf.

Several of his men smiled at him and he ignored them. This didn't mean he was soft where the woman was concerned. Not only were they sharing warmth in a perfectly honorable way, but he was providing her protection, should anyone be foolish enough to attempt to overrun their camp in the middle of the night.

At one point, she drew closer to him, woke, stared at him, smiled a wee bit, and fell back to sleep. He snuggled closer to her, smiling in his wolf way, and then noticed the sword she grasped.

～

THE DARKNESS of the night enveloped the camp. The faint glow of embers from the campfire provided a faint light when rustling noises near the camp alerted Erik. He lifted his head from next to Accalia's sleeping form, his furry ears twisting back and forth, and listened. Non-wolves couldn't move near the camp without being detected by the pack. With his wolf's night vision, Erik made out the shapes of his men as they moved toward the source of the noise. Two wore thick, wolf fur coats while the others gripped their swords.

Staying in wolf form, Erik left Accalia's side to join his men while others moved in to guard her. It didn't take long for them to track down the group of five bandits who had planned to raid their camp.

One of the thieves lunged at Erik with a dagger, but he swiftly dodged it. He danced around the red-bearded man, keeping out of the dagger's reach. His focus remained on the man, his gaze taking the wiry man in, the way he moved with agility and sure-footedness even in the dense bracken.

The man charged him as if he could take on a wolf shifter and win. Angered, Erik raced around him and bit him in the calf. The man fell to his knees. Erik took advantage and grabbed his throat and tore at it. The coppery smell and taste of blood filled his senses.

Once he pawed the man's shoulder and ensured he was dead, he heard sword fighting taking place further away, and momentarily, his brother Finlay caught his eye as he was engaged in a sword fight with another thief nearby, steel clanking against steel. Meanwhile, Logan chased after one who tried to flee. They had to kill these men, unlike the others who hadn't attacked and ran away. These had been sneaking in to catch them unaware and they couldn't let any of them live and chance them returning. Not with Accalia under his watch.

Erik found the rest of his men surveying the bodies of the

thieves they had killed. Five of them. All had been accounted for. All of his men were also unharmed.

Taking the lives of innocent travelers was a task thieves had no qualms about. But when facing fierce wolves and well-armed warriors, their confidence wavered. It became a whole different challenge for them.

Erik shifted. "Bury them in the bog in the morn." Then he shifted and headed to a stream and waded into it, washing his coat of any remnants of the man's blood.

His men soon followed him there and cleaned themselves. He left the stream and shook off the excess water. Then he inclined his head to the men and wolves and loped back to camp.

The air was crisp and cold, carrying the scent of pine and wood smoke from the fire. All he could think of was returning to Accalia and keeping her warm while protecting her.

When he saw her, he was surprised she was awake, standing with two of his guards, her sword in her hands ready for a fight.

"What...what happened?" she asked.

He shifted, not meaning to until she'd asked the question. "We had some difficulty. Thieves were trying to enter the camp. They made a mistake in doing so."

"They're dead?"

"Aye."

"Good." She sighed deeply, lay back down, and pulled his fur around her. She patted the ground next to her. "Guard me." She closed her eyes.

He shifted and snuggled against her again, knowing he had to tell the lass about his boys, but fearing she might not be happy about the arrangement in the least.

Before dawn's first light, the men were packing to leave, and Erik shifted and was pulling on his clothes some distance away.

Once he was dressed, he went to wake her, wondering how long it would take her to be ready. But she was boldly watching him.

"Lass."

She rose from the blanket and stood and stretched.

"Keep the fur cloak as 'tis nippy out this morning."

"Thank you." She wrapped it around her and walked into the woods.

"Keep her in sight, brother," Erik said.

"Aye," Logan said.

"But watch the woods at the same time. The vermin we killed last night willna be the last of them."

"Aye." Logan hurried after her.

"She is tolerable," Finlay, their youngest brother, said.

"At least out here." Erik motioned to the woods. "But I must see that she is good with our people."

Finlay shrugged. "What if she canna produce an heir?"

"Surely she will be able to."

"She is an only child. What if that is all she can produce? Or not even that?"

If she was a suitable mother to his lads, maybe her da would see them as an extension of his pack and not feel the need for her to bear her own children.

"I wondered why you were speaking in our native tongue when you have said we must all speak Gaelic," Finlay said.

Erik shook his head. "Old habits die hard."

"So you dinna intend for her to learn it?"

"We live here now. We must speak the language of the people who live here."

Suddenly off in the woods, Accalia screeched. Half the men, including Erik and Finlay, sprinted for the trees.

The dense ground fog and the smell of a coming rain permeated the air. They scoured the area, heard horses galloping off, and ran to camp to get their horses.

"Where is Accalia? Logan!" Erik shouted.

"We killed one of the men. We havena found Logan or Accalia,"

Finlay yelled, some distance away.

"Here!" Logan called out, his head dripping with blood, his eyes appearing a little out of focus as he stumbled out of the woods to see Erik. "One of the brigands has her. There were six of them. I killed one of them!"

"Her da's men or others?" Erik grabbed his brother's arm to steady him, ready to kill every one of the men who had hurt his brother and taken the lass away.

"Not her da's men. She was struggling against them, and she cut one with her *sgian dubh*."

3

W hat were the chances that two clan leaders would abduct Accalia in two days? Furious that one of Freigard's men was carrying her away from camp on his horse, she was anxious to know if Logan was all right. Four other men were riding through the woods beside them. Six had come for her. Had Logan killed one then?

A steady rain began to fall. The chilly drizzle made it even colder. The men in human form wore heavily padded leather armor and were armed with swords and bows like soldiers. They smelled like gray wolves which was another reason she knew they were Freigard's men and not thieves.

She prayed Erik's brother was alive after he had fought so valiantly to rescue her. But he'd been way outnumbered, six to one. She'd pulled out her *sgian dubh* tucked in her belt and stabbed one of the men in the thigh, but he'd moved before she'd cut him deeply. Another of the villains had wrested the dagger from her hand, twisting her wrist painfully.

She'd kicked and scratched and even bitten one of the men on the arm. His leather was so heavily padded, that she doubted she had injured him in the least. Her wolf's teeth might have torn through it though, had she been able to shift.

The five men rode as fast as they could through the forest, trying to distance themselves from Erik's camp. The one held onto her so tight that she couldn't wriggle free no matter how much she tried. She hated them and was irritated with herself for not alerting Erik sooner.

Horses tromping the ground some distance behind them made her pray that Erik and his men were coming for her. Then again, what if the riders were more of Freigard's men she hadn't seen before?

The heavy, drenching rain turned to a lighter rain shower, but by then both she and her captor were wet and slippery against each other, and she hoped she could break free still. She didn't want them to get away with her and she didn't want Erik to believe she didn't have the wherewithal to stand up for herself.

She tried to wrench free of her captor's iron grip. She nearly got free, felt herself slipping from his grasp before he struck her on the side of the head with his fist hard and she saw a sprinkling of stars. If he thought that would make her compliant, he was gravely mistaken. She threw back her arm at him, striking his black-bearded chin with her elbow as hard as she could while she strained to hear the men coming for her.

He gave a harsh laugh. "You think you can hurt me? Freigard will see you dead before you mate with Norwulf."

She was surprised to hear it as she tried to gain her freedom.

If Erik's men were looking for her, she knew they would smell her scent. But if they were not aware that she had been taken yet and Logan could be injured, dying, or dead, she had to warn them. She howled, knowing her human howl could carry much farther through the woods than her human's cry of distress. Besides, her howl made her feel more in control.

"Shut her up," one of the men shouted.

She was glad she shook him up.

Just then, an arrow flew past her off to her right and hit the rider in the lead in the back. The rider fell from his horse, but the one holding onto her rode on, desperately attempting to outdistance Erik's men.

Another arrow whooshed past them. Another villain in the party cried out, but he remained seated, slumped in his saddle, his horse still racing forward with the others. Aye! She was so grateful to Erik and his men for coming to her aid.

Two more arrows, one man went down, the horse running still. Another injured man struggled to hold onto his horse. Another two arrows targeted him, and he fell to the ground with a thud, his horse still running with them. Then she was alone with her captor.

"They willna get you back," the man growled.

She assumed then that these men's orders were to kill her before she fell back into Erik's hands.

Then white wolves appeared out of the mist, looking like her saviors.

Horses owned and raised by the wolf packs weren't afraid of wolves under normal conditions. But snarling, growling wolves caused the horse she was on to rear up. The man fell, taking Accalia with him. As soon as they hit the ground, she grabbed for her *sgian dubh* tucked in his boot. She yanked it free as he struggled to get to his feet. She jumped away and he unsheathed his sword.

She didn't stand a chance using a dagger against a sword, especially when the man was as tall as Erik and forty pounds heavier. Before they could engage each other, Erik rode up to her and pulled her onto his saddle, holding her tightly in his grasp, protectively, concern etched in his furrowed brow. At once, she felt safe and was glad for the feeling.

"Are you all right?" Erik asked, looking her over and gently touching the area near where she'd been struck.

She was still shaken by the fall and from the brigand hitting her in the side of the head. "Uh, aye." She finally reached down and slipped the *sgian dubh* into her boot.

The wolves surrounding her captor were still growling, but they didn't tear into him. Normally, wolves fought wolves, men fought men. Not all shifters honored the code of the wolf though. And desperate circumstances changed all the rules.

One of Erik's men would kill her captor with his sword. She didn't have any regrets because they could very well have killed her or Eric or any number of his men, his brother included.

"Your brother," she said at once.

"He is well, though he should have called out a warning."

"He was injured while fighting six men!"

"Aye, and he should have called out a warning. They were Freigard's men?"

"They were. The one said Freigard wanted me dead before you could have me. I assume it's because he doesna want you allied with my da." She couldn't believe how comforting Erik felt, how warm, solid, and protective he was, the rain subsiding, his hair wet and rainwater running down his face. She wanted to brush away the droplets with a tender gesture, but she resisted the silly notion.

"Then he is determined to have you. For him to attempt to steal you away from me shows such determination."

"But the man said he would kill me." She realized she was shivering from the danger she had experienced, and Erik must have noticed it too as he held her closer to his hot body and she soaked his warmth in, smelling his manly wolf scent and the air cleansed by the rain.

"Mayhap to keep you in line. I doubt he would have harmed you," Erik said.

"What about you? What do you want?"

"I want what's best for my people. But we are white wolves and you are a gray wolf."

She frowned. "We are all gray wolves, from what I understand.

Then at some point, the gray wolves in the northern regions started changing. It was said so your kind could blend in with the white winters."

"Aye."

"So we are all the same."

"Do you feel this way?"

Erik's white wolves were as beautiful as her kind and she hadn't expected that. "Aye."

"We shall see."

"You havena lived long here." She knew their history. He and his wolves had left their lands, looking for someplace to conquer that was more hospitable. He had taken over the weak chieftain's lands, but then he'd dispersed the residents or turned them as they would have to keep their secret.

So he'd been known as the Great White Wolf Chieftain, even though humans didn't know that the white wolves with him were shifters, nor that he was one. Only that he used the white wolves from his homeland to hunt his prey. Others wouldn't know that he was one of the white wolves on the prowl. But still, she—and her kin—had wondered if there was more to their reason for coming here.

"You shouldna have been so far away from our encampment."

She figured he wouldn't make the same mistake twice. "They wouldna do the same thing twice, would they? The closer we get to your castle, willna they give up?"

"You are no' a warrior, my lady. They willna give up until we reach the castle. Some skulk nearby, I venture to guess, just out of sight."

That didn't make her feel in the least bit comfortable.

They reached the encampment that had been packed up and he dismounted before she could, then he helped her down only to set her on her horse. He was firm but gentle and seemed troubled about all that had occurred. About his brother being injured? Her nearly falling into his enemy's hands, because surely now, Freigard was his enemy? Or concern for her? Maybe a little of each.

Then they were on their way again.

She watched for signs of Freigard's men lurking in the woods they traveled through. Every rustle of a branch or flutter of a bird caught her eye now. As a wolf, her senses were always on higher alert than a human's, but even more so now. She realized then that though she had trained as a warrior in the event they were ever overrun, she didn't know their tactics out in the wild.

Then she saw Logan looking a little pale some distance off, heading in her direction, his head wrapped in a cloth bandage. She caught Logan's eye and mouthed a silent thanks to him. He didn't look pleased. She realized he was probably in trouble with his brother over the matter of her abduction. But he had to fight six men and was lucky to be alive.

Erik had moved ahead to speak with his men and two others were ordered to stay beside her as they made their way through the woods.

With no one to talk to, she rode in silence, wondering what his castle and people would be like now that he had taken it over. All she remembered of the castle was that it had towered over her, dark, and dreary. She had made certain her castle was comfortable, clean, and presentable. Had his kind made any changes? If not, she would make some changes while she stayed there which might not be for long.

Logan rode up and replaced one of her guards, a little blood staining the center of the bandage on his forehead.

"You were valiant, and I thank you," she said, relieved to see him alive, and wanting to hug him for trying to keep her safe.

"Dinna tell the chieftain such."

She scoffed. "Any man who could fight against such odds and come out unscathed"—well, nearly so—"is a warrior and he should be proud of you."

"You were stolen away when I was guarding you."

"Who made the assignment?"

Logan smiled a little at her. "You will have to be stronger, more in charge if you are to interest him. Though your choices—and his —are slim."

She laughed in an annoyed way. "I have no choice in the matter. 'Tis my place to please my da and help my people."

"So you think to have an alliance between your pack and ours if you please Erik?"

"Tis better that, than mating with Freigard and having no alliance. There is no guarantee that Freigard willna attempt to take over our pack later."

"Or sooner. What if he takes over your pack before my brother decides about you?"

"Then I will have to be returned to my people and do what I can to help them through the situation."

"You wouldna want to stay with us?" Logan asked, looking surprised.

"Your brother would have no need of me, and I would have no need of him." But her da and her people would need her, she knew in her heart.

"We will be at Whitehaven Castle by late tomorrow. I would warn you of two things. Cook doesna like Erik, but we lost our own and she is the deposed clan's cook. She prepares good meals so Erik keeps her on."

"She was turned?" She knew the former clan ruling there had been human, though her da and the lord had never been able to agree on an alliance. Even though she'd been but ten moons, the lord had wanted her for his wife and her da wouldn't agree. Not when she and her clan were wolves, and she had been so young. Accalia had liked Cook and many of their staff that she had met.

"Aye, she wanted to leave and didna want to serve the chieftain and his devil wolves, but we had lost our cook, and we had no one else to manage the kitchen staff."

She frowned. "Did you turn the whole staff?"

"Aye. They wanted to be like us."

"I'm surprised she hasna poisoned the chieftain then."

"He requires that she tastes all of his food just in case she intends to poison him."

Accalia shook her head. "So she and the others are white wolves then."

"Aye, devil wolves." Logan smiled. "We have learned you know her, and she has threatened Erik that she will poison him when he's least expecting it if he even hints at turning you."

"She wouldna. Didna you tell her I'm a wolf already?"

"Aye, she wouldna believe us."

"You said there were two things you wanted to tell me."

"Aye. My brother had a mate and lost her."

Accalia couldn't believe it. No one had said anything to her about it. Their kind often mated for life, though if a wolf lost his mate, he or she might take another. Especially in the case of a chieftain who needed an heir.

"How long ago and how did she die?" Accalia couldn't help wanting to know. This was such a shock to her. She had expected to mate with a wolf who had never been mated.

"A year ago. He would have mated before this, but he was waiting until after he conquered Crawford so that he had a castle and lands to call his own."

She didn't say anything. The old chieftain had never allied with her da, but they'd kept the peace between them all these years. When Erik had taken over, they worried he would take her clan over next.

"Erik...has triplet sons," Logan said.

Accalia stared at him.

"They are five summers old."

"How did his mate die?" she asked, saddened for the children and their mother.

"Of a fever. A dozen of our clan members died, and it was dark time for us."

"I'm so sorry to hear this." Not only that Erik had lost his mate, but that her boys had had to live without their mother, like when she had lost her own. How did Erik feel about her loss? How did the boys feel? She felt bad for them.

For her, it took years to learn to live with the loss. Nannies had tried but couldn't take her mother's place. And her da would never remarry. This put the whole situation in a different perspective. Could his boys even love her if she tried to take Erik's mate's place?

She brushed away a wet curl of hair that had blown across her eyes. "Then why does Erik want me for a mate? He doesna need an heir. He has an heir and two spares. Truth be told, goddess forbid if anything were to happen to him but if it did, you or your brother Finlay or some other impressive wolf in the pack would take over, not a young boy."

"Certes. But he still needs a mother for his sons. If you dinna get along with them, he will look elsewhere for a wife. He wants the best for them."

Accalia hadn't expected this and wasn't certain she could handle it. Nurse maids took care of the young ones in her clan. And where did that leave her? Did he not even wish to mate with her, but be a mother to the three boys who might not even like her?

"I see. Well, this trial period may be very short-lived."

Again, Logan smiled. "Your da says you're very good with bairns."

Her da would say anything, it seemed, just to make this happen between them. He should have told her what he had expected of her!

"I dinna know the first thing about bairns," she said, honestly. She wasn't about to lie her way through this. She could see it could be a total catastrophe. They had a few bairns in their clan, but no one had expected her to be a nanny to them.

Logan bowed his head to her. "Then it behooves you to make the effort."

"Mayhap I should look for another prospect."

"Such as?"

"A wolf who desires a mate, no' a nanny, since he has some of those already."

"Aye, my lady. I have said as much. We will speak later." Then Logan turned and rode to the back of her escort and the other guard returned to walk beside her.

She didn't have the faintest clue about raising wolf cubs or bairns. Her da had made her take warrior training if he was off to battle, and she had to lead their people in defense of the castle and how to manage the castle staff. The child-rearing was left to the nannies and nursemaids. The children sat among their people at the meals, and she had seen them playing games and learning their parents' trades, but she was not responsible for them.

Did her father know the situation with Erik? If he did, why didn't he inform her? He probably kept it from her because he feared she would reject Erik if he couldn't move on from his mate's death. The same went for his sons losing their mother.

A sense of unease crept over her. All she could picture was the boys despising her, never getting to know Erik and the consequences that would bring.

4

E rik had seen his brother talking at length to Accalia and had assumed he was warning her about his triplet sons. He hadn't told his brother he couldn't speak to her about it and in a way, he was glad she knew before they arrived home. However, he had intended to mention it before then.

Finlay rode up to speak with him. "What do you think of the lass so far?"

Erik took a deep breath and exhaled. "She has the heart of a warrior." Which he greatly admired. His late wife wouldn't have been armed and fought assailants.

"Aye. Philbin said he and the other guards had to keep her in camp. She felt they needed to be with you to fight the thieves when they tried to sneak into camp."

Erik smiled. "I expected her to provide an alliance, have children with me, and be a mother to my sons. And to run the household staff as she would have been trained. I didna expect her to fight my battles."

Finlay agreed. "How do you think the lads will feel when she arrives?"

Erik shook his head. He was certain his sons would not be on their best behavior when they arrived home, especially since Accalia might become their mother. That meant more rules and another person to enforce those rules. The nannies let them get away with too much nonsense because they were the chief's sons.

When they stopped for the night, he caught Accalia watching him, but then she settled down on his fur and looked away. She had barely eaten anything when they took their earlier break from riding. That worried him. He stalked across the campsite and joined her.

"Are you ill?" he asked.

"I am well. You dinna need a mate, I hear. When were you going to tell me about your sons? Or anything else about this arrangement between us?"

"I dinna need an heir, aye. I want more children by my new mate. But I need a mother for the boys."

"But you dinna need a mate. If I was agreeable, that is."

He let out his breath in exasperation. He'd fought with himself over the notion of mating another she-wolf, feeling he was being disloyal to his deceased wife. He'd even thought to marry a woman, but never mate her, so he thought he would put that out there. "To anyone else, you would be my mate, but we dinna have to consummate the relationship. You would raise my sons as your own and the agreement between your da and me would be secure."

Her mouth gaped. She looked astonished, hurt even. Her da said she would be pleased with the arrangement though her da had suggested that Erik wait to tell her that until he got to know her better. He guessed he should have.

"When I marry a wolf, it will be with a mating. If we dinna suit, fine. But I willna marry you to be your...wife in name only. My mate will be in my bed."

"We can sleep together."

"Och, you canna be so daft as to think I would go along with such an arrangement."

"Daft?" Erik's lips slightly parted in a show of surprise, because he was well and good surprised. His potential mate was calling him daft?

MAYBE ACCALIA SHOULD HAVE CHOSEN her words more carefully since he was the clan chief. Then she smiled at him. No, she couldn't think of another word that said what she had wanted to say.

Accalia had always planned to have children of her own. She couldn't imagine raising someone else's bairns and never having a real mate or her own children.

No way was she going to pretend to be mated to a wolf when it wasn't true.

"With me, this is all about an alliance," she carefully said. "What of your mate? Did you gain an alliance with her mating?" She wondered if he was allied with anyone else because of his mate. Did she have family members who might object to his marrying her? To be the mother of Erik's sons? That could cause all kinds of conflict.

He sighed. "Nay. I met her at a tavern back home. Her parents owned it. She caught my eye, and I was moonstruck. She soon learned that I was a pack leader and told her da who immediately wanted her to marry me."

"You...you had the wolf longing for her and she for you?" Accalia wondered if he had felt forced into it, or if his mate had tricked him, and it hadn't been a case of true love.

"Aye."

She nodded, wishing they hadn't been in love, that it had been an arranged marriage, and that the she-wolf had left a job of working in a tavern for her da to managing a castle, which would have elevated her position. Then if Erik met another she-wolf after his former mate had died, and he and a new mate meant something to one another, it would be all good.

"What about her family? How will they feel about you taking another mate if you do? Some families wouldna like it or would feel they have some say in the matter since mating again can affect your lads."

"They are all gone. She had no siblings, her parents were deceased, and she had no other relations. So there's no one to object to my taking another mate."

"Except for your boys."

He was silent, and she assumed his lads could cause issues with him taking a new mate. As she rode across the rocky landscape, climbing one hill, traversing a loch and a couple of streams, and making their way to a forest, she couldn't stop thinking about what lay ahead.

They arrived at the castle after a half day of traveling without further incidence—to her profound relief—she saw his staff hurry out to greet them. Grooms took their horses, while men and women in the middle of chores came to look her over since she might become the chief's wife. Five wolfhounds hurried out of the castle to greet Erik, perked ears, bristly fur, warm brown eyes, and feet as large as a wolf's.

Three young lads resembling Erik with blond hair and blue eyes gawked at her with open mouths. She couldn't deny they were adorable, but they didn't seem approachable. Their unkempt hair and dirt-smeared faces and hands added to the unwelcoming atmosphere. If these were Erik's sons, she wondered why they hadn't run to him with open arms and big smiles.

Feeling lost and out of place, she had no idea what to say to anyone. She wasn't even supposed to be here since she wasn't mated to Erik. If they had done so at her da's place, she would have a position here. Then she realized the boys were the reason she had to be here beyond all else.

"This is Accalia," Erik said, reaching down to pet the dogs. "Has Cook prepared the meal?"

"I will check on it, my lord," one of the women said and hurried into the castle.

The wolfhounds sniffed at Accalia, checking her out to make sure she could be part of their pack, and she petted them, then smiled at one of the maids. "You are Etta, are you no'?"

"Aye, my lady." The redheaded woman smiled and curtsied.

"I remember you beating a young man at archery when you were a couple of summers older than me when I was here years ago."

"Aye, my lady." Etta blushed.

Then a redheaded maid approached Erik, giving Accalia a cursory glance, and then concentrating on Erik, a smile appeared on her face that made Accalia think of when she was forced to smile in a situation she wasn't happy about. "We're so glad you're home again."

Erik spared her a glance, inclined his head, and quickly looked away.

Accalia's intuition told her the woman was interested in Erik, though Accalia tried to ignore the implication.

Suddenly, a dark-haired, middle-aged woman burst out of the castle and headed straight for Accalia. "You best leave right now. Turn around and return home to your da."

"I'm a wolf too, and so is everyone in my clan," Accalia said, reassuring Cook. "I'm so pleased to see you again."

Cook's mouth gaped.

"Is the meal ready?" Erik asked, sounding annoyed with Cook.

Cook gave him a disdainful look. "Aye. Young Dalton already arrived and told me you were on the way and would be putting people—me in particular—in the dungeon, if I didna have the meal ready for you." Then she frowned at Accalia. "Dinna let him bully you, my lady."

Accalia smiled at her. "He willna."

Then Cook nodded and hurried back into the castle.

"This is Accalia," Erik repeated to his people. "She will be with us for...some time."

He didn't say she was a special guest, or that he would mate her. But she suspected his people knew that was why he had brought her there.

"My lady, I will show you to your bedchamber," Etta said.

"We eat first, and then you can show her where she will stay," Erik said. "These are my boys: Thorfinn, Hendrie, and Johnne."

So the little blond-haired boys *were* Erik's sons, as she had suspected.

The first thought Accalia had was that they desperately needed a bath—before the meal. But she knew she couldn't dictate what anyone would do, and having his servants wash up the boys before the meal when it was about to be served, wouldn't go over well with Erik, she didn't figure. It wasn't any of her business. She didn't believe she would end up being their...mother.

She noticed Erik hadn't told her the name of the woman who stood close to him in a way that said he belonged to her.

Erik said, "Come. We'll eat."

Accalia walked with him into the castle while his staff hurried to join them for the meal. She remembered the grand entryway, and the lanterns on the walls, the only difference was a large tapestry on one wall showing white wolves running through the heather. She smiled to see the beautiful tapestry. The castle was clean, not smelly like before, for which she was grateful.

They entered the great hall where tables were set up vertically from the head table near the fireplace. Erik led her to the head table where she would sit next to him. The redhead sat at one of the lower tables, and Accalia felt smug about it. If she wasn't mistaken and the woman *was* trying to stir up trouble between her and Erik, Accalia would put in her place.

"Who is the woman who came out to welcome you home?" Accalia didn't want to give the woman any space in her thoughts, but the problem was she kept thinking about Uilleam running off with her friend. What if this woman had designs on Erik and his interest in her was mutual?

"Beathag."

"And?" She didn't want to drag it out of him, but if the woman meant anything to him, she needed to know that.

"She's one of the women with the old clan, and she's now a member of mine." He glanced at Accalia as the ale was served. "Why? Do you know her from before?"

"Nay. But she seems to have some interest in you."

Erik's mouth curved up a wee bit. "She might, but 'tis no' important to me."

She sighed. She wasn't about to mention that Uilleam ran out on her before the mating, or mention she was worried about other competition. It would make her look fearful about nothing. If it hadn't been for Uilleam, she wouldn't have worried about it.

Erik turned to speak with his brother Logan.

Erik's boys started chasing each other around their table, trying to catch one another. Why didn't the boys' nannies tell them to sit and behave as any child should at the meal? Finally, they took their seats.

Cook smiled at her as she brought the food to the high table, serving Erik, and then Accalia. "This looks as good as when you cooked for me before," Accalia said to Cook, smiling at her.

Cook beamed with the compliment. She frowned at Erik. "I served the food for Accalia from the same vessel as yours. Do you still intend for me to taste yours?"

Looking *nearly* as serious as could be, Erik motioned to it. "Aye."

Accalia swore he wore the slightest smile, a sparkle in his eyes when he said it and if she hadn't been so observant, she wouldn't have caught it. It was like a secret game between them, and Accalia enjoyed their playful banter. A sense of humor in a partner was a plus for her.

Cook took a taste, stood watching him, and raised her brows.

He motioned for her to leave and get on with serving the meal while the others on the kitchen staff did as well.

Accalia took a bite of her venison. "Your boys looked like they havena bathed in a while." Like weeks, or they had been playing in the dirt all day.

He glanced at them as if he hadn't noticed before. "You can take care of that matter after dinner. I will warn you they might be... quarrelsome for a bit."

She didn't know what to say or to do about it. She would have to see what would happen and take it from there. Unenviable tasks didn't often stump her, but this time might be an exception.

5

While eating her meal, Accalia watched Erik's boys. They were eating a little bit but throwing food at each other or quarreling with each other for the most part. Then they tossed some of their food to the dogs that scrambled to get it before the others did. It was no wonder the dogs were at the boys' table.

Everyone was talking to each other at the lower tables, a few heads turning her way from time to time, the clansmen and women probably trying to determine if she would stay for longer than... some time. Beathag was smiling and laughing with a couple of maids but glanced in Accalia's direction and gave her a haughty look.

Erik said, "You will put the lads to bed tonight. I will warn you, that isna a pleasant task. Their nannies will happily give that chore up to you."

"Are you hopeful I willna succeed?" She felt he was trying to push her away, not solicit an agreement on her part. Was it because he was unsure if he wanted to mate again? She could understand that.

But if they didn't want to mate with each other, she could be stuck with Freigard.

"Nay. I wanted you to know what you're up against. I suspect you'll succeed where I wouldna." Erik smiled imperceptibly.

That made her feel better to know he thought she was up to the task when he couldn't handle it.

She never gave up easily and was willing to do what she could to see if this might work. How difficult could the boys be? Troublesome, she was certain, since their nannies didn't even want to put them to bed at night.

She wanted to ask him about his deceased wife, but she didn't feel comfortable asking him right away. But if she were to mate him, she wanted to know what she'd been like as a mate, a mother, and a pack leader and though she hated to admit it, if Accalia measured up.

After dinner, Erik said, "I have business to conduct with my men. You're free to explore the castle, but since you said you believe the boys should be washed, I'll leave it to you to handle. You will have maids to help, naturally. After that, you will decide when they go to bed."

It was already getting late. As far as she was concerned, they needed to go to bed now. Well, after they washed up.

"All right then," she said, and as they were leaving the table, she motioned to Etta.

Erik hesitated, as if he wanted to say something else, but then thought better of it and headed out of the keep.

The maid hurried over. "Do you want to see your chamber now, my lady?"

"I want to ensure Erik's lads have baths."

Etta's blue eyes widened. "Oh, my, that will be a difficult thing to do."

"Where do they normally bathe?"

"In the loch, when they feel like it. Not so much for a few weeks now."

"It is too late at night. Have the water heated for a bath in their chamber and I will be up presently."

"I will gather three maids to help us."

"We will need that many?" Accalia asked.

"Maybe more, my lady. They are indeed a handful. We quit trying to bathe them because of it."

"Oh, you'll have to show me where their chamber and mine are."

"Aye, my lady. I'll take you there first. I was told you would need gowns. Tailors are working on them now." Then Etta escorted Accalia up the winding stairs to the upper floors of the keep. "We didna expect the lord to bring you home without any bags. We thought he would stay for a week at your da's castle and if you suited each other, he would wed you and bring you here."

"Aye, we believed the same thing."

"This is your chamber," Etta said, showing her the room that featured a bed, chair, small table, and a trunk. A narrow window opened on one wall.

"Where is Erik's chamber?"

Etta's eyes widened.

"Show me." If Accalia were to marry the pack leader, she would be in his bed, not in a guest room. But not right away. She had to know they could love one another and that the boys would be fine with the arrangement.

"Aye, my lady." Etta led her to another set of stairs and showed her a much larger room, a bigger bed, tapestries hanging on the walls, trunks beneath them, and a bathing area.

It would do. "I will take my bath in here while Erik is occupied. But first, we bathe the lads and put them to bed."

"Aye, my lady. Will you sleep in the lord's room?"

"Heaven's no."

Etta nodded perceptively. Then she showed the lads' chamber to Accalia filled with wooden toys—swords, horses, toy soldiers—scattered all over. The beds were unmade, furs on the floor, feathers from pillows scattered around. The room was larger like Erik's for three growing boys.

"I want all the toys removed and the boys' bedding washed. But in the meantime, fresh bedding must be added to the beds," Accalia said. If the boys had no toys in the room, they wouldn't make such a mess of their chamber. And they couldn't play if that was what they did until they fell asleep.

Etta smiled. "Aye, my lady." She hurried off and within minutes, several men entered the chamber and began hauling everything out. Three maids stripped the beds and carried the bedding out of the room. Then others came in with replacement bedding.

"Better." Accalia liked her life and her castle to be nice and orderly. It made her feel more settled.

Then men brought up a tub and women filled it with buckets of water warmed in the kitchen.

Accalia wanted to ask where the hellions were, but suddenly Logan entered the chamber and smiled. He folded his arms. "I heard there was lots of activity going on up here. You'll do." Then he cast her a smirk and left.

She scoffed at him. He wouldn't decide if she would be Erik's mate. She would.

Not much longer after that, three husky Highlanders were pulling three cantankerous boys into the chamber. One of the boys immediately tried to leave, but the burly Highlanders guarded the door. Now that was more like it.

While the door was still open, the five rambunctious wolfhounds ran into the bedchamber. Their claws tapped on the stone floor and echoed through the bedchamber. The wolfhounds ran around, panting and joyfully barking, their large paws creating a chaotic symphony of noise as they stepped on her feet and the boys. They knocked her over and she fell on one of the boys' beds.

The boys laughed. She figured she would have done the same in their place and didn't take it personally.

One of the men came to her aid, but she got to her feet without his help, wanting to show the boys she could manage.

"Out with you," Accalia said, waving her hands at the dogs to leave the bedchamber.

The men herded them out of the room for her, the one saying, "Off with ye now!"

She wondered then if the dogs slept with the lads. If they did, she might have to rethink chasing them off. She wanted them to bathe and sleep and not to remove something that might comfort them.

"It's bathtime," Accalia told the boys. "Whoever wants to take a bath first, remove your clothes and climb in. It's warm and will feel delightful."

"Then you take a bath in it," one of the boys said, folding his arms across his small chest.

"Which one are you?" Accalia asked the impudent lad.

"Hendrie."

"That's Thorfinn," Etta said, shaking her head.

"Aww." So disrespectful and deceitful. Not a good start.

"Who are you?" Thorfinn asked, tilting his head to the side.

"Accalia, like your da told you. I'm staying here for a while. Maybe even forever." Maybe losing their mother was the reason for their behavior. She wanted to demonstrate that she was there for them, even if she had to show a little tough love.

The lads cast glances in each other's direction and then smiled. She suspected that meant they would do whatever they could to make her want to leave right away. They had never met her when she faced a challenge she was determined to overcome. Even if she didn't stay because she didn't want to be with Erik, the boys would be clean and mindful by the time she left.

"Thorfinn, since you're so inquisitive, you get into the bath first." She motioned to the pristine water.

Thorfinn raised his brows. "You canna make me. You're no' my da."

"Do you have a dungeon?" Accalia asked Etta. She knew they did because Cook had mentioned it when Accalia had first arrived.

The boys' eyes widened.

Etta smiled. "Aye, my lady."

"You canna put us in there. Our da wouldna allow it and you would be put in there instead," Thorfinn said, sounding like he knew what he was talking about.

"You are so filthy you are fit for the dungeon. If you dinna wash, you willna sleep in your clean beds. The choice is up to you. Sleep here or sleep in the dungeon." Accalia folded her arms and looked as crossly at the boys as she could.

One of the other boys said, "She wouldna dare to do that. No one would allow her to, and she would be in big trouble with da."

"You are Hendrie, aye?"

"Aye."

"I will count to ten and if the first of you isna in the bath by the time I reach ten, I will march all of you off to the dungeon myself." Accalia had learned the hard way never to bluff.

She hoped Erik would go along with her decision. She didn't intend to leave the boys in the dungeon for long, just long enough for them to get the point and then they would start all over again.

She didn't think it would go that far. But if they were used to sleeping in dirty beds, they might not care if they were sleeping in the dungeon. They might even feel it was a fun adventure.

"She wouldna do it," Thorfinn said, stubbornly resisting the idea.

"Johnne?" Accalia asked, hoping one of the boys would rather bathe than go to the dungeon.

He looked at his brothers as if waiting for them to tell him what to do. Maybe that was the key. Separate the boys. She thought Thorfinn was the hardhead and the leader of the pack of brothers. If they didn't have him telling them what to do, maybe she could get the others to clean up and go to bed. Thorfinn could sleep in the dungeon by himself. Maybe that would have more of an effect on him.

Accalia went to the door, opened it, and said to two of the men, "Remove Thorfinn and Hendrie from the chamber. Keep the boys there until it's their turn to bathe."

"Aye, my lady." Smiling, the guards both looked amused.

Once the lads were removed from the chamber, Accalia told Johnne, "Go ahead and remove your clothes and climb into the bath."

Two maids helped him out of his filthy clothes and Johnne did what he was told. He was much more of a follower, which meant maybe Accalia could reach him first. He seemed a little shy, sweeter than Thorfinn, and not as opposed to bathing. She gave him some soap and a cloth and directed him to wash himself as she began to tell a story.

"When I was a little girl, I was as wild as they come."

One of the maids began to wash his hair.

"I loved to climb trees, play in the meadow, swim in the loch, and on a rainy day, play in the mud near my castle. My mother had fits of course. My da said it was good for me to experience life until I was too old to behave in such a way. But I always bathed and had a clean bed to sleep in. I behaved at meals and was rewarded with many freedoms."

She swore Johnne looked like he was ready to fall asleep in the bathtub. She handed him a large cloth to dry him in and one of the maids had brought out a long shirt for him to sleep in.

Once he dressed, Accalia sat on his bed, had him sit on her lap, and combed out his tangled hair. "You have lovely blond hair like your da," she said. "I imagine your mother had the same beautiful hair."

"She died when we were four."

"I'm so sorry. My mother died when I was young too. I was terribly sad when she died."

"Are...are you supposed to be our mother?"

"Maybe. But we shall see."

He nodded and she urged him up, then pulled aside his furs and he climbed onto the bed. She covered him up and she kissed his forehead.

"What are you going to do with Hendrie and Thorfinn?" Johnne sounded worried about them.

"'Tis up to them. You sleep. I'll see which one wants to bathe next. If neither will, we will see you to break your fast in the great hall in the morn. Your nanny will stay with you tonight."

"No' you?"

She chewed on her bottom lip. "Aye, if you wish it." If it helped her to be closer to the boys, she would.

"I do. Our mother would no' do it. She said she wasna a nanny."

What difference did that make? She had been their mother! Accalia wasn't even their mother, yet she was fine staying with them if it pleased the boys. "All right." Then she opened the door and said, "Who wishes to take their bath next?"

Hendrie looked at Thorfinn and that decided it for her. She took Hendrie's arm, pulled him into the chamber, and shut the door. Hendrie glanced at Johnne half asleep in bed. Johnne gave Hendrie a small smile.

Hendrie didn't look reassured, but then Accalia and Etta helped him out of his clothes and assisted him into the bath.

"When I was a little girl," Accalia said, "my mother had died. I felt lost. My da was away fighting battles often. I only had the maids and nannies to talk to. My mother was everything to me."

"Did you ever get another mother?" Hendrie asked as Etta washed his hair.

Accalia shook her head. "You know how wolves are. They lose a mate and sometimes they dinna want to find another to replace the one they lost and loved."

"So Da isn't going to marry you?" Hendrie asked.

"We will see. It depends on how we feel toward each other. And how you and your brothers feel toward me."

"You were going to lock us in the dungeon," Hendrie said, frowning.

She glanced back at Johnne. He was sound asleep. "Only if you didna bathe. Do you see how nice this is? No' torture at all. Staying in the dungeon would have been uncomfortable and maybe even scary."

Then she helped dry him off, combed his hair out like she had done with Johnne, kissed the top of his head, and covered Hendrie with his furs. "Sleep well, Hendrie."

Like Johnne, he was practically asleep when he climbed under his covers.

The maids smiled. Etta said, "We are very impressed."

But it didn't mean it would stay that way if the troublemaker—Thorfinn—returned to the chamber. She could see him waking his brothers up and causing mayhem, to prove she wasn't in charge of them.

So she had another thought. Now that both boys were asleep, she said, "We heat water for Erik's bath."

"But what about Thorfinn? You dinna plan to put him in the dungeon, do you?" Etta asked.

"He will take a bath in Erik's bedchamber. I dinna want him to disturb his brothers."

Then Accalia and the others left the room, except for a nanny who stayed with the brothers.

"We go to Erik's chamber now," Accalia announced to the guards.

"What did you do to my brothers?" Thorfinn asked.

"Bathed them and put them to bed. They are sound asleep." Accalia led the way.

"I said I wouldna take a bath," Thorfinn said.

Accalia ignored him.

When they headed into Erik's chamber, the servants began to prepare a bath.

"On second thought, hold him outside of the chamber. I want to bathe before he muddies the water as filthy as he is," she told the guards.

"Aye, my lady," one of the guards said.

Then once one of the women brought Accalia a clean night-shift, she took a bath, luxuriating in the feel of the silky warm water on her skin, and washed her hair. She didn't take too long because she wanted to ensure Thorfinn was bathed and put to bed as soon as possible. *Especially* before Erik returned to his chamber and learned what she was up to.

Once she dressed, she had the guard bring Thorfinn into the chamber to bathe. He was looking mutinous, his arms folded across his chest.

"Are you afraid of the water?" she asked, knowing he couldn't be because he swam in the loch. And to her that could be way scarier as dark as a loch could be.

"Of course no'."

"Then get in so we can finish this. Och, Thorfinn, 'tis either the dungeon or a bath. Which will it be? Your brothers are happily sleeping in their beds, so if you go to the dungeon, you'll be alone."

Thorfinn glanced at the guard, who only smiled at him.

"Fine. But I'll tell my da about this." Then Thorfinn tore off his clothes, climbed into the bath, and washed himself. Not his hair though.

One of the maids did that for him.

Accalia was glad she had finally gotten his compliance. They helped dry him off and dressed him in a nightshirt. Accalia didn't believe she could comb his hair like she had the other boys who were so much more cooperative. She didn't ask, sure he would say no. She slipped her hand around his hand, sat on the bed, and pulled him onto her lap.

He looked surprised and started to move off her lap, but she forced him to stay. "I'll comb your hair." She carefully combed out his hair, not wanting to hurt him. His blond hair was silky and fine, curling into coils like his brothers'.

He even relaxed, but once done, he climbed off her lap and headed to the chamber door.

"You will stay here," Accalia announced. "One of the guards will remain here to ensure you comply with my wishes. You can sleep on the trundle bed." Since she was staying with his brothers, she considered that she could make them behave. But after the long journey, she was tired and knew the other boys would sleep if Thorfinn didn't join them.

"My da wouldna approve," Thorfinn said, sounding panicked.

"I willna have you disturbing your brothers who are happily asleep." Accalia began to leave the chamber with the maids and Thorfinn tried to escape.

"You stay. I'm retiring to bed now myself," Accalia said.

The guard, Philbin, looked a little concerned.

Accalia smiled. "Per Erik's orders."

Then the maids and Accalia left the chamber while the one guard stayed behind with Thorfinn. She wondered how that would all turn out. At least she was glad all three boys were clean. And that the two brothers were happily asleep.

When she returned to the boys' chamber, she dismissed the nanny and climbed under the covers of the nanny's bed.

Johnne lifted his head. "You said you would return."

"Aye, and I did." She was surprised he had been awake.

"Where is Thorfinn?"

"He had his bath and is sleeping elsewhere." She didn't want to tell Johnne that Thorfinn was sleeping with their da or he might want to. She suspected Erik would lecture her, but she would do this her way.

6

B y the time Erik was ready to retire to bed that eve, he was surprised to see a guard posted outside his door. "What is this, Philbin?"

"The lady said I would stay here, though others will relieve me during the night."

"Why..." Erik waved his hand in dismissal. "Go where you're needed. I dinna need you here."

"Aye, my lord." Philbin hurried off, looking much relieved.

Erik would have to tell Accalia she had no business posting his guards. He saw the bath had been prepared for him and was delighted that someone had thought to do that since he hadn't asked anyone to. But when he stripped off his clothes and put his foot in the bathwater, the cold water startled him. He frowned and cursed under his breath.

Then he heard a slight snoring off in the corner of the room where the trundle bed had been set up. What the...?

He drew closer to the sound and saw Thorfinn sleeping soundly under the furs on the bed.

That was why a guard had been posted? Accalia! Erik threw on his nightshirt and headed to the guest room where Accalia was supposed to be. But when he reached her chamber and threw the door open, he found the room was empty. Her bed hadn't been slept in either.

God's wounds. The woman was supposed to have bathed and put the boys to bed, not turn his keep upside down. He headed for the boys' chamber, wondering where Hendrie and Johnne were.

When he pulled the door open, he found both boys sound asleep, both clean, the chamber devoid of toys, the beds clean. And there on the nanny's trundle bed slept one angelic-looking Accalia, her golden, luscious hair hanging over her shoulders, her breasts rising with her breath. She looked beautiful. How could such an enticing creature create such a muddle for him?

But then he realized she had done what he had told her—wash the boys and put them to bed. He hadn't told her which beds to put them in. He had to admit he hadn't seen the boys so well-behaved at this time of night in a couple of years.

He quietly closed the door to the chamber and returned to his own. He watched his oldest triplet sleeping there, looking as angelic as the others, when he knew Thorfinn was anything but. He thought of having one of his guards carry him to his bedchamber, but it was late, and it didn't hurt for him to sleep the rest of the night here.

Erik sighed, stripped, and bathed in the cold water in his bath-tub. After washing up, he left the tub, dried off, and climbed onto his bed. For tonight, he would leave things the way they were. But tomorrow night, Thorfinn would sleep in *his* room.

EARLY THE NEXT MORNING, Accalia woke, surprised that Hendrie and Johnne had climbed into bed with her and were snuggled against her under the furs. She was astonished that Erik hadn't given her grief as soon as he learned Thorfinn was sleeping in his chamber.

She wondered if the boys joined their nanny in bed if they became cold. Would Erik even approve? She suspected not, because the boys needed to grow up to be warriors, not coddled. On the other hand, the nanny probably wouldn't have wanted them in her bed as dirty as they had been.

Accalia hadn't realized how easy it was for her to connect with the boys. Well, these two. She wasn't sure about Thorfinn. She slipped out from underneath them, not waking them because they were so tired, and she found a new gown for her to dress in.

Once she was ready for the day, she woke Johnne and Hendrie, helped them dress, and then ushered them out of the chamber. "We're going to break our fast and then you can show me all your sword-fighting skills."

"Do you fight with a sword?" Hendrie sounded surprised.

"Aye. All men and women should be able to protect themselves."

"A wooden one?" Johnne asked.

"A real one. But if you are no' too hard on me, I will practice fighting with you with wooden swords." She loved to do that as a young girl. She hadn't done that in years. She would be a little out of practice and could see the boys ganging up on her to get back at her for threatening to throw them in the dungeon.

They smiled at her, and she was glad she seemed to be winning them over.

They headed downstairs to the great hall, and she saw Thorfinn standing at the table where the lads had eaten last night.

"Will you eat with us?" Hendrie asked.

"Aye, you were our nanny, and the nannies always eat with us," Johnne said.

She wanted to eat with the boys and bond more with Thorfinn.

She figured it might take longer to get through to him as alpha as he was.

"Aye, I will." She went with the boys to their table and Thorfinn's blue eyes widened. "Did you have a good sleep, Thorfinn?"

"You are no' sitting with us," he said, not so much as that he was telling her, she didn't think but was surprised that she might be.

"Aye. Johnne and Hendrie asked me to."

"She slept with us too," Johnne said.

Thorfinn's jaw dropped. "Our mother would never do that."

Everyone was watching her, even Beathag and Accalia assumed they would speculate about why she was sitting with the boys unless they believed she was escorting them to their table. Three nannies waited nearby to see what she would do. She looked over at the head table and saw Erik watching her.

She took her seat with the boys, sitting between Hendrie and Thorfinn.

"Mother never sat with us to eat in the great hall either," Johnne said.

"After we break our fast, she will fight us with swords." Hendrie sounded excited.

Thorfinn eyes widened. "Fighting? With real swords?"

"With wooden. Where did you sleep last night?" Johnne asked him.

"In Da's chamber."

"No' in the dungeon?" Johnne looked like he couldn't believe it.

"He took a bath," Hendrie said, "so he didn't have to go to the dungeon, right?"

"Aye," Accalia said.

"What did Da say about you sleeping with him?" Hendrie asked Thorfinn.

"I was asleep in a trundle bed. I never saw him come or go. You are going to fight us with swords?" Thorfinn asked Accalia.

She thought he was ready to get even with her over forcing him to bathe.

"Aye. If no one throws food at the table or tosses food to the dogs." She ate some of her eggs and was surprised Erik didn't make her sit with him. Maybe he thought this was a better place for her since she seemed to be getting along with the boys—even Thorfinn.

They grinned at each other but when she frowned, they all lost their smiles and nodded in agreement. The dogs waited, hungrily anticipating morsels of food from the boys but were sorely disappointed.

After everyone finished seating, Erik joined her at their table and spoke with her. "Lads, you're dismissed."

They looked disillusioned.

"I'll join you to fight you in a few minutes. Get swords ready for all of us," she said, not about to break her promise to them.

The boys yelled, "Yahoo!" and took off running, the wolfhounds taking chase.

"Swords?" Erik asked.

"To practice sword fighting." Of course.

"Why was Thorfinn in my chamber last night?"

"He's the alpha of the boys and he was stubbornly refusing to take a bath, influencing Johnne and Hendrie, who were fine with taking a bath and going to bed. I didna want him disrupting his brothers' sleep." She brushed some breadcrumbs off her gown.

"And you?"

She smiled. "The lads wanted me to stay with them. I'm making progress with them, so I did."

Erik was frowning at her. "You're not to be their nanny."

"Better than their enemy."

He let out his breath and folded his arms across his broad chest.

She knew where Thorfinn got that mannerism from now.

"Thorfinn is no' to sleep in my chamber any further."

"Aye. I believe he will be fine with sleeping with his brothers and not be up to mischief this time," she said.

"So you'll be sleeping in your bedchamber."

"Aye."

Again, he said, "I dinna want them believing you're another nanny." Then he added with a hint of a smile brightening his dark expression, "I'll see you in the inner bailey."

She thought Erik would give her grief over her decision and was prepared for it. When he didn't, she was glad. But she had planned to swordfight with the boys and hadn't intended to do so in front of their da!

7

A ccalia decided—whether right or wrong—that she was doing well here, taking charge like she wanted to do as she did with her staff at home. She had always found that easy to do, but taking care of the boys, she wasn't sure about that.

Then she headed out to the inner bailey where the boys were waiting for her with wooden swords. Hendrie had two and he ran to her to give her one.

She took it and ruffled his hair. All three lads were smiling. She felt good that they were so eager to play with her.

Several clansmen and women were doing chores but when they saw Accalia coming to fight the boys, they all stopped to watch. When she saw Erik come out to observe the situation, she had a thought. She hoped she wasn't making a mistake that she would later regret.

She walked over to Erik and handed him the wooden sword. "You wear them out a bit and then I'll fight them."

Erik's mouth opened and she thought he would tell her no, but then he gave her a hint of a smile, took the sword, and approached the boys, who appeared a little worried. They probably figured she would be easy to beat. She was proud of Erik for agreeing to play with his sons.

Thorfinn attacked his da first while the other boys waited.

But then she worried that Erik might be too hard on his boys. She was standing off to the side, casting Erik a look like he should take care with them. She didn't want to tell him how to battle his sons. But she didn't want him to beat them so badly to prove his masculinity and to demonstrate something to the rest of his clan. Or maybe even to her.

He caught her eye and Thorfinn struck Erik in the chest, then looked up at him as if he feared he would be in trouble. Erik smiled. She let out the breath she'd been holding up until then.

He motioned to the other boys and fought all three of them. Erik was so fast, sending Thorfinn's sword flying with a whack of his. He ran to retrieve it as Erik hit Johnne's sword and sent it off in a different direction. He raced to get it while Erik struck Hendrie's sword, and it went sailing through the air. Thorfinn rushed back to attack his da again.

Erik's intense expression, a fighter at heart, turned to joyful laughter when his sons' swords were airborne. Erik's reaction melted her heart. He glanced at her and smiled. She smiled back, feeling the more she saw his interactions with his sons, the more she liked the person he truly was.

The boys were so wild and looked eager to beat their da, Accalia was glad he was wearing them down. Sweat dribbled down Erik's face as he readied his sword to fight his tiring boys. Johnne took a break. Hendrie came in swinging but missed Erik's sword. Thorfinn came in for another clash with his da but without his brothers' help distracting him, he lost the advantage.

Forever it seemed they fought.

Everyone was laughing and cheering. Even Accalia couldn't help but laugh and smile to see the battle progressing between da and sons. They were so bent on fighting him but also having a great time, she thought this couldn't have worked out any better.

Erik knocked Thorfinn's sword out of his hand, then Hendrie's, but Johnne was sitting that fight out.

Erik raised his sword, ending the session, and said, "Good work, lads."

Then they looked at Accalia. She had hoped they would be worn out after all the fighting with their da, but the boys looked eager to fight her next. She'd promised.

Erik held his sword out to her and when she reached for it, he grabbed her hand and pulled her close. He leaned over and kissed her mouth, shocking her. She was so startled that she didn't respond at first, not that he probably expected her to. But then she wrapped her arms around his neck, pressed her body against his, and kissed him. No man had ever kissed her like he had, and she wasn't letting him go until he kissed her further.

His eyes widened a bit as he looked down at her. Now she had shocked him! Which was just the effect she was going for. He wrapped his arms around her waist and kissed her back, his masculine lips warm against hers. She parted her lips to take a breath, and he inserted his tongue into her mouth, teasing and tasting hers and that astonished her all over again. But she loved this with him.

She nearly forgot that half his pack was out there watching them kiss and that his sons were too, and she wondered what they were thinking about all of this. More than that though, she couldn't believe her body was reacting to his to such a degree. Her breasts tingled, her heart was beating like crazy like his heart was, and she smelled the scents they were both giving off that said they were highly interested in each other as a mated couple. She hadn't expected that.

Then she broke free from the kiss. She was surprised to connect with him in such a way. Though some wolves didn't take a mate if they had lost one, his actions made her believe he was interested in mating.

His lips parted as if to speak, and then he saw all his people watching and smiled. "You, lass, are a bundle of fascinating contradictions."

"So are you." She was pleased with his praise and realized just how much she craved it—from him. Even if he had room for improvement—just like she had, she looked up to him as a warrior and protective—someone who held his emotions in check most of the time but let them slip for her to enjoy.

He smiled again and stalked off.

Then she faced the boys. They looked worn out, sagging in their stance, their breathing ragged, their hearts beating hard, which was good for her. She waited. Then Thorfinn's body tensed, and she knew he was ready to spring into action. She readied herself as he rushed her. Hendrie and Johnne waited. Which she was glad for. She didn't think she could fight off all three of them at the same time.

Thorfinn struck at her and she smacked his sword with hers, sweeping it away. Unlike when he challenged his da, he held onto it. He was a strong lad, and she assumed he wouldn't want her to show him up. Likewise, she didn't want to be too easy on him when he might not appreciate it. It was different when his da was fighting him. He was so much bigger and stronger than the boys and her. That's why she hadn't wanted Erik to be too hard on them.

Thorfinn hesitated to attack her, and it appeared he was studying her, trying to figure out how to make her lose her sword. What a boon that would be! But she was glad he was thinking about it, not just rushing in, believing he could be the victor with wild, uncontrolled actions.

Again, his whole body came to life as he charged her, and she blocked his sword. But she held her own, and the fight was on. He attacked in a hurry without strategizing and struck her sword several times. She was surprised and impressed that his swings carried so much force, given his youthful age. He hit her sword, and she parried, then pushed him several steps back, neither giving any quarter.

So that his brothers could have their turn, she thought of letting Thorfinn win. She didn't want to, but she needed to end the battle with him. He came at her again, but he wasn't as steady on his feet, his skin sweaty with exertion, his face red from fighting so hard. When he swung his sword, she knocked it from his grasp, and it flew off to the side.

He ran to grab it, and she knew from his determination, that he intended to fight her again. But she motioned for his brothers to take a turn. She hadn't envisioned them both fighting her, but they weren't as hard on her as Thorfinn was.

She was surprised he hadn't inserted himself in the practice battle alongside his brothers. Instead, he stood off to the side, holding his sword, frowning, looking like he wanted to get her back for making him lose his sword. So much for bonding with him.

Now she was tired as Hendrie struck her sword and Johnne came right in following it, striking her sword again. Like Thorfinn, they were trying hard to beat her. She hit Johnne's sword, but as soon as she swept it aside, Hendrie struck again. She pressed the boys forward, getting them to back off, showing them an offensive move, while they were defending themselves the whole way.

But when she concentrated on Johnne as he attacked her with his sword again, Hendrie decisively moved to take her on, striking her weapon from her hands with a hard thwack. Johnne rushed in for the kill, poking his sword into her stomach.

She laughed. "You lads are much skilled in sword fighting."

Hendrie ran to get her sword as if he intended to continue the game, but she curtsied to them before he handed it to her. She was worn out. "Mayhap we can do this again another time." She wasn't about to fight with him again. She was ready to have a respite.

Etta hurried over to her, giving her a mug of honeyed mead. "Well, done, my lady."

"Oh, thanks be to thee." Accalia drank from the mug and noticed Erik had been watching with some of his people. He hadn't left them to their own devices like she thought he had.

He raised his brows, inclined his head, and smiled, then left the "battlefield."

"Young Thorfinn would have returned to battle you if his da hadna told him not to," Etta said.

Accalia laughed. "I wondered. Thorfinn looked like he wanted to fight me again and get even with me for sending his sword flying."

"I'm sure of it. I have never seen the lord playfight with his sons. It was something to behold. And of course, the lads playfighting with you was as amazing. Everyone's talking about how well-behaved they were at the meal. Did you threaten to send them to the dungeon again?" Etta asked.

"Nay. I told them I would playfight with them if they behaved at the meal. It worked."

"It sure did."

The crowds dispersed to do their chores now that the show was over.

"What do the boys do when they're done breaking their fast normally?" she asked Etta.

"They make themselves scarce. No telling what they do."

"Hmm." Accalia saw them watching her and wondered what they were up to now. "Were they like this when their mother was still alive?" She figured they hadn't been until after she had died and maybe no one knew how to deal with them in their grief. She felt bad for them, thinking of how she had felt when she had lost her mother. Maybe that's why she felt such a need to bond with them.

Etta inclined her head. "From what she said, her da believed that they had to learn from their mistakes, just like her father's da and mother had taught him. That their mother wasna to pamper them."

"But she loved on them, aye?" Accalia assumed she would, though in some rare instances, some she-wolves weren't loving, doting mothers. But she'd been lucky with her mother in that regard.

"Uh"—Etta looked around and saw no one was close to hear her speak—"nay. She was young when she and Erik mated. She was upset when she learned she was having the bairns. She did as little as she could with them. Their nannies took care of them always. Even nursing mothers nursed them. She wouldna have anything to do with the task."

Shocked, Accalia glanced back at the boys who were watching her. They couldn't hear them, but she thought she intrigued them. Or they wanted to cause further mischief, didn't want her to catch them at it, and were waiting for her to go off and do something else. All children needed to know they were well-loved.

"What about Erik?"

"Wilma insisted that he didna fuss over the lads either. When she was being indulged, he would play games with the boys. If she learned of it, she would tell him that he was ruining the lads."

"Nonsense." She couldn't fathom him trusting the woman's words. However, she had known a woman who captivated every man's attention and could make them do anything for her. Perhaps his wife possessed that power as well.

"Aye, but, though she wasna...I shouldna say this but...she wasna good with the staff, yet she somehow managed to convince Erik she was the greatest she-wolf in his eyes."

Now that surprised Accalia, until she realized the woman had been working in her family's tavern, so would never have managed a castle's staff. No one had instilled in her how important everyone in the clan was. The woman must have blinded Erik to what was going on.

"All right. Then things are going to change."

Etta smiled. "You have to mate the lord, Accalia."

Wanting to do what was right for everyone, Accalia patted her shoulder. "We would have to love each other first." Then she stalked toward the boys, and their eyes widened. They shared looks and Hendrie glanced at the side as if planning to make his escape.

When she joined them, she said, "What chores do you do around here?" She knew busy hands kept them out of mischief. Even when she was a girl, if she didn't have anything to do, she got herself in trouble.

Thorfinn tilted his head as he looked up at her in an arrogant way. "We are the chief's sons."

"Aye, which means you should show all you can do to prove you are worthy of being the chief's sons."

They looked at each other and frowned at her.

"The strongest, brightest of the wolves will take over once your da no longer leads the pack. Who will the wolves want to lead them then?" she asked.

Hendrie sincerely asked, "You?"

She smiled. "I'm thinking of the distant future—a young person grown."

"Me," Thorfinn said with conviction.

"Nay. The person who wins his clan's heart, protects them when they need his leadership, and proves to them how competent he is. Not someone who shies away from work. Who plays pranks and misbehaves. But someone who proves he has what it takes to lead a pack. Not because he's the pack leader's son, but because he is worthy of the position and can do good by his people," she said. "When we arrived, I saw that the fences were being mended, the south wall was being repaired, and the horses need to be exercised, groomed, and fed. These are worthy chores of a chief-to-be to do."

"I dinna think they will let us work on the wall or the fences," Hendrie said.

"And we have stable hands who care for the horses," Johnne said.

"But you see, you need to learn how to do all these things so that as a leader you can expect the same of your people. If they have never done it, you can teach them," Accalia said. "You can learn skills from the blacksmith, the mason, the carpenter. It will make you more valuable. Or you can even fetch firewood or water. You can herd the sheep or goats, gather nuts and berries, and fish."

"Fishing! We can do that. Will you fish with us? By boat on the loch?" Johnne asked.

"Aye, come with us. A guard escort will have to come with us, but we love to fish," Hendrie said.

"Can you even fish?" Thorfinn asked, cocking his head, his hands on his hips, appearing to doubt that she could.

"Aye, but I need to speak to your da about it."

"Because he is in charge of you?" Thorfinn asked.

"Because I am under his protection while I am here."

"You are no' leaving any time soon, are you?" Hendrie sounded disconcerted at the prospect, and it touched Accalia's heart.

With reassurance, she patted his back. She meant to answer him, but Thorfinn did first.

"Nay." Thorfinn waved his hand at Accalia. "Didna you see the way Da kissed her. He isna letting her leave here." He made a sour face.

She assumed that he felt she was replacing their mother. Which she wasn't, especially not if their mother hadn't been loving toward them. "I'm no' leaving any time soon. I will be right back after I ask Erik for permission to go fishing."

Then she saw Logan and went to speak to him since she had no idea where Erik was. "Do you know where Erik is?"

"Seeing to the mending of the south wall. Do you need something?"

"Permission to take the boys fishing."

Logan smiled. "They want you to fish with them?"

"Aye. Well, at least Hendrie and Johnne do."

"I will see if 'tis all right with Erik and will gather the necessary force to protect you. We dinna oft have trouble, but since we have had issues with Freigard because of you being here, we need to take precautions." Then Logan left to find Erik.

She returned to the boys. "Logan's going to check with your da about us fishing."

It took forever for anyone to return to speak to them. Thorfinn shook his head. "Da isna going along with it. I'm sure he doesna want to lose you, even if you can fight with a wooden sword."

To her and the boys' surprise, they saw Erik headed their way, his chest bare, glistening in the morning sun, streaked with mortar. He was stunning to look at and she had the strongest urge to pull him into her arms and feel his bare skin against her cheek. But she had taken him away from his duties and he didn't look happy about it.

He joined them and looked from her to his boys, though her gaze was on his beautiful, muscled chest. Then he said to the boys, "Logan said you wished to fish with the lady."

"Aye," Johnne and Hendrie said.

"No rocking the boat on the loch," Erik warned, but his gaze was hard on Thorfinn. "If I learn you tipped the boat over on purpose, you will wish you hadna."

"Aye," all three boys said this time.

"You are sure you want to do this with them?" Erik asked Accalia, sounding a little concerned for her safety should the boys do some mischief.

"Aye. We discussed doing chores around the keep. Catching fish is something they wanted to do, so I'm willing to see how well they fish." She smiled.

Erik's mouth quirked up a bit. "And you, lass?"

"Oh, I can fish." She didn't think anyone believed her. The truth was that it was all about luck. If the fish were biting, then she was able to catch fish. But even better? When she was in her wolf coat she could catch fish. Everyone back home knew it, but here, no one knew about all the talents she possessed.

"Good. Then we shall have fish at the meal. Logan is gathering an escort as we speak. If the boys give you any trouble at all, let me know."

"Aye." But unless it was something bad, she wasn't about to say anything and ruin the small beginning she had at befriending the motherless boys. She suspected though, that if men were watching them on the loch, the boys wouldn't do anything to get themselves in trouble with their da.

But she decided she was going as a wolf. "I'll be right out," she said to the boys and headed for the keep. In her guest room, she removed her clothes and shifted into her wolf. Then she raced out of the room, startling a maid.

She tore down the stairs nearly colliding with a guard, who laughed, and she ended up at the bottom. She loved running as a wolf. She moved so much faster than a human could.

She ran outside the keep and into the inner bailey where the boys and their guard escort were waiting. Logan frowned at her and said, "Accalia?"

She howled. Erik came to see what was going on. He hadn't seen her in her wolf coat, so he was probably interested in seeing what she looked like. Not just to know her when she was in her wolf coat, but to see if she appealed to him. It was the wolf way.

"You're going fishing in your wolf coat?" Erik asked.

Though it seemed obvious to her.

"She canna do that, can she?" Thorfinn asked as if he thought she was cheating.

Erik smiled. "If that's the way she wants to fish."

"Then we should shift," Thorfinn said.

"Nay. She thought of it first. You three will row the boat out on the loch," Erik said.

She was glad Erik said that because she hadn't considered that part of the situation. She was too excited about fishing as a wolf.

But then Logan said, "I'll help the boys row."

"You're too easy on them," Erik said. "But none of you are to leave the boat as wolves. Good fishing."

"That's no' fair," Thorfinn said.

Accalia ran out through the gates and headed straight for the loch. Everyone else rode horses down to the water's edge in quick pursuit.

Three boats were waiting for them, fishing poles and buckets in the bottom for the fish. If the boys got into trouble, the men in the other boats could come to rescue them.

She jumped into the boat the boys were going in and Logan joined them. Then he began to paddle out. She almost felt guilty that she wasn't helping to paddle, but the boys should have helped to row. She barked at them.

Logan smiled at her. "Help row, lads."

They groaned, their blond hair caught up in the cool breeze.

She breathed in the scent of fresh water and fish, the sparkling blue waters of the loch stretching for a mile, surrounded by rolling green hills and looming mountains. The sun danced off the surface, creating dazzling patterns and reflections. A river trout broke the surface, and she nearly leaped in after it.

"Woah!" Johnne said. "Someone catch it."

But they hadn't reached the spot where Logan would anchor the boat. The water gently lapped against the sides, the boys peering over the port and starboard, looking for fish. In the distance, birds twitted from the woods near the north shore, and she felt relaxed and happy to be here with the boys.

She was enjoying her time with them when she thought it would always be a fight.

Once they were in the deepest part of the loch, she leaped overboard. With a splash, she dove for fish and soon caught a brown trout. She rose to the surface and Logan took it from her and put it in the bucket.

The boys had been watching for her, and then they began to bait hooks to fish on the other side of the boat so they wouldn't snag their hooks on her.

"The lady caught a fish already. Now it's your turn," Logan said as she dove back under to fish further.

She caught a sea trout, but when she rose to the surface with the fish in her jaws, the boys hadn't caught anything. They eyed her, wearing frowns, looking a little grumbly. Especially Thorfinn.

Before she dove to fish again, she shifted, kicked her feet, and moved her arms to keep herself afloat. The water was much colder when in her human form than when she was wearing her wolf coat. "Let the boys shift and they can try to catch fish as wolves."

"Aye!" the boys cheered and began to strip off their clothes before Logan had a say in whether they shifted. They shifted and jumped into the water.

Smiling, Logan shook his head. "Aye, you can shift."

Accalia hoped it was a good learning experience for the boys. Though she belatedly recalled their da had said they could not shift and fish with her. But earning their trust meant everything to her.

Now she hoped Erik wouldn't be angry with the boys for going against his ruling when she had told them it was all right.

Or cross with her for suggesting it.

8

Erik had not intended to watch Accalia fish with his sons. He had too much work to do, but when she had shifted, he had to see her. She was a beautiful gray wolf with black markings on her face and blond cheeks, throat, and belly that made her stand out. Any wolf would be proud to call her his own.

He certainly hadn't expected her to fish as a wolf, and he was curious how well she could do. To his surprise, she shifted and talked to his boys. The next thing he knew, his boys stripped off their clothes and shifted. Hadn't he told his sons they couldn't?

He realized the lass was usurping his power over the boys with a skill no one else had. She very much had a will and mind of her own. He figured they were bound to clash over it. He hoped the boys would be okay while they swam in the loch and fished. That was his main concern.

None of the boys were catching anything though as she continued to catch fish but stopped periodically to watch them. He was glad Logan had taken the boys out and other boats were on the water in case the lass or his lads got into trouble.

Och, he couldn't stand remaining on shore with the other men.

His brother Finlay joined him. "What are they doing? Fishing as wolves? That's a new idea."

Erik motioned to another man and said to Finlay, "Come on. We're taking another boat out."

Finlay smiled. "Aye."

They soon reached Accalia's boat and Logan smiled at Erik. The boys and Accalia were under the water still and didn't know he had arrived.

Erik said to Logan, "I told the lads they were no' allowed to shift."

"Aye, but the lass overrode your ruling. The boys are having fun and she's bonding with them. Is that no' what you wanted?" Logan asked.

"Aye." He hated to admit it. "Have the lads caught anything?"

"Nay. They dive, come up for air, catch their breaths, and dive again."

Thorfinn came up, saw his da, his eyes growing big, and he dove down again as if he could hide from being in trouble with his da.

Erik sighed and saw Hendrie break the water, who panicked to see his da. "'Tis all right to shift if the lass allows it, *this* time." Erik started to strip off his clothes as the other two boys came up for air this time.

Accalia surfaced with another brown trout. Her eyes were huge when she saw Erik naked on the boat nearby before he shifted and leaped into the water.

Finlay laughed. "You are undoing his chiefdom little by little."

Logan took the fish from her, but she didn't dive this time. The boys looked tired, and Erik thought it was time for them to return to the boat. He assumed Accalia could fish longer, but the boys were still young.

Then Thorfinn came up with his first fish, smaller than anything she had gotten, but he could barely lift it, and she took it from him and offered it to Logan. He shifted and said, "Did you see it? Did you see it?" He was shivering and quickly turned back into his wolf.

Erik joined them, carried Thorfinn by the ruff, and lifted him a little to the boat. Taking his cue, Logan pulled the young wolf aboard.

Then Hendrie came up without a fish, but Erik hauled him to Logan to help him get the lad into the boat. Johnne rose to the surface last, no fish either, and Erik assisted him to Logan. The boys remained in their wolf forms, shaking excess water from their coats all over Logan.

Erik didn't believe Accalia could have lifted the boys to Logan, but he was amazed that she had caught ten good-sized fish.

Treading the water, he shifted and said to Logan, "Take the boys back to the keep. They need to shift, dress, and warm up. We'll go back in the other boat."

Accalia swam away from Erik and headed closer to the other boat. He thought she might be planning to get out too, but she dove under and brought up another fish.

He had never thought about fishing as a wolf in the loch using boats to store their catch. Fishing in rivers and creeks was a common mission, but not as a wolf in a loch after diving off a boat. He was amazed at how well she was doing. Then he saw two of the men in the other boats strip and shift and dive overboard. She had started a new way of fishing for the clan. They would have fish for their next meal.

He caught several of his own and saw her paddling near the boat. He was afraid she was getting tired and needed help to get into the boat.

He offered up the last fish he had caught to Finlay and shifted. "Are you ready to go in, lass?"

She nodded.

"Let's get the lady into the boat," Erik said.

Finlay helped her climb aboard and she sat in the boat

watching Erik. Feeling competitive, he wanted to catch more fish than the lass had. But he wanted to return her to the keep so she could warm up.

He could stay with the men in the other fishing boats but preferred returning to shore with Accalia. She was a bundle of contradictions and astonished him at every turn. But she had livened his life up by leaps and bounds.

He climbed aboard the boat, and she studied his dripping wet, naked body before he began pulling on his shirt, and then his kilt and belt. "Homeward," he said.

Finlay began rowing.

"The lass caught more fish than you, aye?" Finlay said, rubbing it in.

"Aye. We have a new way to fish, thanks to the lass." Erik was beginning to believe she was invaluable. Not just a pretty woman who would give him an alliance if he mated her. Most importantly, she was winning his sons over and showing them affection that his deceased mate had never shown them.

Once they beached the boat on the shore, Accalia jumped out of it and raced up the hill to the castle. Erik climbed out of the boat, mounted his horse, and galloped after her. When they arrived at the inner bailey, Erik dismounted and headed into the keep after Accalia.

She raced through the keep to the stairs and up to her guest chamber, though she hadn't used it last night. He wanted her in his bedchamber tonight. He never expected to feel this way about the lass, but he couldn't get the vision of her out of his mind—both as a woman and as a wolf.

Wolves didn't court for months or years. Once they recognized the attraction between them, the connection they had that went deeper than any human's because of their heightened senses, he knew she was the one for him. Not only because of that, but because of how she treated his sons and the staff.

He reached her guest room and knocked. She didn't answer. He opened the door, believing she wasn't there, but he had to be sure before he looked for her elsewhere. He wanted her to know he wanted her in his bed tonight. When he opened the door, she was standing there naked and she screamed.

He stared at her naked beauty for a moment, her beautiful breasts, her rosy perked nipples ripe for kissing, the thatch of blond curly hair hiding her feminine treasures, her long golden hair, wet and curling in tangles over her shoulders. Then he smiled.

"Apologies, my lady." But his words didn't sound much like an apology to his ears. He couldn't help himself. Accalia intrigued him like no lass ever had. He shut the door and stood on the other side, anticipating her departure from her quarters. He needed to address their living arrangements and inform her of his expectations.

He waited and waited. What in the world was she doing in there? Patience wasn't his strong suit. He knocked on the door again. When she didn't answer, he felt annoyed. This time, he didn't throw the door open. What if she belatedly came to the door and he hit her with it?

He slowly opened the door and found her dressed in a shift, sleeping under the covers. She was glorious whether she was awake or asleep. Fishing as a wolf must have worn her out. For the longest time, he watched her sleep, already wanting her in his bed in the worst way.

Then he closed the door quietly and headed to the boys' chamber to see if they were dressed. He wanted them to know that Thorfinn would be sleeping with his brothers in their chamber and Accalia would be sleeping elsewhere this eve.

He opened the door to their chamber and found all three boys sound asleep on their beds. He couldn't believe it. The she-wolf, well, and he, had worn the lads out. Smiling, he shook his head. He had never seen his boys in this light before Accalia had arrived. It was a welcome change in their behavior. He closed the door and headed back downstairs where he met up with Logan and Finlay.

"So is the lass sleeping with you tonight?" Finlay asked.

"Or is Thorfinn going to?" Logan said.

"The lass is. Thorfinn will sleep with his brothers."

"Where are they all?" Finlay asked.

"Sleeping."

His brothers laughed. Erik smiled.

"Cook said that everyone brought in enough fish for the whole clan to eat at the meal," Finlay said. "Everyone is talking about how they want to fish as wolves now. 'Tis so much faster than fishing with poles."

"I know. I dinna know how none of us ever thought of it before."

"The lass is canny," Logan said.

"That she is. Let's work on the wall until it's time to eat." Erik headed outside.

ACCALIA WOKE and figured it was time to eat. She couldn't believe Erik had barged into her chamber. She'd heard the knock at her door, but she'd been naked and brushing her hair. She hadn't had time to throw on some clothes before he opened the door. She wasn't used to being naked in front of other wolves. Back home, she usually removed her clothes in her chamber and then would shift and run.

She dressed, walked to the lads' room where they had napped, and ensured they were ready for the meal. When she opened the door and peeked inside, she found the boys still asleep. She walked into the chamber and said, "Are you ready to eat?"

Sleepy eyes opened and the boys looked over at her and groaned.

"Come on. They willna hold the meal for us. We dinna want them to eat all our fish."

That stirred the boys, and they hurried to get up and go with her.

"Did you enjoy fishing as wolves?" she asked.

"Aye," Thorfinn said, "though my fish wasn't as big as yours."

"You made a fine catch," Accalia said.

"Aye, but we didna expect Da to join us," Hendrie said, Johnne agreeing.

"He saw how much fun we were having and had to join in." She had been glad he had joined them in the fun activity and hadn't given any of them any grief over it. It wasn't just a way to connect with the boys, it was a food-gathering mission, and the boys needed to learn to catch fish that way too.

"You dinna believe he was angry with us for disobeying him and listening to you, do you?" Thorfinn asked.

"If he is angry with anyone, it will be me for saying you could shift. Have you caught fish in the river before?" she asked.

"It runs too fast, Da said," Johnne said.

"Is there a creek that doesn't flow as fast where we can fish?" She figured maybe catching fish in the loch was too hard for the boys, despite that Thorfinn had caught one. But if they weren't used to grabbing fish in their wolf jaws, she could teach them to in shallower tidal pools and slower-running creeks.

"Aye, but we would have to have a guard force."

"Tomorrow, if the weather is good, we'll do that," she said.

"If Da allows it," Thorfinn reminded her. "Are...are you going to sleep in our room again?"

"Your da wants me to sleep elsewhere. I need to talk to him about it." She didn't want to say he wanted her to stay with him. She didn't want the boys to believe she was replacing their mother, and she had no idea if she would mate Erik or not. It was best not to confuse them.

"He willna allow you to stay with us," Thorfinn said, matter-of-factly.

"We'll see." Then they walked into the great hall where everyone was beginning to gather.

Erik wasn't there yet. She walked the boys to their table.

Beathag joined them and said, "You'll be leaving soon."

"Oh?" Accalia arched a brow.

The boys looked at Accalia as if she truly was leaving.

Beathag smiled at her wickedly and then turned and flounced off, taking her place at another table.

"You're no' leaving, are you?" Johnne asked, tears forming in his eyes.

Irritated by the woman's comments because Beathag had upset Johnne, Accalia hugged him. "Nay. I dinna know why she would say that." But she was going to set her straight.

"She wants da," Thorfinn said.

He was too young to know such things, Accalia thought. "What do you mean?" She wanted to get clarification before she jumped to conclusions.

"She was storming around the castle before you got here," Thorfinn said. "She said Da was bringing some strange woman here to marry him."

"Strange?"

"Aye," Hendrie said. "When we saw you, we didna think you were strange."

"Nay, but we didna believe you would threaten to throw us in the dungeon either," Thorfinn said.

She smiled. "Well, you are clean and none the worse for wear." But then she wondered if the boys liked Beathag and would be disappointed that their da might mate Accalia instead. "You are fond of Beathag then?"

"She doesna pay any attention to us. No' like you do," Johnne said.

"She doesna threaten to throw us in the dungeon," Thorfinn said.

"That's because she doesna care anything about us," Hendrie said, scowling at Thorfinn.

Accalia looked at Thorfinn.

He shrugged. "Aye."

Logan approached Accalia and said, "You're wanted at the high table."

Frowning, the boys looked disappointed, even Thorfinn. She gave them each a hug. The boys smiled at her when she did. "Good. I will tell his lordship what we want to do on the morrow."

Their faces brightened at the idea. Their nannies joined them at their table and Logan escorted her to sit beside Erik's chair. Then Erik stalked into the great hall, his gaze going to his lads first, and then to Accalia at the head table. He smiled.

"You confound Erik, you know," Logan said, smiling down at her. "He doesna know what to make of you."

"'Tis best to keep him guessing, aye?" She smiled brightly at Logan. She wondered if his mate had confounded him or used her feminine wiles on him.

Logan laughed.

Erik joined her and they took their seats. Then the mugs were filled with honeyed mead, and the bread and fish soup served. "You are having a profound effect on my people. And on me."

"Good or no'?" She sipped her mead.

"We dinna want you to leave."

"I...I believe I'm making progress with your sons." She stole a piece of bread from his plate and began eating it. She swore all conversation stopped dead. She hadn't been observing his people, but now she suspected they were watching the two of them and their interactions.

"And me?"

Her cheeks heated. She wasn't used to a man showing her interest. Her da had never allowed it, though she'd flirted with young boys when she was younger, but a fully grown man? No.

For Erik to kiss her was such an incredible experience, and for her to kiss him back and feel her body reacting to his, she hadn't expected it, but she wanted more of it.

"I believe we have made some progress," she said, then changed the subject to one she was more comfortable discussing. "I think the boys are a little young for fishing in the loch as wolves. However, how will they ever learn if no' given the opportunity? And Thorfinn did catch a fish. Do you know how proud he felt of his accomplishment? He was even prouder when he saw you observe him at it."

"I witnessed that. I originally prohibited them from swimming in the loch as wolves while attempting to catch fish because I was concerned for their safety; I thought they might become exhausted and drown. However, after observing how much fun they were having and how determined they were to succeed, I realized my initial order had been incorrect. As you said, they need opportunities to grow and hone their abilities. I agree that practicing fishing as wolves in a creek would be more suitable for them at their age."

She couldn't believe he would agree with her but was glad. The ability to see someone else's input and change his mind made for a better leader. "I must thank you for fighting the boys in practice swordsmanship."

"I didna believe you would put me in that position." He lifted a brow, a hint of a smile in his expression.

"Your lads loved you for it and so did your people. Did you see how many came out to watch you spar with them? You are good with the boys even if you shy away from showing them. Aye, you are the pack leader, but you are still their da and they need to learn from you what you expect from them." She ate some of her soup. "The fish is delicious."

He tapped his knife on his bowl. "You will sleep with me and no' the lads. You are no' their nanny."

"I am bonding with them. Is that no' what you wanted? Why should you care where I sleep anyway? We are no' mated and until that happens, I willna share a bed with you." Och, she didn't mean to say until that happened as if it were a foregone conclusion.

She saw his eyes widen a bit. She could very well imagine where that would lead, and she would have to get to know him better before she made a drastic mistake that couldn't be undone.

She tsked. "You shouldna have barged into my guest chamber."

"I...apologized."

"No' sincerely enough. Your smirk told quite a different story."

"How could I no' have been both surprised to see you standing there naked, and filled with admiration of your beauty at the same time?"

She scoffed.

"When you sleep with me, we willna need pretenses."

She continued to eat her soup. "If I were to sleep with you, what would your people believe? That we are mated. When we are no'. And it would unnecessarily confuse the lads to think that I might become their mother? No' to replace theirs of course. Never to do that."

Erik waved at Cook who hurried over to see to his needs. "I seemed to have lost my bread."

Cook smiled at Accalia, and Accalia knew the woman had seen her steal it from Erik's plate. If she hadn't, the rumor had already circulated throughout the pack. It was amazing how interesting news could be shared so fast.

"Aye, my lord. Do you want some more?" Cook asked Accalia.

"Nay, but thanks. I've had two pieces already. My compliments to the baker, and you for preparing the fish soup."

Cook glowed and hurried off to get Erik some more bread.

"Thank you for allowing the boys to fish as wolves for as long as they did," Accalia said.

Cook brought Erik several more slices of bread, and then she hurried off.

"Do you want another piece of bread?" he asked Accalia.

She figured he wouldn't be able to eat all of them and snatched another from his plate. He chuckled.

He drank some of his mead. "Why are you being so stubborn about staying with me?"

"I have told you why."

"Any number of she-wolves would die for the chance to be in my bed."

"Then you must no' disappoint them." She knew he was bluffing because none of the she-wolves who might want to be in his bed could have the potential of allying with another clan chief. She didn't believe he would do that to his sons either. Though she believed Beathag might still cause trouble for her. Or at least try.

"I dinna want any of them in my bed. Only you."

"But you assigned me a guest chamber."

"Which you didna sleep in last eve. And things have changed between us."

"Nothing has changed between us," she said, though that was far from the truth. His kiss had opened a new level of intimacy between them, and he had been acting differently towards her since she had been doing so well with his sons. "I am still your guest. We'll leave it at that...for now."

"Your da didna tell me how difficult you could be."

She finished her soup. "He didna tell me how difficult you could be either. Besides, I do have other options."

"Oh? Pray tell me what your other options are." He took a bite of his bread, looking like he wasn't worried about the prospect.

She curled a lock of hair that had come loose from her braided hair around her finger. "A Welsh prince."

Erik barely bit back a smile, the rogue. He pointed his piece of bread at her. "Your da mentioned him to me if you brought him up but said the prince lived too far away to make a mutually agreeable alliance with him."

She snatched Erik's partially eaten bread from him and took a bite. She wanted to ask him about his mate, but she thought he was being honorable not to speak of her disparagingly probably because he had loved her and for the sake of their boys.

Then she changed the subject since that approach hadn't been helpful. "Mayhap we can challenge the boys in archery. Or walk the horses, something to teach them skills they need to know as they get older."

She had it in mind to teach them how to track people and animals while the boys wore their wolf coats. It was an important skill to learn, and she wondered if they had been taught it, or self-taught.

"Archery then, but you willna hand a bow off to me to teach them the skill tomorrow. They do know the rudiments, but none of them are very skillful at it. I will have my archers teach them."

"They can instruct me too. I know how to use the bow, but I can always use further instruction." She thought Erik didn't look entirely happy with her.

She suspected it had more to do with her not sleeping with him than with them practicing archery on the morrow.

9

Erik ate another slice of bread and pondered how to convince Accalia to sleep with him. Every time he was around her, the ache in his loins grew. He couldn't believe she had so much spice and distracted him from all his tasks. He wanted her for his own in the worst way.

As much as she was making headway with his boys when he hadn't been able to since their mother had died, he felt more and more like she was the one who should be his mate. Not only because they needed a mother, but she had a way of helping them to see their worth and he was impressed with her innate ability to do it.

Here he had believed she had to prove she was worthy of joining the pack and mating *him*. Now he thought he would have to prove to her that *he* was worthy of her love! He couldn't believe how upside-down his world had gotten once she came to stay with them.

"I...want to say how much I've enjoyed the time spent with you. I hope you are feeling settled here, and not like I tore you away from your family without anyone to object."

"I'm enjoying my time here with you, your sons, and others."

"And staying here." He didn't ask. He didn't want to learn if she wasn't sure about staying here with them.

He was amazed at how she showed them so much affection when their mother had withheld it from them. He could envision all that would lead up to Accalia having bairns with him and loving them.

He eyed the minx. He couldn't believe Accalia would steal his bread from his plate, shocking and amusing his whole pack. He knew they had been watching to see how he would react. After getting over the initial shock—no one would ever dare to steal food from him—he had wanted to laugh.

She didn't look in the least bit guilty either. Like she was amusing herself at his expense. She gave him a little smile. He smiled back. If anyone else had done that, he might have taken them to task, but with her, he wanted to congratulate her for winning another round of challenging him.

He glanced at the boys eating fish soup and bread and observing them. He wondered how they had viewed Accalia stealing his bread. They better not try to do that to him themselves.

He noticed they no longer quarreled or threw food at each other or the dogs. The wolfhounds had moved off to another table where younger bairns were accidentally dropping some of their food, as little ones were known to do. His lads were clean and he appreciated her help with that.

"My bed is more comfortable," Erik said to Accalia, still trying to get her to acquiesce and join him in his bedchamber.

"I was fine on the nanny's bed in the boys' chamber. And the guest chamber was adequate. You need no' worry about me."

He sighed. "Will you run with me as a wolf this eve?"

"With the boys?" she asked.

"Just the two of us. We'll have an escort, but the boys will be asleep."

"Aye, all right. I'll put them to bed and then join you downstairs."

He smiled. "Aye." He ran as a wolf on patrol with other wolves, but running with his potential mate? It was important to be there for each other as wolves and to see how well they worked together. "Dinna tell the boys, or they'll want to go."

She smiled. "I will tell them we are, but we'll do it with them another time."

He feared she would want to run with the boys and not leave them out. He felt for once, he was making a wee bit of progress with Accalia.

"What do you intend to do after we eat?" he asked.

"Run with the boys as wolves, but we'll run with you later."

He chuckled. She was still winning the game.

Once they were done eating, they left the table, and she gathered the boys together. "We run as wolves as soon as your da can gather a guard detail."

"Yay!" the boys shouted and raced off to their chamber.

Erik thought she was utterly amazing.

The boys didn't bother to check if he was okay with it, they just kept moving. Accalia had a natural knack for handling the boys in a way that made them adore her, even Thorfinn who could be obstinate.

Logan joined Erik before he headed outside. "The lass is a handful."

"Tell me about it. She's taking the boys for a run as wolves. Gather a guard force to watch them. You'll go with them and make sure they'll be all right. She and I will run as wolves this eve, and you can arrange a guard force for that as well."

"Aye. You dinna want to go with all of them now?"

"We'll do it later. I want to run with Accalia tonight without worrying about the boys."

Logan smiled. "Aye, I'll get right on it."

So why did Erik wish he was with Accalia and the boys now? But he couldn't change his mind now or he would appear indecisive—not a good look for a pack leader.

THE MORE ACCALIA played with Erik and saw the softer side of his personality, the more she liked him. If he had constantly told her she couldn't do something, she would butt heads with him.

She was almost considering going to his bed tonight but had to ensure she was doing the right thing. What if she let her wild wolf half take over and decided to mate him? Aye, she was strongly attracted to him. She was fighting with herself to keep the status quo. She didn't know him well enough yet.

She arrived at her bedchamber and hurried to remove her clothes. When she was at home, she wasn't allowed to run as a wolf as much as she could here. She was loving this. And she knew the boys were as thrilled that she was taking them for a run.

She shifted and raced out the chamber door, then took the circular stairs to the bottom and ran until she reached the main doors to the keep. A guard hurried to open it for her. She loved seeing all the wolves in their various fur coats, mostly white. If she stayed here, she would eventually know all of them and their howls too. But for now, she was clueless.

She saw the boys chasing each other across the inner bailey. They would wear themselves out before they even went for a run. Two wolves approached her. One she recognized as Logan from his scent. Then Erik's other brother Finlay joined them with eight men on horseback.

She had thought they would all run as wolves, but these men were ready with bows and swords in case they had to fight brigands. And Logan and the other wolf were there to help protect her and the boys as wolves, if they ran into trouble. She appreciated that Erik would let them run and would be fine with allowing some men to guard them when they probably had more important business to attend to.

She ran at the boys and nipped at them, encouraging them to run with her. Panting, they chased after her and Logan. The other wolf followed them.

But then they were in the woods running together, the men on horses riding in front of them, on their flanks, and behind them to protect them. She hoped that all the men weren't necessary, but with Freigard trying to disrupt her da and Erik's plans with her marriage to Erik, if it came to that, she understood the concern.

Also, the boys were young, and being with her would be a worry. But they had to stretch their legs and learn to be capable pack members too even at this age.

She didn't figure they would run as far as she would with Erik tonight, especially after having fishing lessons earlier. She suspected they would be ready for bed tonight and not give the nannies any trouble.

They had run through the woods for some time when the lead guards suddenly slowed down and stopped. She suspected they had heard or seen trouble in the forest. The guard hairs raised on the nape of her neck and down her back.

Logan and the other guard wolf's ears were perked up like hers and the boys' were. The guards behind them had turned around and looked off to their rear. The guards on their flanks were facing out, circularly surrounding the wolves.

Then Logan and the other guard wolf tilted their chins up and howled. She lifted her chin and howled too. The boys followed suit. She loved their little howls. She hoped there was no need for concern, but she worried there was and now she regretted the decision to take them on a wolf run like this, despite it being broad daylight and running on pack territory that should be safe.

She licked each of their faces to make sure they weren't afraid.

She could smell their anxiousness, even Thorfinn's. She thought they should return, but the men weren't moving, and she suspected they felt they could protect them better if they stayed where they were.

But then they heard horses coming in their direction. Her heart and the boys' were beating like crazy. Were the riders friend or foe?

Logan howled and someone coming in their direction howled back.

They saw a dozen riders and a half dozen wolves, Erik in his white fur coat leading the pack. This was the second time he had come to her rescue from villains, though she still hadn't seen or smelled anyone else in the area. He looked magnificent, a leader of men, a wolf to fear.

An arrow whizzed toward them through the trees and instinctively, she flattened herself against the ground, barking at the boys to do the same. She felt her first real sense of fear. She attempted to appear brave in front of the boys, but they could smell her anxiousness.

Another three arrows shot out overhead and the boys skittered. Hendrie whimpered. She nuzzled him and the other pups to show them she was there for them. Five more arrows were set free and then Erik's clansmen sent their arrows through the woods to hit their targets and hopefully take out the brigand archers.

She suspected Erik's guards hadn't done so before because they had been waiting for additional support to ensure they could hit a target. Three men cried out in the woods several yards away and a couple of horses rode away from Accalia and her party.

Erik's men began shooting back. More horses galloped away from Accalia's party. Then some of Erik's men rode off after the brigands in hot pursuit.

Erik, Logan, and the other wolves stayed with her and the boys, which she appreciated. The boys were scared, and she feared for their safety. The men who surrounded them on horseback remained stationary.

After what seemed an eternity, one of Erik's men who had taken off after the archers howled, letting them know it was safe to take her and the boys back to the castle. She hoped he wouldn't be upset with her about running with the boys, even with a guard force, and put them in harm's way. These men were bold. She knew Erik was angry. Hopefully, he was furious with just the men who had attacked their party.

When she saw the castle towers, she had never been so relieved to see a fortification looming before her. They reached the castle gates and ran into the outer bailey. It was one thing to be concerned about the men protecting them and herself, but the little ones were her charges, and she had feared for them. Erik licked Accalia's face, and she realized he wasn't upset with her. She licked him back and then nuzzled each of the boys. They were panting, looking worn out.

Erik barked at them to stay at the castle, and Accalia inclined her head and ushered the boys into the keep. She figured he would go after the brigands and ensure his men weren't injured. To get the boys' minds off the scary wolf run they'd had and onto what they could do in the future to protect themselves, she would elicit help to teach the boys archery skills.

They probably knew some, but after what they had witnessed a short while ago, she suspected they would be eager to practice archery to protect their clansmen and themselves in the future.

She took them to their chamber and then hurried off to hers. Once she had dressed, she returned to their chamber to check on them. They were dressed but sitting on their beds looking worried.

"Come. We're going to archery practice."

They brightened and rose from their beds. "Da will be vexed with us for getting into trouble on the run," Thorfinn said.

"'Twas no' our fault, but the men's who attacked us."

"Where is Da?" Johnne asked.

"He went to help his men take down the brigands who were shooting at us," she said.

"Did he say we can practice archery?" Hendrie asked.

"Aye, though I believe he thought we would do it at another time. But after what happened, I think this is a good time to practice our skills. I need to practice them too."

"We can beat her," Thorfinn said to his brothers, sounding sure of himself.

She laughed. "Aye, you probably can. Let's go find someone who can help teach us archery."

Johnne led the way down the stairs and out of the inner bailey where men were building the wall. "Rob can teach us."

"Teach you what, lad?" Rob asked, scratching his red beard. He glanced at Accalia and winked at her.

She felt her cheeks heat with embarrassment. She wasn't used to men plying their charms on her. At home with her pack, her da wouldn't allow it.

"Archery. And the lady," Hendrie said, his small chin held up high. "She needs it the most."

"She does, does she? Does his lordship approve?" Rob asked Accalia.

"He does. He said we could do this. After what had happened while we were on a run, we need to prove we can protect ourselves when the time comes."

"Aye." Rob slapped another man on his back. "Come, let us teach the lads and lass some archery skills, Fenton."

"Aye."

They all headed to the inner bailey where a couple of older lads set up targets. And then Rob said, "Who wishes to go first?"

Accalia wanted the boys to go first, but they all pointed at her and smiled.

"I guess I'm going to go first." Accalia took the bow. She nocked the arrow and shot at the circle on the target made of straw rolled in a large coil. She hadn't used a bow for a couple of years so she was glad she had shot the arrow near the center. She glanced at the boys and their jaws hung slack.

She wanted to laugh. "Who is up next?"

"I'll go," Thorfinn said. He had a smaller bow designed for the lads and lasses who were beginners at learning archery.

Fenton helped him with his form and then Thorfinn hit the outer coil of the target. "Nay!" He stomped his foot, his brows furrowed. He sounded frustrated. Probably because Accalia had done so well, and she was just a lass.

But she had been practicing on and off since she was their age so she had been doing it for several years. "This is why we're practicing. Rob or Fenton, can you show us how to hit the bullseye?"

"Aye." Rob took up the bow and aimed and hit the bullseye.

Then Fenton did the same thing right next to Rob's arrow.

"Hendrie? Johnne? Are you ready to practice?" she asked.

"Aye." Hendrie lifted the smaller bow, and Rob showed him how to aim. Then Hendrie released his arrow and struck the target in the ring next to the outer ring by Thorfinn's.

Thorfinn folded his arms across his chest, scowling. She needed to teach him to be a better sport when he wasn't coming out on top.

Then Johnne went next and hit the halfway mark inside the target. Pumping the bow in the air, he shouted out with glee.

She was so proud of them. "Let's go again." One time wasn't enough. They had to do it until they were too tired to hold their bow.

She kept wanting to look in the direction of the portcullis, to see if Erik and his men were arriving yet, but she didn't want to worry the boys.

After an hour or more at practice, the boys sagged, but they had improved by the end. She glanced at the entryway to the inner bailey, worried that Erik and the others hadn't returned. She didn't want to concern the boys, but as soon as she looked in that direction, they did too.

Why hadn't the men returned yet?

10

E rik raced back to where the brigands who had attacked Accalia, the boys, and their guard escort were. He listened for any sign of horses moving around in the woods, men's voices, growling wolves, steel striking steel, and arrows whizzing through the trees. Birds tweeted a warning of Erik's presence in the woods, and a breeze stirred the branches of the pines. He smelled the air for the scents of his men and those of their attackers, all gray wolves, though he thought they were in human form and knew they had gone in this direction.

His heart was pounding furiously. His wolf senses were enhanced and sharpened. The scent of blood and sweat permeated the air as Erik came across the body of a man lying prone in the bracken wearing three arrows—all were his brother Finlay's. Erik was grateful the body belonged to one of the villains.

But then he heard swords clashing through the trees. He saw the glint of sunlight off a sword being swung at Finlay. Erik ran in his direction, plowing through bracken and low-hanging branches intent on helping his brother. When he got closer, he witnessed the terror in Finlay's eyes, and the alarm in the grizzled face attacker's gaze when he saw Erik lunge for him.

Adrenaline and a healthy dose of fear emanated from his brother and his brother's attacker before Erik reached the brigand. His muscles tensed as he readied himself to pounce. Finlay stabbed at the distracted brigand's shoulder, drawing his attention back to his brother.

Erik leaped and slammed into the man, biting his sword arm before he could cut him. Bones crunched and the taste of copper filled Erik's mouth as he tasted the blood of his enemy, the taste of victory and justice.

Before he could grab the man's throat and end his life, his brother pierced the villain's heart with his sword. Pack members began howling or shouting. Logan howled, telling them to return to the castle.

Finlay wiped off his sword and sheathed it. "I could have handled him on my own."

Erik nodded but wouldn't have taken the chance that the villain wouldn't have gotten the upper hand with his brother. Erik howled to let Logan know where he was and to gather there.

Men on horseback began riding into the area, then wolves loped through the woods and joined them, until everyone was gathered, including Logan. "All of our men are accounted for. Two of their men got away, but it doesna hurt for them to return to Freigard and tell him how many men he lost over the confrontation. We'll give them a proper burial in the bog," Logan said.

Erik would have rather they all had been killed and Freigard could wonder what had happened to them. But Erik hadn't wanted his men to chase after them and possibly be ambushed. He helped them drag the nine dead men to the bog half a mile away. Once they had finished the task, he headed home with the others.

When they reached the inner bailey, he saw Accalia and his boys holding bows, looking tuckered out, the targets filled with arrows. They were watching for them, and as soon as they saw him and the others return, they joined more of his people who hurried out to greet them after battling the brigands.

To his surprise, Johnne and Hendrie quickly threw their arms around his furry neck. Thorfinn looked unsure whether he should or not. Accalia motioned to him to hug his da. Once he had, she smiled at Erik, tears in her eyes, and he nuzzled her leg with his nose.

She reached down and petted him and then hugged him.

He howled, and she laughed, and he realized just how much he loved hearing her laughter.

Beathag ran out and looked like she wanted to hug him, which would be too bizarre to consider. Before she could, Erik raced off to dress in his chamber. Once he was done, he found his sons and Accalia drinking ale and he joined them.

"I was glad to see everyone returned unharmed. What about those whom you fought?" she asked.

"Dead, though two escaped. They will ride back to Freigard and tell him about their defeat." Erik said to the boys, "You have done well." He was proud of them for practicing archery, and he knew it was all because of Accalia. Though Rob and Fenton were there teaching them the fundamentals.

"The lass shot several areas into the center of the target," Rob said.

"Aye," Fenton said. "I would have her at my back any day."

She smiled at them. "Your teaching skills are excellent."

Erik hadn't had the patience to teach the boys before. Maybe he could work with them now when he had time. But he was glad that Accalia could use a bow so well.

"What do you intend to do now?" he asked Accalia because she always had a plan of action.

She glanced at the boys. "You can play."

"Aye!" Thorfinn said, shouting at Johnne. "You're it."

And off the three boys ran, playing tag.

"Thank you for taking the time to work with the boys on their archery skills. It seems they are no' anxious about what happened earlier."

"They were concerned about your return," Accalia said, "but for the most part, we kept them busy so they wouldn't worry too much."

He took her hand and kissed it, his gaze meeting hers. And then he placed his hands on the sides of her face and kissed her before he changed his mind. She kissed him back, showing she was glad he had returned to the keep safely.

Rob and Fenton had made themselves scarce.

"I need to work on the wall before we break to eat the meal." He wanted to ensure she was well-occupied and not feeling isolated. He never thought he would worry about such a thing with a woman he was interested in courting.

"I planned to help the women making my dresses with the task."

Which made him feel guilty he hadn't allowed her to pack some of her things to bring with them from her home. Then they heard riders approaching the outer gates and he and Accalia watched to see who was coming.

His men quickly assembled to observe the situation in case there was trouble.

Erik was shocked to see Ragnoff arrive with two of his cousins, Gorm and Ivar. They had been three of their brother Leifson's staunchest supporters, despite Erik saving Ragnoff from drowning when their boat sank off the coast back home. Why would they come here?

Ragnoff rode up to Erik and dismounted, his cousins doing the same.

"What brings you here?" Erik asked. He knew Leifson didn't want him and his brothers to return home. Maybe he had died.

Ragnoff looked gruff as he always did. "You need to return home. Leifson isna of sane mind."

"I am home. None of us have any intention of returning there." Erik knew his brother was ruthless, but so did Ragnoff and his cousins yet they supported him against Erik and his remaining brothers.

Ragnoff glanced at Accalia. She stiffened under his hard gaze. He glanced around at the castle. "This is now yours?"

"Aye." The castle was unless he was referring to Accalia.

"She's your woman?" Ragnoff asked.

Before Erik could respond, Accalia folded her arms and said, "He's mine."

Erik smiled a little at her, amused that she would lay claim to him instead of the other way around when he didn't think she meant it but only said so for Ragnoff's sake.

"You may eat with us and then return home," Erik told Ragnoff. He wasn't giving them a place to rest. He didn't trust them. As far as he was concerned, they were still loyal to Leifson. He had men take care of their horses and then waved to Ragnoff and his burly black-haired cousins. "Come. We can talk while working on the wall." He didn't mean for them to have to work on it. Not when he was sending them away with nothing to gain.

He glanced at Accalia. She smiled at him, inclined her head, and returned to the keep.

He met Finlay and Logan at the wall that required immediate repairs after a gale had torn down a section of the stone structure. They had to get it done before they had real trouble with someone like Freigard and his men as much as they were causing problems on his land.

"Hey, brother," Logan said to Erik, helping Finlay place another rock in the mortar.

But they both eyed Ragnoff and his cousins who joined them.

"They want us to return home." Erik carried a rock over.

"Why?" Logan asked, continuing to work on the wall, not looking in their direction as if they weren't even there.

"Leifson has killed five of our men for no good reason. He said they were looking hungrily at his wife. The Gods know he had a hard time getting another one. So he fears any man looking at her will take her away from him," Ragnoff said, watching them rebuild the wall.

"We knew what Leifson was like and you still backed him," Erik said.

"He wasna as bad before you left," Ragnoff said. "He willna admit it, but you and your brothers had the best battle strategies. We have lost several battles with neighboring clans. He fears losing his position."

His life, more likely. "You see what we have here. He gave us no choice but to fight him or leave. This is where our home is now. Naught would make us return."

"Knowing Leifson, he has stirred up the wrong beehive," Logan said, slapping on some mortar.

The other men working on the wall agreed. "We tried to convince the three of you to come with us." "You believed his lies about Erik and his brothers wanting to kill him in his sleep." "You believed his lies about Erik and his brothers wanting his woman." "He created problems with the clans to the north and south of our settlement and we told you that would come back to haunt him."

Erik and Finlay lifted a rock together and put it in place.

"You have your answer," Erik said. Then he motioned to Philbin. "Take Ragnoff and his cousins to the keep and get them some ale."

"Aye." Philbin escorted them back to the keep.

Erik might have sounded like he was offering his hospitality when he didn't want to hear another word from the three men, and he didn't want any of his men to waste their breath explaining their reasoning for leaving their homes.

"The lass is certainly resourceful," Finlay said, changing the subject. "I never imagined she would be practicing archery with your sons."

"I agree. I was proud of her and the boys."

The last time he'd tried to work with them, they were younger and so inept, that he couldn't deal with it, realizing patience wasn't one of his strong suits. Which was the same as his father had been with Erik and his brothers when they were lads.

He suspected Rob and Fenton, who would have been trying to keep up their tough warrior persona with the boys while training them so they wouldn't lose face, changed the way they had treated them when Accalia was watching the process. He realized how much his people behaved differently around her—smiling more, laughing more—as if she brightened their day.

Logan said, "You need to do something...you know, romantic with the bonny lass."

"Willa didna like doing anything like that." Though if it made a difference to Accalia, Erik would do about anything to show her that he wanted her.

"She's no' like Willa, and all women are different. Think on it, brother," Logan said, loving to give him brotherly advice, even though Erik was the oldest of his brothers here.

Erik nodded. "Aye." He wondered if she would like to watch the sunset with him. Or would she think it was a waste of time? Since she was so interested in keeping the boys busy with chores, he wondered if watching sunsets wasn't something she would be interested in.

Logan smiled at him. "I can see you are overthinking this. You can do it. But if you need any ideas, Finlay and I can think of something for you to try."

"I've got this." Erik hoped. He didn't want his brothers telling him how to woo the lass. He helped others to place another stone.

The first time she had taken the boys' side against his, and did what was good for them, he had recognized her innate mothering ability. His mother had been like that until she died of a raging fever when he was about the boys' age. With a wolf's stronger healing genetics, they recovered quickly, but several of his clansmen had come down with the fever and nearly a dozen had succumbed.

"She's doing right by the boys, you know," Finlay said, carrying another stone to the wall.

"Aye." That's all Erik needed was his brothers ganging up on him about his love interest. He paused to drink some ale from his flask.

Before seeing how Accalia worked with the boys, he thought maybe they were too old to need a mother nurturing them, but after seeing how she handled them, he knew now what it meant to the boys.

"I admit she is the woman I want for their mother. Their nannies are loving and caring, but they have a duty to perform. They aren't free-spirited like Accalia. They would never suggest teaching the boys to fish in the loch, run with them as wolves, or encourage them to practice archery."

His brothers nodded.

"Moreover, their mother"—Erik had never admitted his late mate's shortcomings to anyone, his brothers even—"had never done these things with them either."

"Exactly," Logan said, as they all went to work on the wall.

"In the short time Accalia has been here, she has shown us what a real mother should be toward my sons, and she isna even their mother. She has all the natural nurturing instincts though," Erik continued. More than that, he wanted her as his mate with all the benefits.

Logan folded his arms. "*I* would woo her."

Erik cast him a dark look.

Finlay laughed.

Logan slapped Erik on the back. "I know that expression. You want her and no one will have her but you, unless the lass isna agreeable. Which then leads me to the conclusion that you are no' doing something right."

It was true that when wolves decided they were right for each other, they didn't wait a long time before they mated. Erik knew he had to convince Accalia he could have more of a romantic side. But she was shying away from any aspect of that, except for kissing him in the bailey.

They continued to work on the wall, seeing some real progress, lifting another stone with Erik's help.

As far as seeing him as her lover and wolf mate, he felt he wasn't making any headway with her. Well, mayhap a wee bit when he kissed her in the inner bailey the one time. When she kissed him back, she did it with feeling, not like she was forced to, but that she had been as much into the kiss as he had been.

He smiled. He wanted to kiss her like that again. But it was her reluctance to join him in his bed where he could be more intimate with her that she was balking at.

His brothers laughed at him. "What I wouldna give to know what you're thinking that makes you smile so wolfishly," Logan said.

"Have you told the lass that company is coming?" Finlay asked.

"I need to." Erik suspected Alasdair and Isobel had learned he had been bringing Accalia here and they wanted to see who his prospective mate was. He was hopeful they would put in a good word with her concerning his character.

If Alasdair gave him grief—in his typical fashion, as Erik did with him—he hoped he didn't react in a way that showed any unfavorable traits. Normally, they bantered back and forth in a good-natured way, but while he was trying his darndest to impress Accalia, he wasn't sure how that would all play out.

"You know Alasdair will bring his bachelor brothers, Hans and Rory," Finlay said.

Erik would have to keep them far away from Accalia if one of them tried to romance the lass more than he did!

WHEN IT WAS time for the meal, Accalia and the boys headed for the great hall to eat with the rest of the pack. She worried that the three men who had come about Erik's oldest brother were causing trouble. Then Beathag sashayed past her, bumping into her, making Accalia lose her footing.

Accalia could have let the slight go, but not only was she alpha, but if she were to mate Erik, she would manage the staff, and the woman had to know her place.

Then she told the boys, "Go to your seats and enjoy your meal."

"Are you going to join us?" Thorfinn asked, his eyes wide, his voice hopeful.

"I'm sure Erik will expect me to eat with him again. I'll see you off to bed this eve." Accalia hugged each of them and kissed the tops of their heads.

They loved her hugs, and she enjoyed their hugs back. She hadn't expected them to cherish them, but they were now hugging her freely at spontaneous times and she was glad she hadn't thought they were too old for such nonsense. In truth, everyone loved a hug, if they were honest with themselves.

She even wondered how it would feel to be embraced by Erik in a way that was much more of a hug. She thought of being with him in his bed, legs intertwined, his mouth on hers, their bodies naked and pressed against each other. If she kept thinking of it, she'd end up in his bed with him to see.

Erik wasn't in the great hall yet, so Accalia turned and stalked toward Beathag, grabbed her arm, startling her and she gasped.

"Come with me." Accalia pulled her out of the great hall, past Erik as he arrived with his brothers and the other men who had been working on the wall.

He frowned at them and waited to see what was happening, while his brothers and the others walked into the great hall. Accalia had a job to do, but not in front of everyone in the pack.

She shoved Beathag against the wall outside the great hall, her hands on her shoulders, forcing her to stay there. "I dinna know what you are playing at. But you have no chance to mate Erik if you think you do. No' even if I leave here. You willna disrespect me again or you will see a side of me you dinna want to."

Accalia didn't give the woman a chance to explain herself or apologize. Accalia released her, then turned to Erik and smiled. She joined him and he took her hand and they entered the great hall together.

"Do you want to explain to me what that was about?" Erik asked.

"Nay. 'Tis a matter between the two of us." She didn't believe Erik needed to intercede on her behalf. If she had to manage a staff, she needed to do it her way. She sat next to Erik at the head table. "What's going on with the men from your homeland?"

The men who had come to see Erik were sitting at a lower table.

"They are well-trained warriors with our clan," Erik said, as the servers brought them platters of wild boar. "We tried to convince them to come with us, but they stood by Leifson. He can be erratic and moody. And if he doesna like anything you've said or done, he'll fight you to the death."

She ate some of her boar. "You wouldna think of leaving, would you?"

"Nay."

"Good. As to the earlier matter, I'm sorry we were running as wolves when Freigard's men attacked and that I put your sons at risk."

Erik looked surprised she felt that way and leaned over and kissed her cheek. "The men who tried to kill you were the ones strictly at fault. They shouldna have been on my lands in the first place without invitation. None of my people should feel they canna go for a run as a wolf or otherwise in my territory."

"Are you and I still running together this eve?" Accalia asked Erik, suspecting he would say no, worried about her safety.

"Aye, we said we would and these men willna keep us from running through our lands when we wish it unless you dinna want to."

She was surprised he would say *our lands*, this time when they were *his*, and she wasn't even a pack member. "Aye. I look forward to it." She would fight the wolves herself if she had the chance.

"Will you stay with me this eve?" Erik looked directly at her, appealing to her as a man who desired more of a relationship between them.

Liking that he was trying hard to appeal to her, she smiled and stole a slice of his bread from his wooden plate. "Nay. Though 'tis tempting." She had noticed he no longer had Cook sample the food before he ate it.

His smile was wickedly wolfish as if he knew she was considering staying with him.

11

W hile Erik finished a slice of boar, he needed to tell Accalia about the guests visiting them.

"We are having guests on the morrow. Alasdair, his mate, Isobel, and some of his clansmen, including his sister, Bessetta, will stay with us for a few days. His mate is an Icelander, but now one of us. She's a wolf," Erik said to Accalia, again hoping that Alasdair wouldn't bring either of his bachelor brothers with him if one might sway Accalia to look upon him more favorably.

Erik had considered telling Alasdair to leave them behind, but he knew Alasdair would be highly amused and be sure to bring them then.

"Oh, oh, Alasdair? I know him and his clan."

Erik stared at Accalia for a minute. He hadn't thought her da had gotten along with Alasdair's clan or he might have already mated her off to one of Alasdair's brothers.

"Bessetta played with me when they visited my clan." Accalia smiled, appearing pleased with the memory. "Alasdair and his brothers teased us mercilessly, but we always had the last laugh." She chuckled. "Once Alasdair took over his clan, he was all businesslike, much like you. But when he was younger, he was full of mischief."

Was that why Accalia was so good at besting Erik? She'd had the experience of doing so with Bessetta against her brothers?

"They willna give you trouble here," Erik said. He would see to it.

Accalia laughed. "They would never win."

He smiled, loving that she was confident in her abilities. "I thought that mayhap Bessetta could stay in your bedchamber and then you could join me in mine to free up the room while they visit for the next few days."

"Oh, aye, I can give up my room to Bessetta and then stay with the boys."

That *wasn't* what Erik had in mind! And with Alasdair's brothers there, if they came with him, Erik wanted to ensure she was not alone with them at any time, in case they were more in the mood of courting the she-wolf than giving her grief now that they were all older.

"I'll be glad to see Bessetta. I havena visited with her in a couple of years. And I havena met Isobel yet so it will be nice to see her. Was this a planned visit?" Accalia asked.

"When they learned I was bringing you here, they wanted to visit and see you. I didna realize they already knew you. Alasdair made no mention of it. Mayhap they want to see how well we suit."

Accalia laughed. "Oh, Bessetta would want the best for me. I thought you would have already sought her hand in marriage since she was a known quantity. She's good with wee ones, sweet-natured, and beautiful. Taking care of the children of my pack wasna my primary duty back home because my da needed me to supervise the household staff and the castle and its grounds in its entirety when he was away at battle. But Bessetta often works with the children of her pack."

"You are beautiful and manage the boys brilliantly. You are the one who intrigues me. Besides, I already have an alliance with Alasdair. Bessetta is a lovely lass, as willful as you, I realize. She and I are friends, but neither of us is drawn to each other in the way of the wolf."

She nodded.

"And I wanted to make another alliance that would benefit all—your da, Alasdair, us. So you were the perfect choice—unmated, a she-wolf, love bairns—so your da said—and were perfectly agreeable to meet me and learn how we would get along."

"It seems to me, my da exaggerated about my strengths a wee bit when he agreed to this arrangement."

"He knew you would be happy to be here with me." He cast her a hint of a smile.

"You were hopeful."

"I am lucky." Because his wolf craved her like he knew *she* was interested in him. He couldn't understand her reluctance though to take their relationship deeper. She would manage the staff and be a mother to his boys. He would protect her from Freigard and his men, and her da wouldn't have any further say in who he might pawn her off on.

Erik believed he was likable, except when he encountered a devil wolf like Freigard who brought out the worst in him. Then, yes, he could become easily angered, but it was justified. He trusted his ability to be a fantastic partner, to bring pleasure to his mate, and to demonstrate his love for her. So why wasn't he succeeding?

"What about the men who came from your homeland? Are they going to cause trouble for you?"

"Nay. They chose Leifson over us, and they'll have to deal with him."

"Good. I would say the same."

He was glad to hear it because if they thought alike, they could lead the pack more successfully.

"After the meal, how about I gather a guard detail while you put the lads to bed so we can run as wolves?" Erik asked.

Her eyes widened a bit, and he wondered why, then he thought maybe it was because he didn't order her to do it but asked.

Then she smiled. "Of course. But you should say good night to your sons."

She was right.

"I will the next time. I must ensure Ragnoff and his cousins leave the castle after we eat."

She smiled and looked relieved.

Suddenly, there was a flurry of panic from the servers for the meal and some people sitting at the lower tables. They rushed out of the great hall and Accalia got up from her chair, but Erik grabbed her hand and said, "They're shifting."

Her eyes widened and she sat down at the table. "Oh...oh, because you and your pack members turned them."

"Aye, and they canna control the shift during the full moon phase," Erik said. "Likewise, they canna shift into their wolves during the new moon phase. They know to stay here at the castle during the full moon and if the need to shift comes over them, they take care of it."

"But all of your people were born *lupus garous*?"

"Aye."

"Do the others regret having been turned?"

"Nay. They like that they can run as wolves, have longer lives, and their injuries heal in half the time that it takes humans. And they like being part of the pack and members of the clan."

"That is good. Did anyone object to being turned?"

"Cook."

She laughed. "It seems to me that she is happy enough now."

"Aye. She is a good cook, and except for her trouble with shifting during the meal sometimes, she is happy here with us."

He and Accalia finished the meal, and he planned to hug and kiss her before she left. But she jumped out of her chair. "See you." She hurried off to gather the boys and head them out of the hall. They hugged her, and she hugged them back and kissed each of their heads.

He and his kin watched her, and he could tell they approved of her actions as much as he did. Even the original staff turned by his people seemed to love her.

"Well," Logan said, joining him. "It appeared you were going to kiss her but missed the opportunity. I swear no one left the great hall expecting to witness it. Several were disappointed that they didna see you kissing in the bailey. What happened?"

Finlay was right there, overhearing the conversation.

Erik wished he wasn't the center of attention and that no one would know what he had in mind to do—especially when it didn't go the way he had wanted it to. If it had, that would have been another story.

"She was so eager to send the boys off to bed and join me on a wolf run, she hurried off."

Logan smiled. "I assumed that. All right, I'll gather a guard detail then."

"I'll join you in the inner bailey shortly." Erik looked forward to running with her and enjoying the beauty of his lands at night.

"You want me to send Ragnoff and his cousins on their way?" Finlay asked.

"Aye. If Leifson had forced them to remain with him, that would be one thing. But they rallied to his cause and it's up to them to deal with it."

"I agree."

Erik was glad both his brothers were such a help in running the pack. He knew if anything should happen to him and Accalia was his mate, they would take care of her and the boys. He hoped they wouldn't have to deal with more brigands on the run.

ACCALIA HURRIED the boys to bed, eager to join Erik on their wolf run across the land. She wanted to find the perfect fishing spot to take the boys and teach them to fish in their wolf coats in a few days.

She thought Erik had looked like he would kiss her after they finished the meal, but when they kissed the next time—she wanted it to be in a more private setting. That way no one would have any expectations about them if it didn't work out between them.

The nannies soon entered the chamber, looking less stressed now that the boys were much better behaved. She was so glad she could help them.

"What did Da say about what had happened with the brigands?" Thorfinn asked.

"Nine of the villains were killed and two escaped. The goal is to capture one alive, learn who oversees the men, and send them to fight us. So we dinna want to kill all of them."

"After he told you who he worked for, then you kill him?" Thorfinn asked.

"Aye. His loyalty remains with his lord. If we let him go, he would return straight to him and tell him what had happened and then we would face the enemy in another battle." After she spoke, she realized it wasn't the best bedtime story to share with the lads.

Then again, after dealing with what they had, they would probably still have nightmares about it no matter what.

The boys climbed onto their beds, and she kissed each of them on the forehead. "Now sleep tight. Your da and I are running as wolves tonight and then we'll be off to bed after that like all good wolves."

"What if the brigands attack again?" Frowning, Thorfinn sounded worried about them.

"Whoever sent the men will have even fewer. And maybe we

can capture one of them this time. But I suspect they will be too scared to return for another engagement."

"Will you let us know when you return?" Johnne asked.

"Aye, I will. I will kiss each of you, but I willna wake you. Dinna wait up for me to do so." She didn't think they would. They looked drifty-eyed, Johnne rubbing his eyes and Thorfinn yawning, Hendrie following suit. She was glad they had several exciting adventures—though battling brigands was another story. "Get your rest." She hoped they would be all right sleeping with their nannies for tonight after what they'd been through.

"What did you do to Beathag?" Thorfinn asked.

She hesitated to answer. Then she figured they might as well know. "I told her she wouldna cause me grief any longer."

"You didna push her on the floor because she ran into you in a mean way?" Hendrie asked.

"Nay. I didna need to."

"You told her you would send her to the dungeon," Johnne said.

She smiled. "Why, I should have thought of that."

"She only tells *us* she's sending us to the dungeon," Thorfinn said, sounding a little cross.

"If she bothers me any further, that might be the next thing I say," Accalia said, amused that the boys wanted to know how she'd handled the woman.

"What are we going to do on the morrow?" Thorfinn asked, trying to get her to stay a while longer.

She had used that tactic when she was a young lass and hadn't wanted to sleep yet, no matter how tired she'd been. "We'll see when the sun comes up." Then she glanced at the nannies waiting to take over.

They inclined their heads to her. She was glad that the boys were behaving better now for their sake. She gave each of the boys a hug and then left the room.

In her bedchamber, she removed her shawl, belt, gown, and

shoes, and then shifted into her wolf. She dashed out the door but ran into a wolf she didn't recognize in her wolf form, but she knew her scent—Beathag. She never visited this part of the tower that Accalia had seen.

Accalia suspected Beathag planned to give her issue. Maybe Beathag had thought to attack when Accalia was still in her human form, but she'd stripped and shifted too fast and now Beathag was facing a wolf. A wolf bite could cause serious damage. But Accalia knew how to fight as a wolf, which gave her the advantage.

For a moment, she eyed Beathag, waiting for the wolf to make her play. Accalia wasn't going to attack her without provocation. That wasn't a good way to take charge of the staff. The wolf jumped at Accalia, snarling and growling. Accalia immediately attacked, taking the wolf by the throat and pinning her to the floor. Every time Beathag tried to fight Accalia to free herself, Accalia tightened her grip and growled.

The boys and nannies raced out of the bedchamber. They gasped, but no one tried to stop Accalia. She had no plan to hurt the she-wolf, only to make a point.

Accalia finally eased up on Beathag, intending to release her, but if Beathag bit at her, she would bite her back to prove a point—like she would if Beathag was an unruly pup.

Accalia released her. Their hearts beating hard, Beathag stood. Her fierce gaze was on Accalia. Likewise, Accalia waited for the she-wolf's attack. She could predict with certainty it was coming. The woman didn't know when to take her losses and leave.

Beathag lunged at her, going for Accalia's throat this time as if she thought she could manage the same move that Accalia had made against her.

Accalia swiftly tackled Beathag's leg, bringing her down, not breaking it, though she could have easily done so. It would have healed in about three weeks, but Accalia didn't want to take it that far. Beathag fell on her side and yelped in pain. As soon as she swung her head around and tried to bite back, Accalia tightened her hold on her leg. Beathag yelped again and dropped her head on the floor.

Then Accalia saw a wolf running to join her—Erik. She hoped he didn't think she was being mean to Beathag. She released Beathag's leg.

Erik licked Accalia's face in greeting, which delighted her.

He barked at Beathag to leave.

The woman feigned she had been terribly injured. Erik growled at her to move along. She finally got up and walked on three legs. Accalia had not injured her. Maybe she'd hurt Beathag's pride, but Accalia hadn't even drawn blood.

He nudged her to let her know he was saying good night to his sons, and she smiled at him, loving that he had taken her words to heart. He herded them into the bedchamber and licked each of the boys' faces, who were fending him off with scrunched-up expressions and laughter. She loved it. Then she and he left the room, descended the stairs, and loped to the inner bailey where men on horseback and wolves loitered, waiting on them.

The whole party moved into the outer bailey and outside through the gates. The gate guards shut and locked the portcullis after the party was outside.

She was glad she and Erik could run together as wolves without the boys. She wanted to see if he would play with her in a courtship wolf-shifter way, or if he would be all solemn—for fear the brigands would return. She would understand if he treated the run furtively, considering what had happened to her and the boys earlier. But she still wondered what would happen with the issue of Beathag and how Erik viewed it.

They smelled the woods for signs of other wolves, but all they caught were whiffs of the scent of pine, rabbits, red deer, and a wild cat. They loped to a loch that she hadn't seen before and she enjoyed the vision of it, the full moon reflected in the still, dark waters, the trees surrounding it, likewise appearing as though they were part of the water.

With Erik again in the lead, he took her to a cliff. They climbed the path up through the rocks and stopped on a ledge to look over a glen filled with heather and green grass. The view was amazing. Way off in the distance, clouds were forming, and she was mesmerized by the forks of lightning spearing the forests far away. Was it coming in this direction? Or moving another way?

She loved exploring the area with Erik by her side. She had envisioned doing this with him back at her castle. Then she started moving in case the storm overtook them. She wanted to see all the pack's lands with Erik, but she figured they would have to stop early because of the coming storm. When he took her to a burbling stream, she stopped on the bank while he started to cross the water.

When he saw she hadn't followed him, he returned to her. She was looking for fish—somewhere the boys would have more success catching in a shallower creek bed. Then she saw good-sized trout moving downstream, and she smiled. This would be perfect for a future fishing trip.

Then she moved across the stream with Erik, and he nuzzled her face, and she nuzzled his. He almost seemed afraid to be too intimate or playful with her as a wolf. He was a big wolf, and she realized he might never have had the opportunity to play with a female.

She was a big gray wolf, smaller than him. But she could tackle a male. She'd done it so many times with Bessetta's brothers. Yet she wasn't sure that Erik would appreciate it, she realized. He seemed to want to rub his cheek against hers in a wolf way that said he was loving this with her.

But she had to know that he could play with her like he could with his boys. So she licked his face, but that got a lick back on her nose, kissing, not playing, more serious-minded, intrigued in a mating relationship. She sighed and her wolf's breath was frosty on the air, though she hadn't felt it was chilly because of her heavy wolf coat.

She bit the ruff of his neck. He had a thick neck and dense fur, so it was like she'd mouthed him rather than had bitten him. He glanced at her, his smile wickedly fun, like he attempted to figure her out. Poor old wolf. Her da had given up long ago on trying to do so.

She whipped around and went for Erik's tail and nipped it. He glanced back at her as if she had barely tickled him and he was trying to guess what she was doing. A couple of his men on horseback nearby, watching their surroundings for them, chuckled.

She was about to give up on Erik when she realized he was twitching his tail ever so slightly, covertly watching her over his shoulder, and she smiled. Aye! He was waiting for her to initiate the play again—making sure that was what she was up to.

They stood motionless—all except his tail—him watching her, while she was pretending innocence slightly behind him, observing his swishing tail with her peripheral vision, hopefully not indicating she was going for it again. Then she boldly leaped for his tail so he couldn't mistake her intent. He likewise whipped around to grab her, she yelped in joyful surprise and fun and tore off, and the chase was on.

The wolves with them were running full out, keeping up with them, protecting them, while Accalia and Erik were having the time of their lives. She hoped this would never end, yet the old fear of having a potential mate leave her for another woman at the last moment did come to mind.

Why did she even have to think about that at a time like this?

12

W hen Accalia gave Erik's neck a love bite, he was amused and very interested. She had a way of making everyone love her. But when she nipped at his tail with a featherlight touch, he thought she wanted to play with him.

He had never done so with a she-wolf and didn't want to hurt her because of his size or become too enthusiastic during wolf play like he could be when fighting with his brothers or other kin and pack members. Certainly, his late wife had never wanted to.

The notion encouraged him that Accalia wanted to deepen their relationship. She eyed his tail again as covertly as she could. He observed her without being obvious about it. He was ready to play the game. His tail swished back and forth, teasing her, encouraging her to try and make another attempt at nipping at him.

The instant she turned and leaped for him, he swung around to his right and meant to tackle her. Once he turned, she recognized the game was on and dashed off. He wanted to laugh, she was so cute, but he was in hot pursuit. Despite her legs being a little shorter than his because she was a female, she was fast.

All the guard wolves ran off with them, keeping their distance and ensuring Accalia and Erik could play without anyone causing problems for them. Likewise, the soldiers on horseback continued to protect them, smiling at the change in activity.

Again, Erik wasn't sure what to do. He could catch her, but he was afraid he might be considered overzealous or injure her if he pounced on her. She didn't give him a chance to think about it for long. She whipped around to her right and when she did, she opened herself up to an attack and he tackled her.

Catching prey was instinctive. He hadn't given it another thought, just pounced on her since she was within his reach. Down she went, and he was on top of her. She didn't fight him back, her chest heaving with exertion. He listened to her heart pounding, as her tongue lolled out of her mouth. Her lips curved slightly into a grin, while her eyes were bright with excitement.

He still had her pinned down and she didn't even try to unseat him, appearing happy to be under his control—for the moment. He smiled down at her, licked her cheek, and nuzzled her face.

She nipped at his chin and woofed—a happy woof that said she was very pleased with how he played with her. He sighed with relief, his breath turning to fog in the cool night air.

They had been running, loping, and walking for over an hour. Thunder rumbled and he glanced at the storm building off in the distance. Lightning flashed across the dark clouds billowing into a massive storm system, appearing more ominous. The wind began blowing hard and they could smell the rain coming. Thunder followed from a distance again, but the storm was getting closer.

Erik was enjoying the run with Accalia and playing with her, and she didn't appear to want to quit anytime soon. He wished they could have stayed out here longer. But he knew the boys would be afraid of the storm and fear that she and he were still out in it. Maybe not so much that he was, but that Accalia was. They would believe he could manage any adversity.

As much as he loved pinning Accalia down because she

appeared to be content with it and he loved the wolf intimacy between them, they needed to return home. He worried about her safety.

He knew the boys' nannies would do their best to soothe the boys' fears during the storm, though he hoped his sons would overcome them soon enough. It didn't help that a fortnight ago they had been in the stable playing in the hay when lightning had struck the wooden frame and set it on fire.

Between those rescuing the horses and the boys, and others putting out the fire, his sons were well-traumatized. Erik had been upset with them and their nannies that the boys were playing where they weren't supposed to be in the first place and the nannies hadn't been watching the boys. If they'd been safe in the castle, none of that would have happened as far as them being afraid of storms, that was.

He nudged at Accalia to return home with him and let her up and they raced in the direction of the castle. Though she tried her best to beat him to the castle, he was sticking by her side the whole way. He was so glad it had been just the two of them and that they hadn't been running with his sons or they would have wanted him to tackle them instead. Wolf play with his future mate—because Erik wasn't letting her go—was the best thing ever.

Before they reached the portcullis, Erik howled to let the gate guards know they were almost home. They reached the open gates and headed inside, the guards shutting and locking them after the last of the pack members were inside. Everyone howled to let the others know they had returned. They heard a few howls from the barracks and the keep, acknowledging them with a greeting.

Erik and Accalia were near the castle doors when the rain began to fall in a deluge, but their guard hairs kept their soft, downy inner coat dry. Guards hurried to open the doors for them, and they headed inside. Lightning was overhead now, and he was glad they were safely inside.

Accalia sprinted through the castle and up the stairs. Before settling in, Erik ensured everyone who had joined them on their excursion had entered the keep. After completing the task, he wondered if Accalia would stay with him now that she saw he could play with her as a wolf. He sure hoped she would.

He was certain she would check on the boys, but he wanted to guarantee she would come to bed with him afterward. He shifted in his chamber, dressed, and headed for the lads' room. He wouldn't leave it to chance that she would join him.

When he arrived at the chamber, he thought she might still be dressing in her room, but she was trying to coax the boys into their beds. All three were sitting in the corner of the room far away from the shuttered windows where they could see the flashing light from the storm, hear the winds howling, and the rain slamming against the thick stone walls.

"Up with you," Erik said, not about to pamper the boys. He lifted Johnne off the floor.

Before he could put the boy in his bed, Accalia said, "Oh, aye, what an excellent idea. You will take them to bed with you."

He had to have looked at her like he thought she was jesting to make such a suggestion. He wanted *her* in his bed, not his sons! But then he believed he had the best solution of all. "Aye, and Accalia will join us so we can protect her too." He smiled at her. Two could play at this game.

That got the boys off their bums in a hurry, both Hendrie and Thorfinn grasping her hands as if sealing the bargain. She raised her brows at Erik. He smiled again. He had won this engagement between them.

The nannies' jaws hung agape as he carried Johnne to his chamber, Accalia following behind, the other boys holding onto her hands with a death grip. When they reached Erik's chamber, he had this perfectly planned. He would be in the middle of the bed, Accalia to his right where he would snuggle with her, and the boys to his left who would feel safe in his big bed with the two of them showing the lads they had nothing to fear.

But Accalia wasn't about to let Erik dictate bed arrangements and she immediately had the boys go to the center of the bed, which they eagerly did, scrambling under the furs to take their positions. Accalia took the right side of the bed and Erik was obligated to take the left side. The lass had won again.

Though to be sure, he had her in his bed—with him, delighting him. The next time? He planned for it to be a lot less crowded.

THE MORE ACCALIA was around Erik, the more she came to love him. She knew he'd been hesitant to play with her as a wolf, though she wondered if he thought he might hurt her, he didn't believe in playing with a she-wolf, or he was too serious. She'd loved it when he took the chance and had fun.

She wanted to do more of that, but by the time they'd attempted it, she had been too worn out to unsettle him once he had tackled her. So she conceded he had won and she knew he had loved that. But the bed situation?

When she saw the boys were terrified to go to their beds and Erik would force the issue, she knew she had to intervene with a motherly touch. She hadn't expected Erik to agree, but with the caveat that she had to join them in his bed.

She had guessed his intention, so she was glad she had changed the scenario to suit herself. She was ready to join him in bed, but not with the boys. Since the boys were with them, she didn't want Erik to show her affection and intimacy, best shared in private.

She and he settled onto the mattress on opposite sides of the bed and looked across the sea of boys, all three already sound asleep, and she knew that his sons joining their da in bed had been the right thing to do. He raised his brows at her and gave her a devious smile that told her she wouldn't win the game again. She smiled back. Who said she wouldn't?

Then she closed her eyes and thought of all the good—and bad —things that had happened during the day. She wondered how the visit with her friend Bessetta and her brothers would go on the morrow. She suspected Bessetta would want her to sleep with her as they had done as young girls when visiting one another and tell her all that had gone on since they had last seen each other.

Bessetta had gained a sister-in-law, but nothing much had happened in Accalia's life—until she had to travel with Erik to his castle.

Then before she was ready, she heard Erik stir and she wanted to groan. She wasn't ready for the day to begin.

AFTER HAVING pleasant dreams of chasing Accalia while they were wolves, catching her and making her his, Erik woke to find his sons sprawled across his big bed and saw Accalia slipping out the door so she could return to her room and dress. He sighed and rubbed his eyes, wishing he had been able to wish her a good morning before she left.

"Time to get up and break our fast," he told his sons.

They all groaned a little.

"We have visitors today. Come on. Time to get up." Erik climbed off the bed and the boys rose, looking half asleep. "Go to your chamber and your nannies will help you get ready."

"Where is Accalia?" Thorfinn asked, frowning as if he thought she hadn't slept with them all night.

"She left to get dressed in her chamber."

"Did you kiss her?" Johnne asked.

"Of course, he kissed her," Thorfinn said as if he were the expert.

Hendrie watched Erik's expression as if he didn't trust that Thorfinn was correct.

Erik would have loved to have kissed her, cuddled with her, and more, but the boys had been an obstacle three times over. He smiled.

"He did," Johnne said as if Erik's expression said it all.

Hendrie twisted his mouth in thought, then said brightly, "He couldna have reached her. Not over all of us."

Hendrie was smart, Erik would give him that.

"She walked to his side of the bed and then kissed him," Thorfinn said.

Johnne shook his head. "Da would have kissed her first and then she would have kissed him back."

"Da was still in bed with us," Hendrie said.

Accalia walked into the room and said, "What are you lads doing still in your da's room? You need to get dressed at once."

They all looked at Erik. "Do as she says." He was surprised they would get his take on it since they had been listening to her. Besides, he had already told them to return to their chamber and dress.

"He kissed her," Thorfinn said, hurrying out the door.

Johnne agreed and hurried after his brother.

Hendrie waited a moment, then smiled. "You didna." Then he joined his brothers.

She shook her head and was about to follow them out the door when Erik caught her arm and pulled her into his arms for a kiss. "You made sure there were too many obstacles between us last eve so that I couldna very well kiss you. And then this morning, you slipped out before I even had a chance to leave the bed. Are you afraid of me?"

"Nay, I'm afraid of what I might do."

They heard chuckling outside the door. Erik said to the boys, "Go!"

The boys' footfalls ran down the hall.

Then Erik kissed her as thoroughly as they had in the inner bailey. She was as enthusiastic this time as she was the last time. It gave him hope that she was feeling the same way about mating him as he was her.

"Thank you for playing with me on the wolf run," he said, kissing her again.

"By the time we played, I was wearing out or you wouldn't have had such an easy time of it," she said.

"Next time, we'll play first and explore afterward."

"It's a deal."

"And tonight, I want you in my bed—alone with me."

She gave him an exaggerated smile. "Bessetta and I have no' seen each other in ages, and we always sleep together when we visit each other. I had forgotten that when I mentioned she could have my room."

He smiled at her as if he didn't believe her. She raised her brows.

"All right, then they stay one night and no more."

She laughed. "You wouldna have them come all that way and send them home. They will be gone before long and then—"

He hung on her every word, his hands caressing her shoulders.

"We'll see," she said.

"We *will* be together." He would have it no other way. He wanted her and he knew deep down she wanted him. She had already fallen in love with his boys, and they felt the same about her. They were meant to be a family, a mated couple, and she—his pack leader mate. He had to get her to agree. He sighed. "About Beathag—"

"She isna a problem."

"If we mated, she would know she has no chance with me."

Accalia laughed. "I believe she might see that already. I'll join

you downstairs. If you dinna hurry, you may miss your guests."
Then she pulled away and headed for the door.

He was glad she had taken Beathag to task.

He dressed as fast as he could, not wanting Accalia to see Alasdair's brothers before he could be at her side, showing all of them that he had every intention of making her his mate.

ACCALIA LOVED how things had changed so drastically between her and Erik. He had come off so forceful and in charge. At first, he felt she had to prove *she* was right for *him*. But now, he desperately wanted her to be in his bed, sharing more.

That was more like it. She'd seen the panic on his face when she left him alone and headed downstairs and she knew it wouldn't take long for him to join her. She was sure it had to do a lot with his worrying about Alasdair's brothers' interest in her. If they showed any interest in her this time, she was sure it would only be to irk Erik in a brotherly way.

When she arrived downstairs, everyone was gathered around to meet their guests as soon as they arrived. The boys hurried to greet her and gave her hugs, which she reciprocated. Then Erik was searching for them, and everyone moved aside so he could join them.

"Alasdair, Isobel, and their kin are here," Logan said, walking into the castle.

Erik, Accalia, and the boys moved outside with other clansmen to greet the newcomers in the inner bailey. Even the wolfhounds joined them, eager to join in on the excitement.

As soon as Accalia saw Alasdair and his kin, she observed Isobel wearing a sword and a bow and carrying a shield, looking like she was prepared for battle, her blond hair as golden as the sun, hanging in braids down her back, her blue eyes sparkling with humor.

Even though Alasdair leaped down from his horse and gallantly headed to help her down from her horse, Isobel jumped down on her own. Together, they were a striking couple—where she was fair, he was dark-haired and eyed.

Instantly, Accalia liked Isobel. Then she saw Bessetta and couldn't hold back, dashing forth to hug her. Bessetta had reddish blond hair but was a blond wolf in her wolf form, like Erik's pack members. She hugged Accalia and whispered, "You are mating the white wolf lord, aye?"

Accalia glanced back at him, standing proud with his lads as if waiting for her answer, though she knew he couldn't have heard Bessetta's words. But he was smiling maybe hopeful he could still convince her to stay with him instead. Now he had to prove something—not only with his people but with his friends.

Alasdair and Isobel and Alasdair's brothers joined Erik. Accalia wished she could hear what *they* had to say.

13

"Is it a done deal?" Alasdair asked Erik as they enjoyed watching Bessetta and Accalia visiting with each other.

Before Erik could respond to Alasdair's question, wishing he could give him a resounding aye, Thorfinn said, "She adores us." He acted as if Alasdair hadn't proposed the question to Erik.

"All of you or just you three lads?" Alasdair's brother Hans asked with a twinkle in his eye.

"He kissed her, and she kissed him back," Thorfinn said, puffing his chest out.

Alasdair laughed.

"Aye," Erik said, glancing at Alasdair's brothers to show them that the lass was with him. "'Tis true."

"And we all slept with da in his bed last night," Thorfinn added.

All the men and Isobel laughed.

That, Erik hadn't wanted anyone to share.

Both Erik's and Alasdair's brothers were smiling at the lasses. So was Isobel. Now he was afraid Bessetta and Accalia would stay with each other until Bessetta, and her family left here.

Then Bessetta and Accalia hurried over to join the men and Isobel and Alasdair introduced Accalia to his mate.

Looking eager to welcome her with open arms, Accalia hugged Isobel. "I'm so pleased to meet you. I didna think that Alasdair would find a mate who would be his match."

Seemingly pleased by the gesture, Isobel smiled broadly. "Ja, we are." Thankfully, she didn't ask how things were going between Accalia and Erik.

Then Erik hurried to escort them inside the castle to break their fast, taking Accalia by the arm to show she was with him. Isobel smiled at Accalia to show her support for whatever she decided.

Bessetta followed behind them as if she knew when to give Accalia and Erik the time to be together alone. Then everyone was seated at the head table, the boys looking a little disappointed that they couldn't be there.

Alasdair and Isobel sat on Erik's left, and Accalia and Bessetta sat to his right. He knew the two women would want to sit together, and he wanted to do everything he could to show he supported her friendship with Bessetta. Accalia had shown a keen interest in being friends with Isobel, for which he was glad.

Alasdair leaned over and inquired of Erik, "How is Accalia getting along with your sons? I feared when you found a mate, she might not be content with the situation. But it seems they have a genuine affection for her."

"She's fantastic with the boys. I couldn't have chosen anyone better to bond with them."

"Except that they join you in bed at night."

Erik laughed. He knew that would come back to bite him. "Only because of the bad storm we had last night."

"Understandable after what had happened when they were playing in the stable and lightning struck it and set it on fire. Even for us, we had a time calming the horses last eve during the storm before we reached Whitehaven Castle," Alasdair said.

"I had wished you hadna been out in it."

"I had wished the lasses hadna had to go through it. So about the sleeping arrangements tonight..."

"Bessetta will have Accalia's bedchamber. You and Isobel will have your own. Your brothers can bunk with mine."

"And Accalia?" Alasdair asked with a smirk.

"If it were up to me, she would be asleep in my bed—without the hindrance of my sons. But if it is up to her, there is no telling."

"What seems to be the difficulty? She seems interested in you and if she is as good with your sons as you say she is, then mate her already. I wouldna hold back."

"She said you and your brothers plagued her and your sister when you were younger," Erik said, changing the topic.

Alasdair laughed. "Aye, you wouldna believe the shenanigans the two of them pulled. They were no' the innocents."

"Oh?" Now that was a surprise to Erik. He thought the brothers had been the mischief makers entirely. He was amused.

"Aye, when we went swimming at the loch, they would steal our clothes off the bank. We never even saw them, but we smelled their scents and of course we would vow payback."

"So they initiated the mischief?"

"Sometimes. Sometimes we did. Those were carefree times."

"From what I understood, they bested you any number of times." If Accalia had been honest with him and he knew she had been.

Alasdair smiled. "Aye, they did. Why? Has she done so to you?"

Aye, but not that Erik wanted to share with his friend. Still, he gave his position away when Alasdair caught him smiling.

"Well, she is a bonny lass, skilled at organizing the staff back home, and I dinna know how her da will manage without her. If she is good with your boys and you care for her, she would make a good mate and be good for your people," Alasdair said.

Erik knew that already.

Then the ale was served with bread, venison, and chunks of cheese. Before Erik could eat a slice of his bread, Accalia snatched it from his plate. Bessetta laughed.

Alasdair had thankfully missed the action while eating his food, but Isobel had caught a glimpse and laughed too. But this time Cook was prepared and brought Erik two more slices of bread.

That's when Alasdair took notice. Erik realized so did lots of his kinsmen.

"A playful mate is a treasure to have." Alasdair squeezed Isobel's hand, leaned down, and kissed her.

Erik completely agreed with Alasdair. Accalia had made a significant, positive impact on his life.

ACCALIA WOULDN'T PRETEND to be serious at the meal just because they had guests, especially when she wouldn't have any pretenses in front of Alasdair and his kin. And she wanted to show Erik she would be her usual fun-loving self with him. She loved how he smiled at her, showing he was amused and not embarrassed by her actions. She swore he was anticipating she would do that very thing.

"You are predictable"—he leaned over and kissed her cheek—"until you are no'. And I love you the way you are."

She was so surprised when Erik professed his love to her, though she knew he was being sincere. She sighed and finished his slice of bread. "If we were to mate, how would your sons feel about it?"

His jaw dropped. Then he smiled.

"They already adore you. I've never seen them so well-behaved since they lost their mother. Even Thorfinn, the most stubborn of the lads, is thoroughly in your court. If you were to leave us and return home to your da, they would want to leave with you."

Her eyes sparkled with tears.

"I propose we travel to your home with the boys and wed. I love you and no other she-wolf will do. What say you, Accalia? Can you live with a wolf like me and love me like I know you do the boys?"

Erik looked so hopeful she would say yes.

"Are you trying to get me in your bed tonight?"

He smiled. "Only if you wish it."

"We will see." She was considering it when he confessed his love to her.

But she still didn't want to sound too eager until she'd had a chance to speak to the boys about their da and her and how they would feel about it. She wouldn't ignore how she wanted to be with Erik in a mated way, but she wanted the boys to know she cared about their feelings.

"'Tis an aye," he said, smiling down at her.

She loved how self-assured he was and felt he was right this time. "What is planned for after the meal?"

"Practice sword fighting," he said. "Alasdair and his brothers always spar with us when they visit. 'Tis a good way to learn our strengths and weaknesses against others in a different pack when normally we only practice with those in our pack."

"True. Then Bessetta and Isobel and I can practice."

Erik looked a little surprised.

"I believe Isobel is a warrior at heart. I'm sure Bessetta and I will learn some good fighting techniques from her," Accalia said, "right, Bessetta?"

"Oh, aye." Bessetta had been eating her meal in silence until now, but Accalia noticed she'd been leaning in her direction, attempting to overhear everything she and Erik had said.

Had Bessetta heard him profess his love to Accalia? Probably. He hadn't spoken for her ears only and she only realized the great hall was quiet compared to how it normally was. She glanced at the boys and saw them watching her with elevated interest.

Erik leaned over to speak with Alasdair and Isobel about the sword practice while Bessetta said to Accalia, "You didna profess your undying love to *him*."

"I wish to speak to Erik's sons first."

"Aye, I see your point. You would be a good mother to them."

"I'm surprised Erik didna mate you," Accalia said.

"Me? Nay. He is like a brother to me. We dinna have the wolfish need to mate and procreate with one another. I've seen the boys misbehaving at the meal before and knew they were a holy terror at bedtime. But they are so well-behaved and I dinna believe it had to do with Erik or they wouldna have misbehaved before. And clean? They are spotless."

Accalia smiled. "I didna believe in miracles before I started to lay down the law."

"Better you than me. I wouldna have known where to begin."

"Threatening to send them to the dungeon helped."

Bessetta laughed. "You never cease to amaze me. I wouldna have thought of that."

After the meal, everyone dispersed from the great hall to do chores, or to walk out to the inner bailey to begin sparring with their guests. The lads went with them too, the wolfhounds following them out.

Accalia didn't want the boys to feel left out but wanted to learn pointers from Isobel since she was an Icelander and had trained differently than her people. She and Bessetta took her aside while the men were getting ready to spar with each other.

"Would you teach us some of your swordsmanship?" Accalia asked.

Isobel smiled brightly. "I will be happy to."

"I...hate to ask, but can we practice some with Erik's lads? I dinna want to leave them out," Accalia said.

Isobel smiled at Bessetta, and she shared the same expression with her. "I will be honored, as long as they dinna feel fighting a woman isna as satisfying as fighting with the men."

"They couldna wait to beat me," Accalia said.

Isobel raised her brows.

"Aye and use the bow as well."

"We can do that too while we're here. So the question on everyone's mind is are you going to mate the wolf?" Isobel asked.

Accalia liked that she was upfront about it. "I want to speak with the boys about it first."

Isobel nodded sagely. "You have already won them over. They will love that you consider their feelings. I hope that when I am with child—or in our case bairns—I will be as good with my own as you are with Erik's sons. They will be devoted to you always."

"You will be successful with your own." Accalia was sure of it because she had taken her family to safety against untold danger through stormy seas and with the threat of their new chief having them eliminated once he had killed the rest of her family. "I will tell the boys you will teach us all your amazing warrior skills."

Then she hurried off to speak to the boys standing with a couple of nannies, looking mutinous, like everyone believed they were too young to participate in the exercise.

As soon as she headed for the boys, their expressions brightened, bordering on hopeful that she would spend time with them. "Go get your wooden swords and shields and spare wooden swords for three."

Their eyes grew wide.

"A well-trained warrior woman will show you her special fighting skills. You should be honored. I am. And Bessetta will fight. Go, hurry. We are eager to show the men how impressive we are."

The boys didn't wait a second longer and raced off.

"See, that's what I mean," Isobel said. "I have never seen Erik's boys so eager to do anything the two times I've met them. When you talk with them, they listen. I can take some lessons from you on child-rearing."

Accalia didn't believe it, but she loved Isobel's praise. Maybe her da knew her better than she'd known herself.

The boys raced back outside with swords and shields and passed around the swords to each of the ladies then, still trying to catch their breaths, they waited to see what Accalia would say.

"All right, since Isobel is an expert on a different kind of swordsmanship, we'll let her show us some of the movements." Accalia swept her arm at her, giving her the go-ahead.

Isobel began to show them some of her sweeping sword movements, demonstrating her fancy footwork, illustrating how to use her shield to protect herself, and even how to use it as a weapon.

The boys and Accalia were impressed. Even Bessetta was watching with keen interest. Accalia wondered if anyone had asked Isobel to teach them to fight in her way.

Then Isobel took on Thorfinn and Bessetta fought against Hendrie. Accalia fought against Johnne while the men were having a splendid time showing off their skills and muscles, looking like they were in battle, not just sparring for practice.

At some point, the bailey grew quiet, and Accalia realized quite a few men had ceased fighting while they watched the women and the boys. She was glad the boys had been eager to fight with the women.

When the boys were tired of fighting, Accalia playfought against Isobel. She was much harder on Accalia than Thorfinn, naturally. But Accalia was glad for the challenge. Accalia was holding her own—barely—because she hadn't been trained as a warrior woman from a very young age, but rather to run a household.

The weapons training she'd had was rudimentary at best. Her da had wanted her skilled with using the *sgian dubh* to protect herself, and to a lesser degree—a short sword. Archery had been more her idea, and she had loved practicing at it. But fighting against Isobel's sound thrusts and decisive slashes, Accalia felt she was barely holding her own.

She wasn't one to give up though and stubbornly faced the challenges head on. She could tell Isobel respected her for it as she gave her small smiles whenever Accalia looked like she was faltering but came back with renewed energy and even forced Isobel back a few times.

Isobel wasn't about to give in and took the offensive, forcing Accalia back even more steps than she'd gained. At one point, Isobel struck Accalia with her shield in a frontal assault, catching her off-guard, and Accalia fell back on her arse.

Pronounced gasps rent the air as Isobel looked a wee bit worried that she had gone too far with her practice. Beathag laughed out loud though. Accalia ignored her.

Thorfinn and then his brothers raced to help Accalia. Before they reached her, Accalia was back on her feet, smiling at Isobel.

"You are as good a warrior as I thought you would be. Thanks be to thee for showing me some of your skills. I would love for you to show me more later." Accalia knew when it was time to quit. She was so worn out, she wouldn't make a good showing from now on, she figured.

"Thank you. I didna mean to knock you down with such force."

"I was getting tired, but I hope to give a better presentation next time."

"You did an excellent practice fight with me when you havena been trained in the art of war since you were little like I had been."

"Thanks for telling me that. Would you like to go fishing as wolves?" Accalia thought of fishing at the shallower creek she had seen on her wolf run with Erik.

"Aye!" Thorfinn and his brothers said. "In the loch from the boats."

"As wolves?" Isobel asked, sounding surprised.

"Aye," Accalia said, glad the boys wanted to try it again. "We can have the fish for the nooning meal." She glanced at Erik, who nodded at her, smiling.

He would have to have a guard detail for them, but what she didn't expect was that Alasdair and his brothers were eager to try such a thing, and before long, boats were rowed out across the loch, and a person would stay with each boat, while the others stripped and shifted and jumped into the loch.

Even though Accalia had thought to go with the women, Isobel and Bessetta went with Alasdair and his brothers. Erik, his sons, Accalia, and Logan went together in another boat, while a mix of wolves from both packs accompanied them in other boats.

She considered asking the boys what they thought about her and Erik mating while they rowed out across the loch, but she wanted to speak to them alone. She was worried they might feel intimidated by their da if he was present while she spoke to them.

"About tonight," Erik said to his boys, "you will sleep with your nannies."

They watched him, not saying a word.

Thorfinn said, "Aye."

"You fought well against Isobel," Erik told Thorfinn. "She has bested male wolves twice her size."

Accalia hadn't known that and realized then that Isobel had to have been holding back when she fought her.

"Truly?" Thorfinn asked.

"Aye. Did you learn anything from her?" Erik asked, dipping the oars into the water and pulling the water behind them.

"Aye, that her shield is a weapon. I never saw anyone use it to knock someone down," Thorfinn said, sounding much impressed.

"I was proud of you boys for going to Accalia's aid."

Accalia was too. "I appreciated it too. I was getting tired but even so, she would have been able to knock me down because I wasn't prepared for it. But in a fight like that, you must get back up and defend yourself, not give up or you've lost the battle."

"Aye, Accalia is right," Erik said, then paused and cleared his throat. "She wishes to join me in bed tonight. How do you feel about that?"

Erik did *not* just say that!

"Will you be our mother?" Hendrie asked, sounding hopeful.

Johnne waited to learn if it was true. Thorfinn was frowning and she wasn't sure he was ready for her to be his mother, if ever.

"I will speak with you boys alone about it first," she said, giving Erik a sharp look.

He looked a little guilty that he had brought it up instead of letting her handle it herself, but she assumed he thought she wouldn't do it soon enough for his liking.

The boys waited expectantly. Everyone else was already stripping, shifting, diving into the water, and fishing, their boats scattered across the loch while Erik, the boys, and she remained seated in the boat.

"All right, how do you feel about me staying with your da tonight?" she asked.

"Every night?" Thorfinn asked, wanting clarification. "Not just one night? It doesna count if 'tis just one night."

Erik smiled at her, putting her on the spot where he wanted her.

The other boys were silent, watching her, waiting for her answer.

What if they made love but not all the way and found they didn't suit? How could she agree that they would stay together forever if they weren't the right wolves for each other?

"Just the one night," she said, unwilling to make more of a concession than that and regretting it later.

"Aye!" Erik shouted, his voice carrying across the loch, wolves and those not in their wolf coats watching them.

The boys smiled and Hendrie asked, "Can we go fishing now?"

The notion of her being their mother or anything about mating their da all but forgotten. Fishing in their wolf coats was all that occupied their thoughts now.

"Aye," Erik said.

The boys stripped off their clothes and shifted, then leaped overboard.

Erik pulled Accalia into a hug and kissed her thoroughly. "You willna regret it."

She smiled. "I dinna fight as well as Isobel."

"I canna emphasize all your important qualities enough. I am the one who is sorely lacking in so many of your skills."

She laughed and kissed him back, loving how he always made her feel cherished, a far cry from when they had first traveled together to his castle.

They stripped off their clothes, shifted, and she leaped overboard, while he followed her and they were soon fishing to their heart's content, while Logan monitored the shore and them in case anyone had any trouble.

She was glad Erik had agreed to fishing as wolves, and that his sons could try again. It was important to show he trusted them as far as fishing from the boat. And in truth, all three boys caught a fish each this time, proving that practice did make a difference.

The whole idea was so novel for the other wolf pack too, that they were having a wonderful time. She was glad they were doing this. Maybe they could practice archery tomorrow. She was sure they could do a wolf run tonight, and that would be enough to do today.

She wasn't sure about taking the boys. They would all run with a larger force to protect them. And she still wanted to run with the boys and their da like a family like she had planned for a later excursion.

She hoped they wouldn't run into any trouble with Freigard and his men.

14

———

Once they'd caught enough fish for a grand feast for the nooning meal, everyone returned to the keep. Still, Erik was a little worried that Accalia was perturbed with him over talking to the boys about being with her when she wanted to do that herself without *his* interference.

Erik was over the moon when Accalia had agreed to stay with him. He had to prove to her that she would remain with him not only this eve but from then on moving forward. He meant it when he said he loved her. He'd never felt that way about another she-wolf after his mate had died and he had every intention of not losing Accalia. And he still wanted to take her to see the sunset when he could.

At the meal, his sons were excitedly talking to each other, and he was curious how they felt about Accalia staying with him tonight. Accalia had enjoyed fishing with him and the boys, but she was quiet at the meal now.

He reached over, took hold of her hand, and squeezed it, showing how he felt about her. Was she upset with him for not giving her a chance to talk to the boys beforehand about staying with him? He hoped his impatience hadn't ruined things between them.

"I'm sorry I spoke in front of the boys about you staying with me this eve before you had a chance to," he said.

"Nay, you are no'," she said matter-of-factly.

All right, she was correct. He hadn't been.

"'Tis all right though. I worried they would believe it was a mating between us and would be disappointed if it wasna. I didna want them to get their hopes up if it didna work out between us."

He was certain it *would* work out between them, but he understood her concern. "Aye, lass. I'm sorry. I want it so much, I wasna thinking."

She let out her breath then, and he was sure something else was on her mind. "Since my da seemed to have told you everything about me, did he tell you I was to be married, but the cad took off with one of my companions instead on our wedding day?"

Erik closed his gaping mouth and shook his head. "He didna mention it."

"That's why I didna have a maid with me when you came and stole me away."

He hadn't even considered that when he had seen her sitting upon her horse looking as regal as a queen.

"My da was afraid you would fall for the maid instead of me."

Erik scoffed. "The man is daft to give up such a treasure as you. No other lass would have stolen my attention like you have done."

She relaxed her shoulders a bit. "My da said it was my fault."

Erik shook his head. "He is wrong. If the wolf was so callous as to mate another lass when he pledged his love to you, he is the one to blame. Is that why you were worried about Beathag?"

"A little."

"I've never shown any interest in her."

She nodded and changed the subject then. "I had fun today,

both at the sparring competition and fishing. We could run as wolves this eve."

"Aye, we would have double our forces, and Alasdair and his people would love it."

"What about your sons? I promised them we would all run together the next time."

"As a family. Aye, we will do so."

Then she smiled. *Good.* She didn't seem too miffed with him for telling the boys that she would stay with him tonight before she'd had a chance to talk to them privately about it. And he noted she didn't correct him when he called them a family.

"After we return from the run and have our meal, I will speak to the boys alone," she said.

"Of course. If"—he let out his breath—"if they are unsettled about us staying together tonight, we can hold off." But it was killing him to suggest it.

She chuckled. "You are stuck with me in your bed tonight. And they would be disappointed if we went back on our word."

He smiled broadly. "Aye, as you say." He was sure glad for it.

After the meal, the ladies visited while the men discussed politics and other matters. Not that the women weren't interested in what the men were discussing, but they wanted to talk about different things for now. The wolfhounds had gone after the boys, and she wondered if they were playing with them.

"So, is Alasdair looking to find a mate for you, Bessetta?" Accalia assumed he would want her married off soon because of her age.

"We've been discussing possibilities, but nothing is written in stone," Bessetta said, "but Isobel has some noteworthy news."

Accalia glanced at her.

Isobel smiled. "Aye, I'm with child. I thought so a few days ago, but 'twas your midwife confirmed it after we went fishing."

"Oh, how wonderful. How many?" Accalia asked, surprised she

had practiced fighting when she carried bairns in her belly and glad she hadn't hurt Isobel during the practice.

"'Tis too early to say, though the midwife believes 'tis more than one as big as I'm growing so early on. Alasdair was having fits when he tried to help me into the boat and saw my expanding belly."

The ladies laughed.

"Can you run with us this eve?" Accalia believed so. They often ran as wolves until they were about to deliver. It seemed to make the delivery easier for them.

"Aye, up until the last week or so. It depends on the wolf. Some canna manage, some might move more slowly, but they continue to walk as a wolf until the end. Knowing Alasdair, he will watch me constantly until I have the babies."

"What about you?" Bessetta asked Accalia. "She's staying with Erik tonight," she told Isobel.

"Oooh," Isobel said, smiling.

"It will no' be a mating, just a way to see if we are...uhm, compatible."

Bessetta and Isobel shared smiles. "I dinna believe there is any chance you willna be 'compatible,' the way the two of you give off pheromones so hotly when you're around each other," Isobel said.

"I worry about the boys and how they feel," Accalia said.

"Believe me, they will be all for it," Isobel said. "You have proven to them how much you care about them, and they have shown how they feel about you. I was afraid when I knocked you down with my shield—which I hadna planned—they would have all three taken me to task."

The ladies laughed.

"Thorfinn first," Bessetta said. "He is the alpha of the brothers. The others waited until he went to Accalia's aid first."

"Aye," Isobel said.

"How do you feel about having bairns with Erik who will be half-siblings with the boys, Accalia?" Bessetta asked.

"I want them to know the bairns will be needy when they are first born and I will have to take care of them a lot when they are tiny, but I will love the boys just as much. If Erik and I have bairns together, they will not replace my affection for the lads. I must ensure they know that I have enough love to go around," she said. "But I doubt they will believe it until I prove to them it is so. And that willna happen unless I mate their da and we have bairns of our own."

"Aye," Isobel said.

"Did either of you ever meet Erik's previous mate?" Accalia couldn't help being curious about the woman, even though Etta had told her what she knew about Willa. But had her friends seen what she was like?

"No' me," Isobel said. "She had died before I met Erik."

Accalia and Isobel looked at Bessetta. She smoothed her gown on her lap, her eyes cast downward as if she was trying to figure out what to say that wouldn't be too inappropriate.

"You are among friends," Accalia said. "And we have known each other since we were wee lasses. Tell me the truth."

"She wasna like you," Bessetta said, "and I mean that in the best way possible. I asked some of the maids, like Etta, but I didna have to. I saw the way she was. She wasna nice to the staff, making the servants redo her bathwater because it wasna hot enough, or cool enough. She treated them like they were beneath her when she should have treated them like her kin, her packmates, and cherished what they were doing for her. Like you do. Just like any of us do."

"Aye," both Isobel and Accalia agreed.

"Erik had to have me make peace with the staff secretly because they were ready to quit. Anyway, she was as bad about the boys. She never ran with them as wolves. They had nannies to do that with them, but of course, she wouldna let them because then they would be having fun. Yet she didna have the boys do chores. She was"—Bessetta shrugged—"all over the place when disciplining them or showing affection. But with Erik? That was a whole other story. I swear she bewitched him with her overly sexy moves whenever he was with his staff, at the head table—"

"Insincere?" Accalia asked.

"We felt that she was. Etta said she thought he was in love with her, but then she became pregnant with the triplets and that was the end of her ability to be the center of attention. Instead—"

"Erik's sons were," Accalia guessed.

Isobel nodded. "And the whole pack would have doted on them."

"Aye," Accalia and Bessetta said.

"Worse, when so many people in the clan became sick and twelve died, including his wife, no one mourned her. The boys didna even cry. Why should they? She had never been affectionate to them. When I saw them and she was with Erik, she wouldna allow them to approach him."

"I dinna understand it," Accalia said.

"Me either," Isobel agreed.

"I didna know why he wouldna have said something about it but I'm sure it was because she held so much sway over him. You are the perfect wife for him and mother to his sons." Bessetta smiled with tears in her eyes. "They deserve what you can offer."

"Thanks, Bessetta, for telling me. Erik has never said anything about her, but I suspect it's because he doesna want to sully her name."

"Aye, though maybe he will tell you how much he loves you for being you and not being anything like her. Um, have you had trouble with Beathag?" Bessetta asked. "I believe everyone was shocked when Isobel knocked you down with her shield and she laughed."

Accalia nodded. "I've had some trouble with her. I think she realizes she's no' chasing me off."

"She would be crazy to believe she has a chance with Erik," Bessetta said. "I only mentioned it because I've seen how she has tried to intrigue Erik when he has never shown interest in her. Even if he doesna want to mate you, he wouldna mate her."

"I have told her that." Accalia didn't go into any details about how she showed her that either. She suspected the nannies and the lads, who had witnessed the wolf fight between her and Beathag, might have shared the news with others in the pack.

Isobel and Bessetta smiled.

"As to this matter with Freigard, what is his problem? How can he want you for his mate, but not want an alliance with your da? Is he mad?" Isobel asked.

"He believes he will make me his mate and take over my pack. He willna wish my da or uncle to be in command, but instead, replace them with someone of his choosing. Whoever goes along with his new rule will remain with the pack. Anyone who doesna, will be eliminated."

"He willna be successful. Alasdair told me Erik had had trouble with him on his lands. Alasdair vowed our fighting force to battle any of Freigard's brigands while we are here," Isobel said.

"We appreciate it." Accalia wondered if Alasdair would want Isobel fighting now that he had learned she was carrying their bairns. Most likely not and she wouldn't blame him.

"Are we taking the boys with us on the wolf run?" Isobel asked.

"Aye. 'Tis important for them to feel they can do this with their da. The last time, archers attacked us, so they need to prove they have what it takes to run with us."

"I so agree," Bessetta said.

"Ja, that's the way of our life and the best way to prepare for it is to prove ourselves worthy," Isobel said.

Accalia could only imagine the hardships that Isobel had gone through while growing up. Accalia had to admit she was torn between wanting a lovely wolf run with the two packs and the boys feeling perfectly secure, *and* the chance to take down more of Freigard's men should they try to fight them further.

But before she went on the run with the other wolves, she went to speak with the boys in private.

Their room was as neat as when she had first moved everything out of the chamber and the boys hadn't once complained about wanting their things back. She suspected she had kept them so busy that they were worn out when they returned to their chamber at night, retired to their beds, and playing with toys didn't cross their minds. She figured it was time to return their toys to the room.

She wasn't sure what they had been doing while she had visited with the ladies, but as soon as she walked into the room, she dismissed the nannies so they could take a break, and the boys ran to give her hugs.

"We fed all the horses," Hendrie proudly said, looking up at her, his eyes bright with pride.

"And cleaned out their stalls," Johnne said, wrinkling his nose.

"And walked them too," Thorfinn said, all eager to tell her how they were sharing in doing chores at the castle, waiting for her praise.

"My, you have been busy." She didn't want to praise them for a job they would normally do without any thought of praise, but she couldn't help herself and hugged them. "Well done." They beamed with joy. "You are coming on a run with us as wolves tonight."

"Aye!" the boys shouted.

"Your da and the other pack wolves and your own will run together. Should we have any trouble with any brigands—"

"We willna cower and whimper," Thorfinn said.

"You will stay with the ladies and me, and we'll all get low to the ground to protect ourselves. As wolves, we canna attack the arrows, if they fight that way again. And if they are on horseback, we stay low, away from the sweeps of their swords." She would leap up to unseat a rider, but she didn't want the boys doing that. They were too little. "I want to speak about tonight."

"You mean when you sleep with Da?" Thorfinn asked.

"Aye. You do understand about a mating, right?"

They waited to hear what she had to say about it. As soon as she mentioned it, she realized she had bitten off more than she could chew. She had thought they knew all about it!

"All right, well, wolves mate for life. Your da and I are going to sleep together, but we're no' going to mate. No' tonight."

"He will kiss her for sure," Thorfinn said to his brothers.

"Aye," they both said.

"But you will be our mother?" Hendrie asked, his voice hopeful.

"We will see."

"He better want you to be our mother," Thorfinn said, sounding angry, as if he would have to persuade his da if he wasn't already convinced.

Their da wasn't the holdout. Accalia was, but she didn't know how to explain it. "I believe with all my heart that it will all work out." But she was beyond pleased that Thorfinn and his brothers wanted her to be their mother and tried to hide the sudden tears glistening in her eyes.

"Aye, we knew it would," Thorfinn said, assuredly, his brothers agreeing. "Did Da get mad at Beathag or you for the wolf fight outside our chamber?"

"Your da was mad at Beathag. She had no business attacking me first. All right, well, let's go for a wolf run, shall we?" she asked.

They immediately began to strip off their clothes.

"I'll meet you downstairs." This had been a fun day for them all. She hoped tonight wouldn't be filled with danger.

15

Hoping they had no trouble from Freigard's men, Erik realized how much he loved running with Accalia and his sons tonight with Alasdair and his pack. He was glad to show others that he had someone to care about again, whom he wanted to mate.

He hadn't realized how much Alasdair's mating Isobel had affected him. But now he could see that he'd longed for what Alasdair had in a mate. Erik thought it wouldn't have mattered if he had found another because he'd loved his first mate, though not many people had seen her like that.

Accalia's inner beauty radiated just as brightly as her physical appearance, setting her apart from his previous mate. She had a natural ease with his sons and everyone else she met. He would have had difficulty connecting with her if she hadn't treated his sons with kindness, respect, and affection.

He was glad Alasdair and Isobel were having their bairns in a few months.

The boys were playing with each other at first, tackling each other, play-biting, and then running to catch up with Erik and

Accalia. They had so much energy, but he was sure they would wear themselves out before long.

Alasdair was running with Isobel near them, and he glanced at Erik and Accalia and smiled, knowing Erik was in heaven now that he had Accalia in his life. He had noticed that Hans and Rory had been careful not to tease Accalia and he suspected they realized Erik was now serving as her protector and they would get hell for it.

The boys were trying their darndest to keep up with the longer-legged wolves, but they were now falling behind. Immediately, Accalia slowed down to accommodate them, and Erik did too. She was always anxious about them, and he adored her for it. She always acted like a concerned momma wolf.

Although he wanted to keep her in his bed tonight, he wanted her to be there because she wanted to be with him as desperately as he wanted to be with her. She licked his face and then nuzzled each of the boys' faces and they licked hers back, looking thrilled that she wasn't going to leave them behind.

Others would have watched them, wolves guarding the mix of members from both packs. But Accalia was the one who made all the difference to them. Their tails lifted, their spirits raised, the boys were thrilled when she paid attention to them.

Then she licked Erik's face telling him she loved him too. He wagged his tail, his sons watching their interaction, eager to see them together like that.

They ran all over the territory, but then the boys were no longer loping or running, but walking, taking deep breaths, tongues lolling out, showing how worn out they were. They would sleep well tonight.

Erik howled for everyone to return to the keep, and they all headed that way, the guards still riding on horses or running as wolves on either side of the families, leading the way, or following behind them. Erik had noticed that Isobel had slowed down a little and appeared to have been glad the boys were running at more of a reduced speed so they had to slow down on the run.

When they reached the outer bailey, he was glad they hadn't encountered any trouble with any brigands. Then they went into the inner bailey and those who needed to enter the keep, while others went off to the barracks.

Again, Erik hoped that Accalia didn't change her mind about staying with him. Bessetta and she ran off together toward her chamber and he was afraid she might have. The boys stood with him, looking disheartened.

Erik urged them to their chamber and shifted. "Dress and get ready for bed. I'll return." Then he shifted and hurried out of the chamber, intent on dressing and returning to the boys' chamber before Accalia did so that they both could wish the boys a good night. He hoped she would join him while showing the boys he was staying with her.

He reached his chamber, shifted, dressed, and headed to the boys' chamber. Both Bessetta and Accalia were there, and he feared that he had been thwarted.

But Thorfinn said to Bessetta, "Accalia is staying with Da tonight."

Hendrie agreed. "But if you get scared by anything while you're in your chamber alone, you can come and see us, and we'll take care of you."

"Aye," Johnne said. "We'll protect you."

Bessetta smiled at the boys and hugged Accalia. "I'll handle everything here. The two of you have a good night."

Accalia's cheeks blushed beautifully, and she leaned down and hugged and kissed the boys. "You behave yourselves and dinna give Bessetta any trouble. I'm the only one who is allowed to."

They all laughed. Erik was smiling. He couldn't help it. Accalia was coming to his bed tonight. Then he hugged his sons, something he'd been neglectful in doing because he'd felt they didn't need him anymore. But they hugged him back as much as they had hugged Accalia, and he knew they still needed his affection.

Then he took hold of Accalia's hand, walked her out of the chamber, and headed to his own, feeling like he'd climbed the highest mountain ever. "You dinna feel pressured that I want you in my bed this eve, do you?"

"I was going to come whether you were ready for me or no'."

He looked down at her, not believing her.

"Aye, you didna think I could hold off much longer, did you?"

He swept her into his arms and hurried to his chamber a few feet away.

She laughed. "'Tis no' a mating, mind you."

He would make her want a mating, he hoped. "Aye. You let me know how far you want to go."

"I will. It was fun running with the boys and Alasdair and Isobel's pack."

"Aye." He carried Accalia into his chamber and set her on her feet, though he wanted to dump her on his bed and ravage her. He shut the door after them.

"I believe Isobel was getting a little tired." She unbuckled his belt and pulled away his great kilt.

"Aye. I think she was glad that the boys were wearing out." He removed her belt and shawl.

Then they were wearing only their long shirt-like léines, and he could see her breasts through the thin material. He cupped her breasts with his hands and breathed in her heavenly scent of the pines and meadow flowers. "You are beautiful."

"As are you, Erik."

"In your wolf coat or without." He was still worried his paler wolf coat might not appeal to her.

"Bessetta's coat is light, but I had never seen so many white wolves. Yours is very distinguished with your gray highlights. Your sons have the same beautiful markings."

"So that means you are ready to mate me, aye?" He smiled his most winning smile, he thought, though he suspected it might look a little wolfish.

She smiled back. "Only time will tell."

Not the words he wanted to hear but he believed she was still considering a mating and maybe wouldn't take too long to decide. Though he hoped she would decide to do so before his friends left.

She climbed onto his bed wearing her léine when he had hoped she would strip naked, but if she wasn't ready to be with him in that way, he would accommodate her. To an extent. Except when the boys slept with them, he wore his long shirt, but never did otherwise. He pulled off his shirt and she smiled at him. So far so good. She didn't seem upset with him for getting naked.

He climbed on the other side of the bed and moved in her direction. He had no plans to sleep with her.

She moved toward him—aye!—indicating she was of like mind.

Then they were close, him kissing her mouth, her kissing him back, closed mouth at first, then open-mouthed, tongues teasing and caressing each other's, just what he had in mind. His hand roamed over her hip, her léine sliding with his touch. She cupped his face and looked into his eyes.

"You have the most beautiful sea-blue eyes. They are entrancing," she said, her voice seductive.

"Your forest-green eyes are just as beautiful." He kissed her again, but this time, he moved his hand to her breast and squeezed the soft mound gently with his hand. Then he moved his head down to lick her nipple through her léine, feeling the nipple protrude against the light fabric. She shivered and he smelled her pheromones kick up a notch, which only enticed him all the more.

"Your sons realize this isna a mating," she whispered against his head.

"They would be happiest if they learned it was." He returned his lips to hers and reached down to hike up her léine around her hips. He wouldn't remove it if she felt uneasy about it, but he wanted to pleasure her if she was willing.

She stilled, but then began kissing his mouth as if his pulling up her gown was all right with her.

He slipped his hand between her legs and at first, she wouldn't give him access, as if she concerned that he did intend to mate her, but she wasn't ready for it.

"Can you part your legs for me? I only intend to pleasure you with my fingers."

Then she tentatively moved onto her back and spread her legs, just a wee bit. He smiled down at her, hoping she would love this between them and not be timid always. Then he plied his skill with his fingers, finding the bud among her dewy curls, smelling her scent that told him she was so wet and ready for him if she had wanted a mating.

He stroked her, listening to their heartbeats thundering, their pheromones racing in circles, and she was barely breathing. "Breathe," he said, and kissed her mouth, continuing to stroke her, inserting a finger into her wetness and she cried out with surprise and glee—he thought.

Once she had come, he rubbed his full erection against her thigh, cupping a breast, molding his hand to it, and continued to kiss her for all it was worth.

"That...that was amazing. What...what about you?" she asked.

He wanted to suggest a mating, but he suspected she would have said so if that was the case. "I will be fine"—suffer gravely, he wanted to say but it didn't sound heroic—"until you decide if you want a mating."

"Is there...some other way I can help you out...to...relieve the pressure?"

"I wouldna presume to ask a lady to..." He couldn't even think of a way to say it without sounding crude.

"If you could show me what to do, mayhap I could help?"

"If you are sure…"

"Aye." She sounded so sincere.

He hoped she wouldn't regret offering and kissed her then and moved her hand down to his staff, his hand over hers, making a fist around his erection. Then he slid her hand up and down until she felt comfortable doing it herself. While she was, he was running his hand through her silky hair, kissing her delicious mouth, and mesmerized by her skillful strokes as if she had been doing this all her life. She was a quick learner.

He stopped kissing her when he was about to come and she took over then, tonguing him, her eyes filled with lust just as much as his probably were. She was taking him to the top, still kissing his mouth with tenderness and passion combined, and then he came, and she watched, smiling, looking a little incredulous. He was glad now that she had seen him come, that she hadn't been embarrassed, but fascinated.

"I'll be right back." He left the bed to clean up, then returned to her and pulled her into his arms, her léine still hiked up above her hips, their naked legs intertwined, and she seemed content to sleep with him in that way. Though he was glad they had pleasured each other, and she had become more comfortable with being intimate with him, he hoped it wouldn't be too long before she wanted to mate him and make their relationship permanent for all time.

Then, though he didn't want to sleep, but to breathe her in and listen to her heart beating and her soft exhales of breath, he fell asleep with the she-wolf of his dreams cradled in his arms for the rest of the night, until the morning came, and he had the greatest fear of losing her.

ACCALIA LOVED everything about last night and if Erik hadn't given her another way to bring him pleasure, she would have gone ahead and mated him, knowing he would suffer overly much otherwise. But she was glad he had been willing to show her another way and she believed he was the only one for her.

She hadn't expected to feel embarrassed about seeing his people this morn when they broke their fast, but now she was anxious. She thought she would feel like she did any other day, but she knew everyone would be looking at them in a way that said they wondered if they had gone ahead and mated, maybe even hoped that would be the case.

Except for Beathag. She was casting her a chilling glower.

Accalia felt bad that she hadn't agreed when Erik wanted it. And she realized she was making it hard on the boys when that wasn't her intention. Besides, after the way Erik had pleasured her, she didn't want to give him up for anything.

She would tell him they might mate tonight, but then there was a tentative knock on the door, and she hurried out of bed to dress. Erik was out of bed, threw on his long shirt, and answered the door. Thorfinn was at the door, his brothers standing a way off as if they were afraid their da would be mad at them if they intruded on their da and Accalia's privacy.

"Cook said the meal is ready and everyone's waiting on you. Uncle Logan sent us to tell you."

"We are headed down."

"Can we wait for you?" Thorfinn asked.

Erik let his breath out. "Aye." Then he closed the door and finished dressing.

Accalia smiled. "Was your brother afraid to wake you because I was with you?"

"Aye." Erik smiled. "That is a first though." He fastened her belt, and she sheathed her sword and slipped her *sgian dubh* into her boot.

Once they were dressed, they walked out of the chamber and found the boys waiting for them in the hallway. Thorfinn looked hopefully at Accalia, and she rubbed his head, smiled at him, and hugged the boys. She wasn't going to tell them she was staying again with their da tonight at this point. She planned to but she couldn't until she spoke to Erik first. Tonight, she was certain.

But she did take Erik's hand. The boys smiled to see it. They all headed to the stairs and arrived at the great hall where everyone waited for them. Och, Accalia was more than a little uncomfortable. Then she hugged the boys at their seats and she and Erik sat at the head table.

The meal was being served—eggs, bread, fish, and ale—and Bessetta leaned over and smiled at Accalia. "I spoke with the lads until they fell asleep, which wasn't long considering all the activities they'd taken part in. They were so hopeful you would mate their da."

"Oh, I agree. I'm glad you dinna have any trouble with them," Accalia said, though she figured it wouldn't be long and Bessetta would ask how the night had gone with Erik.

Bessetta cleared her throat and raised her brow, waiting to hear what had happened.

Accalia laughed. "'Twas exceptionally nice."

"Do tell."

Accalia hugged her friend. Some things were not meant to be talked about. Not even though they were best of friends and were in a private chamber. When Bessetta found the wolf for her, she would learn what it was all about—if the wolf was as braw and caring as Erik was.

"No mating?" Bessetta whispered.

Accalia smiled. "No' because of Erik, mind you."

"How long are you going to hold off?"

Accalia glanced at Erik. He was speaking with Alasdair about having archery practice after they ate. Then she turned back to Bessetta. "No' long."

"This eve?" Bessetta asked, her brows raised, smiling impishly.

Accalia chuckled and shook her head. Not to say no, but because she was so amused with her friend for being so curious. Though she probably would be the same way with Bessetta if the roles were reversed.

"This eve, then," Bessetta said, sure of it.

"We are practicing archery. Will you do it?" Accalia asked, changing the subject.

"Aye, of course. You know me. I will participate in anything. And I have been practicing back home. Isobel is as good at archery as she is at swordsmanship. Though I wouldna have wanted her hard life, I wish I had trained more since I was little like she had to prepare myself in case of a fight. But now with her carrying the bairns, I doubt she will be sharing much more of her skills with us," Bessetta said.

"Aye. Her time will be spent preparing for the baby...well, babies. I'm so happy for her and for Alasdair. I know they are overjoyed. And I know you are too."

"Oh, aye. I canna wait to hold the wee ones in my arms and play with them when they are pups."

"I will come and visit when the time comes." Accalia couldn't wait.

"You and I can share a room like old—uhm, oh, by then, things will be perfectly different."

Accalia smiled. For certain, she thought, if Erik didn't change *his* mind.

fter Accalia had finished talking to Bessetta, she began eating more fish stew and Erik turned to speak with her. "Archery competition between the packs is next on the agenda. Are you game?"

"Aye. And the lads?" Accalia asked.

"Certes. And tonight?"

She smiled. "I'll stay with you. 'Twas a pleasant eve we had."

He smiled. "Aye, I will do everything to ensure it is as enjoyable as last eve."

"Oh, aye, you had better, and I will do the same for you."

If he could make her happy, he would be pleased.

They finished breaking their fast and then Erik's people went off to do their work while Erik, Accalia, and the boys went out to practice archery with the others.

Isobel showed the ladies and the boys how to use the bow this time while the men were shooting at other targets, trying to beat each other. Erik loved the competition but enjoyed seeing Accalia and his boys working hard to improve their archery skills.

Isobel loved teaching them and she was helping them to do better. He was glad she wasn't so far along in her pregnancy, that she could still show off her skills. He knew Isobel loved that she could. The boys were enjoying learning more too.

After that, they all ate the nooning meal. Then they planned to take the boys as wolves to a creek to fish and everyone had fun doing that. While Erik was ensuring they had a proper guard escort, with some men from Alasdair's pack offering to guard the families, Accalia had slipped away to strip off her clothes, shift, and ensure the boys were ready to go. Even the wolfhounds were joining them this time.

Erik had missed the opportunity to be alone with her in his chamber until after the evening meal.

When they reached the stream, the boys pounced on several fish but often lost them. Even so, they caught more than they did while fishing in the loch. Swimming, diving, and trying to catch fish in the loch had been a lot more strenuous.

But now they were struggling to keep hold of the fish they had pounced on, the slippery-scaled trout getting away. Accalia, Bessetta, and Isobel watched the boys in their wolf coats, appearing amused.

The dogs were splashing in the stream, playing with each other, scaring some fish a little way off.

Erik continued to help the boys catch the fish, enjoying showing them how to do it. Everyone participating caught enough for their pack and the visiting one for the evening meal. He was glad he had taken the time to work with his sons. They were so determined to catch the most fish.

He glanced at Accalia and saw her standing with Bessetta and Isobel on the rocky shore, smiling at him and the boys as wolves would. He smiled back at Accalia, figuring he had impressed her while working with his sons on this fishing excursion, and showing he could be patient with them for once. For the first time, he realized he had never worked so hard to impress a she-wolf as he wanted to with Accalia.

Once they had enough fish in the baskets carried on the horses' saddles, they all gathered to return to the castle.

Erik ran with Accalia and his sons with the others, while she nipped at his neck and then tackled the boys each in turn. Which made the trip back take quite a bit longer, but everyone seemed to enjoy watching the five of them in wolf play. Even Erik had played with Accalia and the boys, careful not to be too rough.

They reached the outer bailey, and the portcullis and double gates were shut for the night. Inside the keep, Cook hurried to prepare the fish for the evening meal while everyone who had gone fishing as wolves retired to shift and dress, then join each other downstairs. Again, Erik missed being alone with Accalia when Logan took him aside to discuss work on some of the fortifications that needed to be done.

When he managed to shift and dress, he found that Accalia and the boys had already left their chamber, and he met them in the great hall. "Fantastic catches," he told the boys before he led Accalia to the high table. "At your age, I didna catch half as many fish."

They glowed with pride and Accalia smiled at him as if she thought the world of him for praising his sons. He realized he didn't do that often with them and he would be better at it in the future. Especially when he saw how happy the boys and Accalia were that he had done so.

Then he ruffled the boys' hair, took Accalia's hand, and led her to the head table.

"About this eve," Erik said to Accalia.

She glanced at him and gave him the most mischievous smile. "Aye?"

"You still plan to sleep with me, aye?"

"I willna have it any other way. You already told me that you would make it worth my while. Just as I said I would do the same for you."

"Aye." He couldn't be gladder for it.

"You did well with the boys while teaching them how to fish."

"They needed more practice."

"Aye, and they loved proving how good they could be. Did you know they worked hard in the stables—cleaning it out, feeding the horses, and exercising them?"

"Aye, they have you to thank for that. Everyone has seen how helpful they are and willing to have the boys do various tasks to make them better men someday."

"If we mate and marry, what will I wear?" Accalia asked as Cook set fish soup out for them.

Cook gasped but then smiled. "Etta has made a gown for you since *he* didna allow you the time to prepare for this." She emphasized that the "he" was Erik, the brute.

Erik hadn't thought that far in advance. But then he realized what Accalia was saying. She meant to mate him and wanted a wedding. He smiled and took her hand and kissed it. "You will make the most beautiful bride."

She smiled. "Thank you. We must have two wedding ceremonies. My da and my kin will want to celebrate this mating and marriage."

Even though wolves didn't need them to profess their love to each other by having a wedding, for outsiders, it was important to show they were together for other reasons. And he would sign an agreement with her da that he and her da had an alliance through marriage.

"Aye, of course."

"I already have a wedding gown back home."

He felt remorseful because he took her away from her home without staying there to learn if they suited each other and then married her. But he couldn't have. Not when he had to know if she would be a good mother to his sons.

"Aye. I will do anything to make you happy."

She smiled at his comment.

Bessetta poked her in the side. "Well?"

Accalia laughed. "We'll announce it on the morrow."

"Cook will have a thing to say about that." Bessetta was smiling and shook her head.

Then they wrapped up the meal and instead of having ale with his brothers and Alasdair and his brothers this eve before he retired to bed, he told them, "I have an important duty to perform, and we'll celebrate tomorrow."

Accalia slipped out of the great hall to take the boys to their bedchamber. He wondered if he should intrude or what she intended to do. Tell the boys? Should he be there?

He headed up the stairs and took the route to the boys' chamber.

Beathag was heading that way and he said, "Hold!"

Beathag whipped her around, her red hair flying, her green eyes wide, surprised to see Erik coming up behind her.

"Do you wish a stay in the dungeon? I dinna usually send our women down there, but in your case, it would be well-deserved."

"Nay. I...um, just, um, wanted to tell Accalia that I was sorry for troubling her."

Accalia stepped out of the boys' chamber, the boys and the nannies joining her. "Aye?"

"I'm um, sorry."

"No more, aye?"

Beathag glanced back at Erik and he gave her one of his sternest looks that said she would end up in the dungeon if she continued to harass Accalia.

"Nay, no more." Then Beathag looked back at Erik to see if she was free to go.

Accalia said, "You may go. But I dinna want to see you in this tower again."

Beathag nodded, hurried off as fast as she could, and rushed down the stairs.

Then the nannies ushered the boys into their chamber to bathe. Accalia took Erik's hand, and they walked inside.

Thorfinn was first in the tub. They all looked a little surprised to see their da join them. He was surprised to see Thorfinn in the tub first.

"Your da and I have some news," Accalia said. "We're mating tonight and we're getting married."

The boys' mouths hung agape for a moment, then Hendrie and Johnne looked at Thorfinn as if he should show them how they should feel about it and he whooped and splashed water out of the tub accidentally. His brothers whooped and hollered then too and hugged her.

The nannies were all smiling.

Thorfinn left the tub, and the nanny wrapped him in a towel. He hurried over to give Accalia a wet embrace, and the boys hugged their da. Erik pulled them all into a warm hug, including Accalia, showing them they were all his family.

Erik couldn't have been happier to see the boys and Accalia desire this.

"I willna replace your mother. She will always be the one who birthed you and loved you. But I will do all I can to be that for you as I love you to the moon and back. 'Tis entirely up to you if you want to call me mother, or if you want to refer to me as Accalia."

"Mother," Hendrie and Johnne said, not waiting for Thorfinn to decide.

"You are our mother," Thorfinn said, agreeing with his brothers.

Erik was thrilled that his sons were accepting Accalia to be their mother, and she was crying as she hugged them. He ruffled his sons' hair and said, "Finish your baths, dress, and go to bed. We're off to bed now."

"To mate," Thorfinn said, smiling.

His brothers smiled too.

"Aye, and we wish you the most pleasant of dreams." Then Accalia kissed them on the cheeks, took hold of Erik this time, and pulled him out of the bedchamber.

The boys whooped again, and Erik hoped they would go to bed without giving their nannies any difficulty. Down below, they heard people laughing and talking, already celebrating the momentous occasion which was to be expected.

Erik smiled down at Accalia, hurrying him toward his bedchamber. He scooped her up in his arms and was so glad she hadn't delayed a mating with him any longer. He knew this was the way it should be. His sons had shown him just how important Accalia was to them and he loved them for wanting her to be their mother.

When he reached his bedchamber, he sat Accalia on the bed. She laughed at him. "You wanted me here right away."

"Aye, as soon as I could, once I realized you were the one for me." Then he began removing his clothes and she removed hers, only this time, she took off her léine so that they were both completely naked.

She was beautiful in both her human form and her wolf coat. He ran his hands over her skin and touched her rigid, rosy nipples, and she sighed with happiness. He licked her nipples and kissed them, loving how intimate they could become now. "Beautiful, lass."

She slid her hands over his chest, touching his nipples in the same way. Now that was an amazing sensation, he didn't think he would ever have felt. He smiled, lifted her face to his, and kissed her warm and luscious mouth.

"You are the only one for me. I love you, Accalia," Erik said, kissing her cheeks, forehead, and mouth.

"I love you with all my heart." She took hold of his hand and pulled him toward the bed. "I couldna imagine anyone being more perfect for me than you are."

She climbed onto the bed, and he joined her, pulling her into his arms, and began to kiss her. She wrapped her legs around his, opening herself to him. But he wanted to pleasure her like he had done previously before she became his mate. He kissed her neck, making her shiver, and she licked his ear and ran her fingers over his nipple. His pheromones and hers spiked in an instant.

She rubbed her soft heel against the back of his calf. His staff rose in anticipation as she continued to rub her graceful body against his. She was amazing and made him feel that way too.

He started to stroke her between her legs, enjoying the way she moaned and writhed under his touch. He met her mouth with his, then deepened the kiss, while she sucked on his tongue, firing up his blood as hot as the armorer's fire in his forge. Her hands clung to his shoulders with a death grip as he continued to caress her. Need and desire were coursing through his blood as he smelled her pheromones reach a fever pitch, matching the wildness of his own.

He couldn't imagine not taking her for his mate and how terrible it would have been had he not convinced her they were right for each other. She groaned out loud and he kissed her soft, warm breast, ready to make this mating official. But was she?

ACCALIA LOVED how Erik always made her feel so good first, and she was ready for this mating to go forth. She pulled at his hip, to encourage him to join her. His eyes glistened with hunger, and she knew he couldn't wait to mate her.

Just like she couldn't wait for their union either. He pushed slowly into her, then he began to thrust deeply. His hot hard body was making her body hotter. She wrapped her legs around him, wanting to hold him even closer, wanting to show him that he was hers. Her legs tightened around his, and he groaned.

They were kissing each other gently at first, and then more like he was claiming her, and she swore his kissing her was even more passionate than usual if that was possible. Her heart and his raced and she was feeling a little lightheaded, but she enjoyed the feeling of him deep inside of her, their bodies joined, a union made in heaven. His kiss deepened and she sucked on his tongue like she had before, which made him pump into her even faster.

He slowed down, and she thought he was finished, but then he started thrusting into her again. She slipped her hands onto his hips and felt his powerful thrusts. She hadn't realized that mating her wolf would feel this amazing. But then she felt the delicious climax lift her and shatter her. At the same time, he exploded deep inside her, and he groaned with a heavy sigh of relief.

He was still inside her when he rolled over on his back, taking her with him and then he stroked her hair. "I never could have hoped for a more beautiful mate than you. You make me feel complete and so blissful."

She smiled and kissed his chest. "You are an amazing lover. I never thought being mated to a wolf would be this astonishing. You make my world complete as well. I'm glad we are mated."

"Aye." He smiled. "How long did it take for you to realize I was the right wolf for you?" Erik asked her, gently running his hand over her arm.

"Hmm," she said, snuggling against him, and kissing his chin. "No' long. I was more concerned about how the boys would feel if we mated."

"They love you."

"And I love them, and you too."

"The feeling is mutual."

She ran her fingers over his chest with a light caress. "When do you want to have a wedding?"

"As soon as possible. I dinna know when Alasdair, Isobel, and their pack are returning home, and I want them to be here when we celebrate. 'Tis time, dinna you think?"

"Aye. Everyone will already know we are mated. There's no sense in waiting. And the boys are ready for it."

"We'll most likely travel with Alasdair's pack as we return to your home, and then they'll split off and travel to their home. Or even come to your kin's celebration, if they have time and are so inclined. They may need to return to their pack though."

She kissed his cheek. "We celebrate our marriage today and then tomorrow, we travel to my home"—she smiled—"former home, and then we will have their company and they can come to both celebrations. My da would be delighted since he is in alliance with them."

"All right. I'll talk to them about it then. I...well, I want to tell you something about Willa, my late wife. I'm sure some of the staff might have told you something about her."

"You and she loved each other. You have already said so." Accalia realized she didn't need Erik to tell her anything more about his deceased mate than that.

"If I'd had the pleasure of meeting you first, everything for the last five years would have been even better. She didna hold a candle to you in so many ways. The boys feel the same way even though she was their mother. I couldna be any happier that we mated. We were meant to be together."

She sighed. "Aye, some told me a little about her. The boys deserve all the love in the world, just as you do. And your kin are my kin and deserve to be treated with respect and dignity." She patted his leg. "Let's dress and make the announcement."

"Aye. We'll get the boys too." Erik sounded relieved that he had gotten that off his chest. She was glad that he felt he could and that it had made him feel better. She felt better about it too.

Then they dressed, headed to the boys' chamber, and found them still asleep.

"What? No celebrating today?" Erik asked, in a teasing manner. He had changed so much in his reaction to them from when she had first arrived here. She thought she was helping him to see that he was as important in their lives.

The boys scrambled out of bed in a hurry and dressed. Then they gave their da and Accalia hugs. She cherished them and could see from Erik's smile, that he did too.

"You are our mother now?" Hendrie asked.

"Aye, that I am. Forever and ever."

The boys hugged her again. Erik and Accalia left the room. The boys ran past them and bounded down the stairs.

"We made the right choice," Accalia said, holding Erik's hand and he leaned down and kissed her. She was so glad he had stolen her away to his castle. If he hadn't, she might not have agreed to mating him.

"There was no doubt in my mind."

She laughed. She thought he'd had a wee bit of doubt about it when he'd tried so hard to get her to join him in bed and she had been fighting the notion.

When they arrived in the great hall, everyone waited, and they cheered. The boys were ecstatically cheering with the rest of them. Accalia knew this was where she belonged and Erik kissed her in front of his pack to show them how much she was one of them, cherished and home.

She hoped when they traveled to her home, they wouldn't run into trouble with Freigard and his men though.

17

A ccalia was so glad that everyone was happy with her union with Erik. She worried that her uncle might be displeased when they returned to her castle and he learned of it, though he should be glad that Erik was allying with her da. But he could be a tyrant when he didn't get his way, and she could see him treating Erik and his kin poorly. She intended to do everything in her power to keep that from happening.

Then Erik sat down with Accalia at the head table and Bessetta hugged her. "Congratulations. I'm so glad the two of you mated. You're perfect for each other. And the boys adore you. In case you two were headed for a mating, Isobel and I brought pretty gowns to wear to your wedding."

"You knew it would happen all along, didna you?" Accalia asked, so glad that Bessetta and Isobel were here to celebrate with them. She drank some of her honeyed mead.

"Aye. Though I had to see it for myself, it was clear that you loved each other once we saw you together," Bessetta said. "Before that, I told Isobel how sweet you were and how you would be so good with Erik."

"But I was never a nanny for any of the bairns in the pack."

Bessetta laughed. "You were always responsible for the whole of the pack, but even when you were young if a wee one was hurt, you were there to take care of scratches and more. If one was crying, you had to learn what was the matter. You have always shown you cared about the children in your pack. Even in mine!"

Anyone would have done that, Accalia was thinking. It didn't mean she would have made a good mother to any of them.

"Remember the time a little girl had lost her mother in a boating mishap, and you let her sleep with us that night? I was fine with it of course, but I was surprised when you were the one who offered. We talked for so long about...well, I canna even remember any longer, but we fell asleep. And until you left to return home, she sought you out as if you had become her best friend in the world."

"She cried to see me go." She had forgotten all about that.

"Aye, and I had to be there for her once you left. But you had a special knack for making a lass or lad feel loved." Bessetta tore off a piece of her bread and began eating it.

"How is she now?"

"Married to a wolf who treasures her, and they have wee bairns of her own—twin boys. They have a croft and raise sheep."

"I'm so glad." Accalia hadn't seen her when she had visited with Bessetta some years ago. "On another subject, Erik wants to have the wedding this day and then on the morrow we could travel to my castle to celebrate with my pack." She couldn't wait to do it.

"Aye, Alasdair will agree to it. My brother and Isobel would be honored to celebrate with your da and the rest of your kin," Bessetta said.

"I'm thrilled." She was ecstatic that her best friend and her family would celebrate with them again.

"Next, you'll tell me that little wolf pups are coming." Bessetta took a bite of her mutton stew.

"Isobel had been married to Alasdair for some time before she was with child." Accalia figured it would be the same with her.

"Aye, but it might no' be long for you. You never know."

Accalia glanced at Erik to see if he had heard that part of their conversation, her body warming with embarrassment.

Then Erik leaned over and kissed Accalia. "Alasdair and Isobel are delighted to enjoy a second wedding with your family's pack."

"I'm so glad." She hoped Alasdair's presence, as an ally of her da, would help to subdue any objections her uncle might have to her marriage to Erik.

Erik handed her a piece of his bread. She smiled and took it.

"I've sent a messenger to your da to let him know we're mated and coming. He'll learn about it a day before we arrive."

"Good. He will have everything prepared for us then." She hoped her da would speak with her uncle and tell him to welcome Erik and his kin as he should. He would act one of two ways if his past actions indicated how he would treat them. He would make himself scarce, showing his contempt for the situation, or he would give Erik and his people grief, which she thought was more likely.

Once they finished the meal, everyone left to put on their best clothes while Etta, Bessetta, and Isobel helped Accalia into a blue cotehardie, a woolen gown with embroidered trim around the neckline and sleeves that Etta and some of the other ladies had made for her which she so appreciated.

"We began working on it the moment we learned Erik was bringing you here," Etta said.

"'Tis beautiful."

Then they attached a floral garland to Accalia's hair.

"I've got to make sure the lads are ready." Etta rushed off to check on them.

Cook had enlisted several of her kitchen staff to make small cakes stacked on top of each other. Erik and Accalia had to kiss each other over the cakes. Accalia knew the ritual and hoped she and Erik didn't knock them over because that could be bad luck.

Then the ladies walked her down to the great hall, everyone dressed in their finery, waiting for Accalia to join Erik. She felt like a princess as bagpipes, a viol, flutes, and drums played when she walked into the hall. They stopped playing the music, and she joined Erik, who was smiling at her and took hold of her hands. She was on top of the moon.

His gaze was warm and intense on her, his mouth curved up a hint. "Behold my oath, I will take no other she-wolf to be my wife."

She smiled brightly at him and his smile grew. "Behold my oath, I will take no other wolf to be my husband."

Erik placed a gold ring on her finger that he had made for the occasion. "I love you, lass."

"As much as I love you."

Since they had already consummated the relationship and consented to marriage to one another in front of witnesses, they were now married—which for wolves, meant forever.

Everyone cheered them. Then Cook brought out the stacked cakes. All the chatter and laughter ceased as Erik and Accalia very carefully—so as not to knock them over—kissed each other in front of his pack and Alasdair's and Isobel's. Her breasts touched the cakes and there was a hush of worried conversation.

But then Erik and Accalia separated from the kiss, wanting more, but not wanting to upset the cakes and create a disaster.

The cake was offered to Erik and Accalia first, though Erik glanced at Cook with a twinkle in his eye and she looked crossways at him. "Dinna tell me you want me to taste your cake first."

He chuckled and took the cake. "I have finally won you over."

Cook scoffed, but tears of joy filled her eyes, and she even cast him an elusive smile.

Then he fed some of the cake to Accalia, and she did the same to him. It was delicious. The wolfhounds thought so as they scarfed up any crumbs they'd dropped.

"The best as always," Accalia said to Cook, who looked grateful for the compliment.

Erik and Accalia joined their friends and his brothers as the cake was served. "That's what I always love about you, Accalia," Erik said. "You always take a moment to thank or compliment people for their work. Coming from you means the world to them."

"It is well deserved."

The musicians began to play music again, and Erik and Accalia helped form a circle, men and women holding each other's fingers and moving to the left, then moving their right foot to strike their left foot gracefully while dancing in the Carole. Dancers would sing at the same time. She loved doing this with Erik, for the first time.

Accalia broke free of Erik and said, "We've got to get the boys to join us."

"Of course we do." Erik was as eager to dance with them.

They both dragged the boys into the line, and all of them were laughing as the boys messed up the steps a few times, even though the dance was simple to learn. But it made it even more fun.

Servers brought tankards of mulled wines, ale, and honeyed mead and offered them to those watching the dancing. Cook was busy preparing capons and muttons on the spit, while others were baking bread, and beaten eggs were used for thickening sauces.

For hours, pack members danced, drank, and sang in celebration. And then when the meal was cooked, everyone took their seats and feasted to their hearts' content.

"You are beautiful," Erik told Accalia. "I'm glad that Etta had the foresight to make a gown for your wedding."

"Etta had been hopeful. I knew her from before when she was human. Like Cook, she and the others on the original staff didna know that I was a wolf like you, so they were afraid you would turn me. But since they knew me, she wanted me to be your mate. She liked me. She wasna sure who else you might end up mating otherwise and they all knew it could affect how they did their jobs if they didn't like the woman you ended up with."

Erik smiled. "I wouldna have ever married anyone who wasna good with my staff and the boys this time. I learned my lesson the last time. That was one of the reasons I brought you to my keep. To see how you interacted with everyone."

"That makes you a good pack leader. Someone else might no' have cared."

"No' me."

"I felt the same way about you."

"Oh?"

"Aye. If you had treated your staff poorly, I wouldna have mated you."

He laughed. "Then we both found the perfect mate."

She kissed him. "We did. The boys seem happy."

"They are. Ever since you've been here, they've been happy, barely quarrelsome, clean, and helpful. Everyone has said so and they know 'tis all because of you. The boys are excited about the journey to your castle. They've never traveled that far on horseback."

"I hope they can manage."

"We might be taking it a little slower is all. We'll have tents also to make the journey easier."

"You didna have them when you ferreted me away from my castle."

He leaned over and kissed her. "I hadna decided to steal you away until the very last moment and then I made up my mind. The men and I hadna needed the tents. But I would have brought one for you if I had thought I would take you with me. On this journey, we will bring them."

"You hadna thought to take me with you? I had believed you had intended to do it from the onset."

"The closer I got to your home, the more I thought about it, and the more I realized I needed to have you meet my sons first."

"Which I understood once I had met them. Their fondness for me helped me to decide to mate you even sooner. Though I wouldna have waited much longer."

He smiled. "I'm glad for that. How will your da feel about us mating and marrying here?"

"He will have allied with you and be glad for it. My uncle was the only one who was the holdout. He didna want me to marry you."

"Will he have changed his mind, do you think?"

"I hope so, as I'm fond of my uncle. But if he doesna still agree, mayhap he will change his feelings after some time. All that matters is Da approves and he will. When we return to my castle, I will pack my clothes and bring them to Whitehaven." She couldn't help but worry that her uncle might cause trouble for Erik though.

The tips of Erik's ears reddened. "Uh, aye, that was another miscalculation on my part. We will bring your things with us."

After everyone offered their congratulations and enjoyed the ale and food, several of the pack members from both packs went on a wolf run with the newly married couple. A few wolves were a little drunk, so more sober wolves were watching out for them.

Those on guard duty hadn't had as much to drink to be sure they could serve and protect the families. The boys enjoyed playing as wolves like they had the night before, chasing each other, tackling one another, nipping tails and necks in a show of juvenile dominance.

Even Alasdair's and Erik's brothers spent time roughhousing with each other, something that Erik and Alasdair would have joined in on. But now that they had mates, they were playing with them and not with their brothers. Though not wanting to leave Bessetta out of all the fun, Accalia played with her too.

That was another reason Erik loved Accalia. She was fun to be with and loyal to her friends.

Once the boys had worn themselves out, everyone returned to the keep. It had been a nice night out, stars filling the dark void, a light breeze blowing, a grand way to celebrate their mating and marriage as a mated couple in their wolf coats.

But now it was time to settle in for the night and tomorrow they would prepare to leave after breaking their fast. After putting the boys to bed, Erik and Accalia returned to their bedchamber to make love, though Erik was concerned that Accalia's uncle might cause trouble for him when they arrived at her home.

He hoped he could maintain his composure and not lash out at the man, should that occur. He wanted Accalia and his sons to see the good side of him, but if pushed into action, he wouldn't hesitate to act.

18

E arly the next morn, Accalia was eager to see her da and the rest of her pack members, but she was so tired. She worried about everything—how the boys would manage on the long journey, how Isobel would do. And ultimately, the reception that her uncle would give her mate.

They needed to get on their way that morning, and after Erik and she dressed, kissed, and hugged, Erik said, "I'm going to give some more orders to those who will be going with us."

"I'll get the boys ready."

"You will have the tougher time of it."

Accalia chuckled. "Aye, I know I will. After our wild night last night, the lads will be tired. Do you want to switch tasks?"

"I would never manage it."

She loved him. No alpha male would ever admit she had the harder job, and he couldn't handle it. He followed her out of the bedchamber, and she turned down the hall to wake the boys.

Bessetta hurried to join her. "I should have gone to bed earlier. I probably fell asleep before you and Erik did though."

Accalia laughed. She knew Bessetta wanted details, but she wasn't giving her any. Then they reached the boys' chamber and peered inside. The boys were sprawled out on their beds, sound asleep.

"Who's ready to take a trip and have more fun?" Accalia asked.

The boys opened their eyes slowly and groaned, stretched, rubbed their eyes, and yawned.

"Come, come, 'tis time to break our fast and get on our way. You dinna want to be left behind, do you?" Accalia asked.

The boys started getting out of bed and dressing in a hurry.

Accalia and Bessetta began helping the boys to dress. Once they were done, the boys tore out of the bedchamber, raced down the hall, and hit the stairs running.

Accalia and Bessetta hurried off after them. "I hope they dinna waste all that energy before we get to where we're going for the night." Accalia was sure their burst of liveliness would wane on the long ride.

Bessetta smiled. "I wish I had all their vigor."

"'Tis wasted on youth."

"I agree."

As soon as they reached the great hall, the boys were already at their table, ready to eat. She hoped they wouldn't get too tired on the long journey ahead.

"We'll take turns carrying the boys once they are too tired to ride on their own." Erik ate some of his capons. "I was surprised to see the boys down here ahead of you."

"All I had to say was that we would leave them behind if they didna hurry and dress."

Erik laughed. "You have such a wonderful way of persuasion."

She smiled. "You have to know the right words to say."

Cook came up to the table and said, "The food is packed for your journey."

"Thanks be to thee," Erik said.

"I did it for the lasses...and your lads." Cook winked at Accalia, then hurried off.

"I'm glad she at least likes you," Erik said.

"You know she likes you, but she doesna see how to show it."

"Aye. On the journey, the boys and you will sleep together in a tent. Isobel and Bessetta, if they would like."

"What about you?"

"I will be sleeping outside the tent as a wolf for any eventuality."

"Aye, okay." She and the boys might sleep as wolves then. They would be warmer on the chilly nights.

After the meal, there was a flurry of activity as they prepared to saddle up and leave.

They left as the sun was beginning to rise. Accalia was excited about seeing her da and the rest of her kin. But she had to admit she wasn't looking forward to the long journey. Then they would have to return here again. It was important to see her da and finalize his alliance though.

Their guard detail surrounded them while the women and children rode in the middle. The weather was fair, and chilly, the sky lightening with every step they took, the boys talking away to each other, happy, excited. For now, they were sitting tall in their saddles. She wondered how long that would last.

Erik told Accalia, "I'm watching our surroundings if you could keep an eye on the lads. They'll stay in formation, and probably be good for a while, but I dinna want them falling from their saddles should they go to sleep."

"Aye. Bessetta, Isobel, and I will keep an eye on them. You watch for any brigands."

"Aye." Then he moved away from her and continued to guard them.

"What do you think your da will say about..." Bessetta inclined her head toward the boys.

"I dinna know. He may welcome them as his kin, or no'. He will for certes want me to have my own. But I'm hoping he will love them too."

"What about Freigard?" Bessetta asked.

"Word will spread that I have mated and wed Erik and that he has allied with my da, though I'm sure that's why Erik and the others are being so vigilant. They want to ensure that he doesna attack us on our journey."

"He might no' know that you have two packs in alliance riding together."

"Aye, but if he knows about the marriage, he might know you were visiting us." Accalia hoped Freigard wouldn't try anything on their journey to her pack's home. She wanted this to be a joyous journey, not filled with danger. Especially with the lads and her friends traveling with them.

"True."

They had traveled for miles when Erik said it was time to stop, water the horses at a loch, and rest them. Everyone took the opportunity to eat bread and cheese and drink mead. The boys had done well until now, but once they had to mount their horses again, they groaned and moaned.

"'Tis a shorter distance to return home, if you wish," Accalia told them, Erik smiling at her.

"Will you return with us?" Thorfinn asked.

"Nay. We must see my da and give him the good news. He needs to meet you."

"Aye," Thorfinn said, though he didn't sound enthusiastic about it.

Then they began riding again, but only an hour into the ride, Accalia noticed Johnne was nodding off. "Johnne, wake up, lad," Accalia said, and his eyes popped open.

But then she saw that Hendrie was fighting falling asleep, and she called out to Erik. "Your sons are getting sleepy."

"Aye." Erik called to Logan, "Can you take Hendrie on your saddle?"

Logan rode over to remove him from his horse and sat him on

his lap, while another man rode up and took hold of Hendrie's horse's reins.

"Finlay! Johnne needs a lift."

"Aye, coming!" Finlay rode up to Johnne's horse and pulled him onto his horse, one of Alasdair's men grabbing Johnne's horse's reins.

Thorfinn sat up taller on his saddle and Erik smiled at him, and they began riding again. But Accalia watched him like a hawk, sure he would drift off before long. He had to prove to his brothers that he was stronger than them. He was still young, and his eyes began to drift shut.

"Erik," she called out, but he was riding closer to them now and she assumed it was because he figured his eldest triplet would fall asleep in his saddle eventually.

Erik took hold of Thorfinn who didn't protest—though she had thought he might—and he settled his son on his lap while another man took control of Thorfinn's horse.

Other than chasing off some red deer, they didn't see any sign of anything in the woods that would be a danger to them. Not during the day. As darkness settled in, that could be another story. They found a clearing and some of the men prepared campfires when a wild boar ran through one of the tents they were setting up.

Then the chase was on as several men on foot and Erik and Alasdair on horseback raced off to take down the boar for this eve's meal. The boys wanted to go with their da, but he wouldn't allow it. They were too little for such a dangerous hunt.

Instead, they had to help the others in camp set up the tents. Some of the men gathered water. The women and the lads remained in camp so that no one would grab them, or a wild boar would charge them. After they had nearly set up all the tents, and the boys and the ladies had gathered more twigs and branches for the fire—their wolves' night vision helping them see what they needed to without the aid of lanterns—the men returned from the hunt.

They had enough smoked food to see them through to her da's castle, but it was nice that they had fresh meat for this eve.

The boys were eyeing the boar on the spit in anticipation of eating their share of the meat.

She was amused because as hungry as they looked, she knew they wouldn't have enough room in their bellies to eat a lot.

Everyone was talking about battles they'd been in, fascinating the boys. Accalia asked Isobel how she was doing, worried a little about her traveling such long distances when she was pregnant.

"Good. Thanks for asking. Alasdair has been way too anxious. We can ride for months until it gets closer to when the baby, uh, babies are born. No' that I would probably be riding too late into the pregnancy. I'm sure Alasdair wouldna allow it, even if I thought I could ride. I understand his concern and I would do naught to harm our bairns."

They all enjoyed their dinner and retired for the night, most of the men sleeping outside of the tents, some as wolves, others on guard duty as humans. Isobel, Accalia, and Bessetta slept with the exhausted lads. Despite that, they were so excited that they were able to sleep with the ladies in the tent, they had a time getting them to settle down and fell asleep. Accalia wished she was snuggling with her mate though. Once she had him, she wanted to be with him always.

But she loved being with the boys and her she-wolf friends too. It didn't seem long before she smelled cooking, and she glanced at Isobel who smiled at her. "Time to rise, it appears."

"Aye." Accalia hoped *she* didn't fall asleep on her horse while traveling this time. She'd been up so late making love to Erik the two nights earlier and then last eve, stopping so late after riding most of the day, she was exhausted.

"Is it me, or are the two of you ladies as tired as I am?" Bessetta asked, plaiting her hair.

"Oh, I am," Accalia said.

"I am, but only because of the bairns I'm carrying," Isobel said.

"Oh, aye, I imagine that's tiring." Poor Isobel. Accalia had seen a woman with child who was tired in the beginning, then seemed to get over the tiredness after a few weeks. "Are you feeling well enough to travel otherwise?"

"*Ja.* 'Tis naught. I'll be back to my old self soon."

"Good." Then they woke the boys and helped them to dress.

They were tired, grumbly, and it wasn't easy getting them up this morn. She hoped they would feel better once they had something to eat.

As soon as they stepped out of the tent, Erik and Alasdair were waiting for them, and each gave their respective mates hugs and kisses, appearing as though they had missed being with them last night.

Accalia loved that Erik was always loving toward her. She had never seen Alasdair in that light either when it came to being with a mate. He ran his hand over his mate's belly, the first time she had seen him do that and she smiled. So did Bessetta.

Erik looked at his sons who were rubbing their eyes, looking angry at the world.

"Come on, lads. We eat and then we ride again." Erik ruffled their hair.

They sat with everyone, ate porridge and bread, packed camp, and left.

"While you watch the boys and make sure they dinna fall asleep on their saddles, can you do the same for me?" Isobel asked.

Accalia laughed. "Aye, as long as Bessetta watches me."

Logan said, "I'll keep an eye on you lasses."

"You will have us to watch then," Accalia said.

"It will be my honor to keep all of you upright in your saddles."

Accalia glanced at the boys. They had hardly started their ride when they looked about to drift off.

Erik joined Logan and the ladies and the boys. "How is everyone doing this morn?"

"Could we have no' have started later in the day to ride?" Thorfinn asked, surprising Accalia.

She had assumed he would try to let on that he was the toughest of the triplets.

Hendrie and Johnne agreed.

"Nay," Erik said. "We need to get a good day's ride in today, and we'll be there tomorrow."

"Tomorrow? Aye!" Johnne said.

Accalia suspected it would be later in the day, unlike when they had arrived at Whitehaven because they hadn't had to stop as much as they had with the boys. She had hoped they would get in early, partly because she worried about the boys and Isobel.

Isobel, Alasdair, and their pack would have to return to their castle after the celebration, which would mean another couple of days of travel. Accalia assumed if Isobel hadn't been carrying twins, she could have ridden forever without any trouble.

Halfway along the way, the boys were already drifting off, unable to stay awake. But this time, Logan had some other men carry them on their saddles while he watched the lasses to make sure they would make it fine until the next break. Which they appreciated.

At one point, they saw some men take off into the woods. Accalia was on high alert then. Isobel had readied her bow, and Accalia was amazed that she could ride and shoot, simultaneously. Accalia couldn't do that. She had only practiced shooting at a stationary target. But she suspected Isobel assumed there was trouble, not that the men had gone on a hunt for the next meal.

Bessetta glanced at Isobel. "Do you think there is trouble?"

"Aye. The men wouldna have taken off like they did."

Erik stayed with the women, boys, and most other men, but when the scouting party returned, he called for everyone to take a break. Some men took care of the horses, while the boys woke and, Thorfinn asked, "Are we eating soon?"

Erik laughed. "You have been sleeping half of the journey today."

"You woke me too early this morn."

Smiling, Erik shook his head.

"What happened when the scouting party took off through the woods?" Accalia asked.

"A couple of the men thought they had seen something in the woods, but when they looked, they couldna find anyone. 'Twas a good thing." Erik offered Accalia a slice of his bread.

"Thank you." Accalia took the bread, amused that he offered it to her even while they were journeying to her castle. "They would have smelled someone if men or wolves had followed us."

"Aye." Erik glanced at his sons. "Can you stay on your horses until we stop for the night?"

"Aye," the boys all said, looking a little sheepish that they had fallen asleep so early on their journey.

But Accalia would watch them so they didn't fall asleep again.

Then they ate dried fish and bread, without campfires this time. They would have them this eve when they stopped for the night.

Once the horses had enough of a break and everyone had had their fill of food, they continued their journey, the boys riding on their horses again.

Logan stayed nearby, but only a short while into their journey, Isobel said she had to take a break. Once Alasdair helped her down from her horse, which was a first that Accalia had witnessed, she couldn't keep down the meal that she had eaten earlier.

"Are you all right?" Accalia asked her, rubbing her back gently.

"Aye, 'tis the bairns in my belly giving me issue." Then Isobel smiled. "I feel better. Let's ride."

Alasdair looked worried about her, but she patted his chest. "I'm fine. I wish to travel as far as we can the rest of the day so tomorrow will be a much shorter journey."

That's what Accalia had hoped for, and a nice rest at her family's castle when they arrived on the morrow before they began celebrating again. She had envisioned only one marriage would have been celebrated—at Hillshire Castle—when she was mated to a wolf.

Never that she would have two celebrations at two different castles. She figured that if she and Erik had married at her castle first, he would have wanted to do the same at his castle with his pack afterward.

The boys seemed well-rested for the journey, though Accalia, Bessetta, and Isobel were worn out. By the time they stopped to camp, Accalia was ready for Erik to help her down from her horse. Some of the men took care of the boys, and Rory lifted his sister from her saddle and set her on the ground.

"Alasdair told you it would be a long journey," Rory said.

Bessetta shook her head. "I wouldna have missed out on either of Accalia's marriage celebrations for the world."

"Will we get in early tomorrow?" Thorfinn asked as the boys and lasses and some of the men helped them erect tents. Or at least Bessetta and Accalia did. Alasdair made Isobel sit down and watch all the activities as others made campfires or set up a perimeter watch.

"Only if we can leave early in the morn," Accalia told him.

Hendrie groaned. "We willna see you married again and then travel home, will we?"

"Nay," Erik said, joining them. "We will stay a while and visit with Accalia's pack."

Accalia was glad to hear it. She feared he would want to return home as soon as possible to rejoin his people. "When you sent word that we were mated and married and visiting with Da and my people, did you mention we were bringing Alasdair, Isobel, and some of their pack members?"

"Nay," Erik said, "but we will all fish and hunt to help bring enough food to feed all of us."

"Oh, good. I imagine my uncle having fits over all the extra mouths to feed." Accalia's da would be fine with it, particularly since he was allied with Alasdair's pack. If her da were to take some of his pack members and drop in on Alasdair's territory, Alasdair and Isobel would be as gracious about it.

They ate their meals and rushed the lads off to bed, Bessetta going with them, while Isobel had a moment with her mate, and Accalia had the same with hers. She heard Isobel say, "Aye, aye, I'm fine. And I could have helped Accalia and Bessetta set up the tents."

Erik smiled at Accalia and led her to her tent. "I wish I could sleep with you this eve."

"I wish the same." And she knew Isobel and Alasdair wanted the same with each other. But Accalia knew Erik and Alasdair had their safety in mind. "The scouts didna find anything amiss?"

"They didna or I would have told you."

"Aye." But Accalia worried the same.

"Get your sleep, lass. I love you and I'll see you in the morn."

Too early, she was thinking. "I love you too, Erik. On the morrow, we'll be able to stay in my bedchamber for the night." She so looked forward to it.

"Aye, I canna wait." Then he hugged her and kissed her cheeks, forehead, nose, and then her mouth.

She kissed him deeply, then gave him a parting kiss. "Night, my love."

"Night, sweeting."

Then she ducked into the tent and saw the boys' eyes open as they watched for her to enter the tent. She had thought they would be asleep by now.

"Do you think someone is out to harm us?" Thorfinn asked.

"No one smelled anyone—wolves or humans—in the area. Remember to use your nose to identify trouble. Now go to sleep before it's time to wake and you're all grouchy because you didna get enough sleep."

"We willna need help staying awake tomorrow on the ride," Hendrie said.

"Aye, we'll be wide awake, watching to see your castle," Johnne said.

"Sleep, boys. The morn will be here before you're ready." Accalia pulled her furs over her shoulder. "Pleasant dreams."

"Is your castle as big as ours?" Thorfinn asked.

But Accalia didn't answer him as she thought of being with her wolf mate—playing with him as wolves in the woods and then making love to him in his bed, knowing if she continued to speak with the boys, none of them would sleep.

A sense of dread filled her though. They'd been lucky so far, but what if Freigard tried to intercept them on the last day of their journey before they reached the safety of her da's castle?

19

E rik sat by one of the campfires near the women's and boys' tent, listening to the crackle of the logs burning, everyone silent, watching for any signs of trouble. He was in his human form, sword and bow ready for action.

When he wasn't on guard duty in a couple of hours, he would sleep in his wolf coat outside their tent. That way he could howl a warning and tear into anyone who might be a threat to any of them without a moment's hesitation.

Logan joined him at the fire and inclined his head, not saying a word. Like Erik, he was listening for anything that would clue them in that trouble was on their way. Erik would be glad when they arrived at Accalia's castle.

As much as he wanted her to enjoy a celebration of their marriage with her kin, he wanted more to be with her at White-haven. He hoped for their sake that everything would go smoothly as far as making the alliance and welcoming her pack as an extension of his own.

If they could leave in a few hours, they would get there by the midday meal. That's what he was hoping for. Isobel looked like she needed to rest, and the boys did. He wasn't sure how long they would stay, but hopefully long enough for everyone to feel rested up before they journeyed home, and not too long that they would irritate her da and his people.

"Are you worried you might no' be welcome for spiriting the lass away like you did?" Logan said.

Erik smiled at his brother. He had risked a war with her da when he did it, but he knew he had to do it. Well, mayhap he should have discussed the matter with her da first. But he hadn't wanted him to say no to the plan. Erik could be a wee bit impulsive when he came up with an objective at times, he had to admit.

"I would be," Logan said, tossing a few sticks onto the fire.

"The outcome is all he'll care about. He gets an alliance, his daughter has a mate, and if he cares, which I hope he does, he'll be glad we are happy with each other."

"Aye, I'm sure he will be. If we were just human, it wouldna be an issue. Young girls and boys would be promised to each other and usually wouldna even meet until it was time for them to marry on their wedding day. But as wolves, we mate for life, and it's important that we are there for each other forever."

"Aye, true."

They stopped talking and once they were relieved of guard duty, Logan and Erik stripped off their clothes and shifted into their wolves. Logan went to the other side of the tent and stretched out. Erik stayed near the opening.

It was quiet during the night, though Erik had trouble falling asleep. He was anxious to get to Hillshire Castle and get this over with. Unable to sleep, he barked to let everyone know it was time to get up. It might be a wee bit early. He heard groans coming from inside the tent—from the lasses. The boys were still sound asleep. Getting them up would be a chore, he figured.

Then he shifted and dressed. Isobel came out of the tent, looking tired. "Do we have to get up so early?"

"Aye, to get on our way so we can rest at the castle."

Isobel groaned.

"Up, up, all three of you," Accalia said.

"Listen to your mother," Erik said, poking his head inside the tent.

They hurried to clamber out from under their furs and dressed.

Accalia smiled at him and joined him outside the tent to give him a good morning kiss. "I'm glad you said something. I dinna think any coaxing or threatening would have gotten them up like a word from you."

He laughed. "You have been able to motivate them much more than I have since you joined us."

Then she kissed him and whispered, "Mayhap they're not ready to call me mother yet."

"Aye, but we shall never know if we dinna try it out."

Then Bessetta ushered the boys out of the tent and followed them out.

"Let's eat," Erik said. He hurried the boys to the closest campfire.

Everyone ate smoked boar, then they packed the camp, and headed out.

Even though everyone was tired, they were sitting higher on their horses, ready to finish the journey.

"Are you all right, Isobel?" Accalia asked.

"I feel better this morn. And knowing we're going to be arriving at your da's keep by the nooning meal makes me even more cheerful."

"Oh, aye, me too."

"Count me in for that," Bessetta said.

They all glanced at the boys, but they didn't look happy at all. Accalia smiled at them. "You dinna have to ride a horse for days once we arrive at my da's castle."

"Aye," Thorfinn said.

The other boys nodded. They took breaks to water the horses

and let them rest, but when they were a couple of hours from the castle, a redheaded, bearded man rode toward them. Accalia recognized him as one of the men with Erik's wolf pack. Hers now, she had to remind herself.

He must have been the messenger Erik had sent to tell her da they were coming. The man looked anxious; his brow furrowed. She didn't think he would return to speak with Erik, but he would have remained at Hillshire Castle until they arrived.

"What news have you, Colin?" Erik asked, sounding concerned as everyone waited to learn what he had to say.

"I didna reach the castle to give the message to Accalia's da's that you were coming with his daughter to make the alliance and to tell him you were wed. As soon as one of the farmers saw me riding toward his croft on my way to the castle, he learned who I was and my reason for being there. He warned me that Freigard and his men are at the castle."

"Nay," Accalia said. This was so not good. Were they holding her people hostage? Her da wouldn't be entertaining the man, she didn't believe. "Does he know we're coming to see my da?"

"No' from me. Mayhap Freigard believed you would mate and marry since he'd failed at carrying you off before, and this is the only way to change the way of things," Colin said.

"By killing Erik and his men when we arrived," Accalia said, horrified. Not only because of Freigard's deviousness but because they had the boys with them and Freigard would not hesitate to kill them, she was certain.

"We are still a couple of hours from your da's castle. You stay here with the ladies and our lads with a small force to protect you," Erik said.

"I'll go with you. You canna lay siege to the castle. What if Freigard starts throwing my people off the parapet? I wouldna put it past him to command it and then I would have to stop it."

"We have to free your wolf pack," Erik said.

"Through a secret passage. Only my da, uncle, aunt, cousin, and I know the way in and out of there. Once we're inside, I'll know those who are members of my pack and those who are no'. If Freigard doesna know we're coming yet, he wouldna believe we would be sneaking into the castle."

Alasdair said, "I believe Accalia has a good plan. My mate and sister will stay with your lads and a guard force."

"We canna take horses. They could hear them and see them. We need to keep out of their sight, in the event they're watching. We'll find the passageway at a croft nearer the castle," Accalia said.

"We'll ride for an hour and then a couple of riders will return our horses to the camp," Erik said. "It would take us too long to reach the castle otherwise."

"Let's go then," Accalia said.

ERIK DIDN'T WANT Accalia in harm's way, but he knew she was right about knowing her people and how to secretly gain entrance into the castle, hopefully giving them the advantage. Though he didn't want her with them in harm's way.

He spoke to Alasdair about who they would leave behind and who they would take with them.

Isobel said, "If I wasna carrying our bairns, I would go too."

Erik knew she would. If Alasdair hadn't been with them, she probably would have joined them. With her sword-fighting skill, she would have been welcome. But she could protect the boys and Bessetta by remaining at the camp.

Once Erik's brother Finlay agreed to stay and help protect the lasses and his lads, Logan gathered the rest of the men who would go with them. Alasdair was taking his brother Rory with them and Hans would stay behind to help organize Alasdair's men, though

Isobel was right there giving her advice on what they needed for protection.

Accalia gave the boys hugs. "Turn into your wolves if anyone enters the camp and make yourselves scarce."

"All right," Thorfinn said. "And we'll bite the brigands."

"You hide," Accalia said. Then she hugged Bessetta. "Keep yourself safe."

"Aye, you as well."

Last, Accalia hugged Isobel, who took a moment to wish her well. Then Erik helped Accalia onto her saddle, and they headed out.

"When we get within an hour of the castle, it will take us a while to walk the last hour," Erik warned Accalia.

"Aye, that's why I'll run as a wolf. Someone can carry my clothes. I willna slow you down that way."

No, she would be well ahead of them if she ran as a wolf. "I will also," Erik said.

She inclined her head.

"I dinna want you hurt," Erik said.

"Aye, and I dinna want you harmed either."

"I was ready to go straight into the fray."

She smiled at him. "I knew you would. I can be sneakier."

He chuckled. "You would be right in doing so. We dinna know how many men Freigard has at his beck and call. Or if some of your people are dead or injured."

"I canna imagine my da allowing Freigard into the castle without a fight, but I'm trying no' to think about what might have happened."

In silence, they rode for an hour, and then when they were an hour away from the castle, the men going with Erik and Accalia grabbed their weapons and anything else they required off their saddles.

Erik glanced at Logan, and he said, "I'll take your things."

"I'll take the lass's," Rory said, smiling at her.

"Dinna drop them along the way to get back at me for the mischief your sister and I played on you over the years," Accalia warned as she stripped out of her clothes.

Rory smiled. "I wouldna think of it, no' when you now have a mate, and Erik is no' one to cross words—or swords—with."

Then she finished stripping and shifted. Erik finished removing his clothes, and so did five other men. They turned into wolves and Accalia and Erik led the way.

The wolves moved much faster, able to stay low and well hidden in the bracken and woods. They managed to reach the croft that was out of view of the castle. A farmer was mending a fence when he saw them.

When he noticed Accalia, he raced to his croft and opened the door, waving at her and her companions to go inside.

The wolves ran toward the croft and loped inside the small abode where the crofter's wife was preparing a meal, and the children were helping her.

The woman, her daughter, and her son were wide-eyed as they saw Accalia and the male wolves enter the croft. She grabbed a fur blanket off the bed and waited for Accalia to shift.

Accalia shifted, took the fur blanket she offered her, and wrapped it around herself. "Tell us what has happened."

"Freigard and his men went to the castle. We do no' know why, but they were allowed into the castle and the gates have been locked ever since. We believe everyone inside has been taken hostage."

Erik shifted. "We were coming to celebrate my mating to Accalia and to agree on an alliance with her da, but we were warned this had come to pass. No' exactly how or why, but we have men following us in their human form, some from Alasdair's pack."

"You are going through the secret tunnels?" the woman asked.

"Aye. You know about them?" Accalia asked.

"No' where they are but that they exist. Most castles have escape routes, aye?" the woman asked.

Erik nodded.

"What can we do?" the crofter asked.

"Take care of your family," Accalia said. "If any of Freigard's men manage to escape the castle and come this way, do what you must to keep your family safe."

"Aye," the crofter said. "May you be successful, my lady, my lord."

Erik prayed no harm would come to his mate or any of the rest of their people, that no one was guarding the tunnel, and that they could free her people without too much bloodshed.

20

With trepidation, Accalia and Erik shifted back into their fur coats, and the wolves left the croft. Accalia led them to a tall cairn. She followed it farther west, stopped, sniffed the ground, and pawed at the dirt.

Erik hoped they didn't need shovels to find the entrance. But then he and the other wolves began digging and soon their nails scratched something metal. Erik shifted and found the rung on a trapdoor and pulled it, opening the entrance to the dark tunnel below. He knew the other men would eventually catch up to them and smell their scents and where they led. He shifted again into his wolf.

Thankfully, with their wolf vision, they climbed the stairs into the abyss and saw the tunnel ahead despite how dark it was. Once the other wolves had descended the steps, Accalia led the way.

Erik hoped the rest of the men would find them soon because he didn't want such a small force to come upon the brigands. Then again, if they were to fight using their swords, they needed to have their clothes and weapons.

They wandered through the tunnels forever, the moss-covered stones damp with moisture. Erik was afraid Accalia had forgotten how to navigate to the castle entrance, but she sat down on the stairs and looked up. She shifted. "That leads to my chamber. We should wait here for the others to catch up. They'll smell our scent and know the way to go." Then she shifted back into her wolf.

They waited for what seemed like forever, hearing naught in the underground tunnels, which probably meant no one could hear them down below.

Then they heard footfalls and heavy breathing. Erik prayed it was his kin and Alasdair's men, not Freigard's. Logan was leading the pack. Erik smiled and shifted.

"'Tis about time. I thought we would have to send someone to show you the way," Erik jovially said.

"You ran as wolves. If we had, we would have been here already," Logan said with the same lightheartedness, as he and Rory gave them their clothes and weapons.

Then Erik dressed and so did Accalia. They armed themselves and she pointed to the stairs. "My chamber is beyond the door. There's a secret wall behind my bed. It looks like part of my bed. We'll be able to listen and make sure no one is in my chamber. We dinna want to alert anyone that we're slipping in this way."

Erik agreed. He was so glad Accalia was his mate. She was not only goodhearted but also clever when it came to battle plans.

Erik preceded her into the secret wall, followed by Logan, Alasdair, and Rory. They listened but didn't hear any sounds at all. At this time of day, unless a maid was cleaning a room or someone was sick, there wouldn't be anyone in the bedchamber. He wouldn't put it past Freigard to be using the bedchambers for his people though.

Accalia squeezed in to show them how to open the compartment on her bed and Erik went first, followed by the other men. Accalia went last, though he wanted to keep her safe in the tunnels. He couldn't leave her behind should Freigard or his men find her. But she was right about identifying who her people were as opposed to Freigard's men.

They went over to her chamber door and listened. They could hear voices from far away, most likely in the great hall. The hallway seemed clear. Erik opened the door and didn't see anyone. "The hallway is clear," he whispered.

"My da's chamber is straight down there on the right."

"We'll check each of the chambers on the way." Erik didn't want anyone coming out of a chamber they might pass by, strike them from behind, and alert Freigard they had trouble.

They went to a chamber on their right and Erik peeked in. The chamber was empty.

"My uncle's chamber," she said.

At least he had seen her da and uncle, so he knew who they were. They moved down the hall. There was no one in the chamber on the left up ahead.

"That is my aunt's chamber. Davina is my da's and my uncle's sister."

So they would know a woman was supposed to be sleeping in there and he smelled her scent. But also men's scents.

"And that is my younger cousin, Cameron's bedchamber. He's four and ten summers."

Everyone would know he would be a young man, not a full-grown warrior, should one of them come into the chamber in the night.

He suspected everyone in her pack was in the great hall. Or they could be in the dungeons. Though he was hopeful Freigard hadn't killed anyone.

They reached her da's chamber and Erik heard Accalia's breath hitch. He opened the door, but no one was in there either. They heard talking down below and he was certain everyone was down there until nightfall.

"We could wait in all the chambers and if Freigard's men show up, we'll deal with them," Accalia said, her hand on the hilt of her sword.

"And if 'tis your people?" Erik asked.

"We move them into the tunnel. They'll be safe there," she said.

Erik glanced at Alasdair. He inclined his head. "We'll divide up and lay in wait."

Erik smiled. "Aye. They willna know what hit them."

"What about our scents in the hallway?" Accalia asked.

"He wouldna know any of us, but you," Erik said, "aye?"

"I didna think of that. Though he would have smelled me in the castle anyway since I have lived here since I was born."

"Aye, do you want to return to the tunnel or—"

"I will stay with you so I know if the person or people coming into the room are friends or foe."

Then they divided up into groups of six in each of the five bedchambers. As soon as Erik, Accalia, and four other men joined them in her da's chamber, they closed the door and took up positions around the room.

They were sitting on the floor next to the bed on either side, next to a large chest, against a wall, hidden by clothes hung on pegs on another wall. Everyone was hidden from the view of the door. Erik and Accalia stayed on one side of the bed together.

He kissed her. "Are you all right?" He listened to her rapid heartbeat and smelled her anxiousness.

"Aye. I hope my da is fine and comes here to sleep."

"I wish that would be so." Erik pulled her into his arms and held her tight so they could rest until someone arrived.

They waited for what seemed like hours but probably only an hour or so when they heard footfalls head past the bedchamber. "The others willna know if the ones going to the bedchambers are my people or no'," she said.

"Logan saw your uncle when we came for you, so he knows him. If a grown man enters any of the other chambers, yours, your aunt's, or your cousin's, they willna belong there. Even so, they willna kill them, no' until they know for sure."

"Aye."

Then they grew quiet and waited. It seemed like forever before they heard more footfalls coming up the stairs and down the hallway toward the bedchambers.

"He has killed enough of my men already," a man said.

"Freigard," she whispered to Erik, her heart beating like crazy.

"I told you he was one to watch out for. If you had allied with my brother, that would have kept him from our gates," another man said, and Erik recognized his voice as her uncle's.

Accalia's eyes widened and she took hold of Erik's hand. "My uncle. Dunbar's...he's in league with Freigard?"

Erik whispered back, "It appears that way."

That's how Freigard and his men were allowed into the castle so easily, Erik suspected. Her da wasn't with them in the hallway, or he didn't make a sound if he was.

"On the morrow, I want you to send out some of your men with a couple of mine to learn if Accalia is still at Whitehaven. Your people can infiltrate them and learn their plans," Freigard said.

"Aye, that I will."

"Dinna change your mind about being with me on this," Freigard told her uncle.

"You are putting me in charge of the pack. I wouldna do anything to sabotage that," Uncle Dunbar said.

Then Freigard said, "You'll stay in your chamber, Baldur, until your daughter returns here."

Her da was with them, but he was a hostage! Erik needed to know how many of Freigard's men they had to fight. If they could solicit Baldur's people to battle Freigard's, they stood a chance to defeat Freigard and his men. He hoped that Baldur's kinsmen weren't siding with his brother.

Erik motioned to the other men in the bedchamber that the person entering the room was Accalia's da and no' to make a sound or harm him.

They all nodded their assent.

"You'll have a guard posted at your door at all times, so dinna get any ideas," Freigard said.

"I canna believe you would go along with this, Dunbar," Baldur said.

"Why no'? I always should have been the one to take over the clan," Dunbar said.

Then the door opened, and Baldur walked inside, looking weary as a guard shut the door behind him. But then Baldur's eyes widened as he sniffed the air. Thankfully, he said nothing and moved deeper into the room. "Accalia?" he whispered.

"Aye." She hurried from her hiding place, throwing her arms around him and hugging him to pieces.

Erik shook his hand and said, "I've mated and wed your daughter. We have an alliance. We will do everything to free your people and eliminate Freigard and his men."

The other men with Erik and Accalia showed themselves and Baldur's eyes filled with tears.

"Uncle Dunbar was involved in this?" Accalia asked.

"Aye," her da said. "He let Freigard and his men in."

Accalia shook her head. "Does he have our people's backing?"

"Only a few because Dunbar has promised his friends elevated positions in the pack. If we eliminate Freigard and his men, Dunbar willna have any sway over the rest of our people."

"Where is Aunt Davina and my cousin, Cameron?"

"They sleep in their chambers so that when you arrived with Erik to tell me your decision about mating him or no', everything would look normal."

"Except Freigard and his men are here."

"Aye. They hoped to stop you before you entered the castle, but Freigard has grown impatient and is sending a group of men to Whitehaven to learn when you'll be coming here," Baldur said.

"We heard. He's sending some of our men also."

"Aye, so that you believe everything is all right when they reach Whitehaven."

"Would our men no' turn on Freigard's men when they are away from our castle?" Accalia asked.

"They have families here and Freigard told them if they give anything away, their families will be the first to die."

"Och," Accalia said. "We have men in each of the chambers. Mayhap they can take Uncle Dunbar and Freigard into custody."

"Freigard isna staying in any of the chambers. He'll go back downstairs to speak with his men and stay below. He wants to be there if you and Erik show up." Baldur gave each of them a hug. "I'm pleased you have mated and married."

"We hoped to have a celebration here also. We didna expect this," Accalia said.

"Neither did we," her da said. "But I welcome the alliance, and I hope you are happy with each other."

"Aye, we love each other," Accalia said.

"Do you have only one guard outside your room?" Erik asked.

"Aye. They've taken all my weapons." Baldur smiled at Erik. "But you have enough for yourself and me, it appears."

Erik smiled at him. He didn't want her da fighting, but he knew he needed to prove to his people that he could lead the pack.

Since Baldur knew his pack members best, Erik asked, "What do you suggest we do?"

"If we kill my guard, that will be the only one up here and he willna be relieved until early in the morn. My sister and nephew dinna have guards. Neither would be brave enough to leave their bedchambers for the night. But you say you have men in each of the bedchambers?" Baldur asked.

"Aye."

"We must do this before anyone is aware of the deception. What about my brother?" Baldur asked.

"He will be held hostage until you decide what will become of him." Erik felt it was best if Baldur, as pack leader, and because Dunbar was his brother, made the decision.

Baldur nodded. "I will go to the door and ask for ale. Then—"

"We will take care of the guard." Erik moved into place next to the door.

Another one of Erik's men moved to the opposite side of the door.

Baldur removed his belt and great kilt. Dressed in his long shirt as if he had gone to bed and then realized he was thirsty, he would use the ruse that he had gotten up and went to the door to ask for something to drink. He took a deep breath, then walked to the door and carefully opened it, so as not to startle the guard or reveal that Erik and his man were waiting to take the man out.

"What do you want?" The guard was still seated on a chair outside the door as if he couldn't be bothered to stand in the lord's presence.

"Some ale, my good man. If you please."

"Drink your own piss. Now close the door and be off with you or you'll wish you hadna bothered me." The guard had turned to look away as if he expected Baldur to do what he told him to do. Immediately, Erik moved past Accalia's da, grabbed the guard, and pulled him into the bedchamber. He quickly broke the man's neck and dragged him behind the bed.

"We'll take your aunt and your nephew into the tunnels," Erik said. "But we also need to carry the guard there so that no one knows what happened to him."

"Aye," Baldur agreed.

"How many men does Freigard have?" Erik asked.

"Mayhap forty. He didna need that many because Dunbar helped him. But he could have as many as fifty. I dinna know for certain."

"All right." That would be a force to reckon with. "We have

twenty-six, counting you and Accalia," Erik said. Though he didn't intend for Accalia to be in the middle of a battle.

"My nephew will want to fight," Baldur assured them.

"Good." Her cousin was practically a grown man.

Baldur pulled off his shirt and shifted into his wolf.

Erik hadn't expected that. He glanced at Accalia. "Will you go with your aunt and cousin to protect them?"

"Aye," she said.

He was relieved she wouldn't run through the castle, trying to take down Freigard and his men.

Then they went out into the hallway and headed toward the other chambers. First, they went into Davina's room. Some of Erik's men were in the room, waiting to do battle with the new arrivals. But as soon as Erik opened the door, Davina looked terrified like she expected a fight between Erik's men and Freigard's.

But when she saw Baldur and Accalia, she gave them both hugs. She was a pretty dark-haired woman, her eyes as dark as brown, and slightly built. Baldur wagged his tail at her and licked her tear-laden cheeks.

"I'm taking you to the tunnels," Accalia said to her aunt. "I'm sure the men here with you have already told you we are here to free our people."

"Aye, and I'm grateful for it."

Accalia began pulling clothes off hooks on the wall and helped her dress in something warm for their journey.

Then they moved to Accalia's cousin's bedchamber, everyone's hearts beating hard. When they opened the door, Cameron looked as stricken, while Erik's men with him were ready for a fight, but everyone was glad to see Baldur, his aunt, and Accalia with Erik and the others. Cameron had the same dark hair as Accalia and his aunt, gangly, not fully muscled yet, his eyes blue and wide with expression.

"If you wish to fight, you can do so, either as a wolf or a man," Accalia said. "I'm hiding our aunt from harm."

Her cousin nodded. "I will fight." Cameron began to strip out of his clothes and shifted into his wolf. Which was the best thing he could do because he didn't have any weapons. Neither did Accalia's aunt.

Erik assumed Freigard's men had confiscated them. "We are going to Dunbar's chamber next. Alasdair and his men should have taken Dunbar into custody already. Accalia will escort Davina to the tunnels after that."

Once they reached Dunbar's chamber, Baldur shifted and knocked on the door. "'Tis me, Baldur." Then he shifted back into his wolf.

Even though Erik knew they should have Dunbar in custody, they had to pretend they didn't, in case something had gone wrong.

A bearded, graying-haired man opened the door. Alasdair had a sword at his throat, keeping him silent. The man had glacial blue eyes and Erik assumed he was Dunbar.

All of them entered his chamber and shut the door. "I was only trying to buy you time until Erik arrived with Accalia, Brother," Dunbar sputtered, trying to spin a tale that would get him out of trouble.

Baldur didn't shift. He didn't bother to waste any words on his brother. A traitor was always a traitor.

Baldur tore into Dunbar as a wolf, targeting his throat, and killing him instantly. His brother had been willing to sacrifice their kin for the sake of power, and he could never be trusted again. Erik understood that, but at the same time, he knew it had to weigh heavy on Baldur's mind.

The aunt sobbed. Her nephew licked her hand and Accalia hugged her. "Come, I must get you to safety."

Erik could smell Accalia's concern and didn't want to leave her alone.

"Aye. Are you sure you want to fight, Cameron?" Getting her emotions under control, Davina wiped away the tears on her cheeks. "You could protect Accalia and me."

He shifted. "I'll fight with the men." Determined to battle with the brigands, he shifted back into his wolf.

The men led Accalia and her aunt to Accalia's chamber and when they opened the door, the men there were ready to take them down, but smiled to see it was Erik and Accalia and the others in their party.

The three other men with Erik retrieved the bodies and pulled them toward the secret wall.

Erik explained the situation, telling them Dunbar was dead, and who the two wolves were. Then Accalia said, "We'll no' stay in the tunnels. If some of their men learn of it, they will hunt us down. My aunt and I will travel as wolves to the camp."

Erik didn't want them traveling alone but needed every man he could muster. Still, he said, "Logan—"

"Nay," Accalia said sharply, her brow furrowed. "You will need every man to help you fight. My aunt and I will be fine."

"We will be," her aunt said, then hugged her nephew and Baldur. She warmly embraced Erik, pleasing him to no end. "Take care." Then she went behind the bed into the secret tunnel.

Accalia hugged and kissed Erik. "May the gods be with you."

"And also with you." He kissed her soundly back, not wanting to let her go. But he did, and she disappeared behind the wall with her aunt. His focus had to be on freeing her people, but he thought of Accalia, her aunt, and their safety.

Four men helped lug the dead guard and Dunbar's body into the tunnel, then returned to help Erik and the others fight the battle they were faced with next.

Now Erik had to finish what he had begun and prayed that Accalia and her aunt would safely return to their camp.

21

"Do you think they'll find us?" Davina asked as Accalia led her through the tunnels of her da's castle. She sounded and smelled anxious.

Accalia hoped she would be all right. "Hopefully no', but we will fight them if we must. Is Niamh all right?" Accalia had every intention of killing Freigard's men who rode with her own to Whitehaven. She would make her men owe allegiance to her da again. Or she would kill them also. She wasn't sure if her aunt would be resilient enough. To withstand the journey, aye. To fight the men? Maybe not. But she was also concerned about her friend.

"She's with the others being held in the great hall. She's fine."

"Good." Accalia couldn't wait to hear that she was freed and be able to hug her for the ordeal she'd gone through. "Freigard is sending some of our men and a couple of his clansmen to White-haven to learn what we are up to."

"I had overheard their plan. You dinna plan to return to camp, do you?" Davina always knew when Accalia was up to something.

"We must eliminate the threat."

"I agree. Our people are being forced to do this. Five of

Dunbar's friends, some who hope for more power in the pack, are also involved in this mess."

"As I suspected. But none of them are with the group Freigard is sending to Whitehaven, aye?"

"One. The one they call Horse because he was practically born on the saddle. He and two of Freigard's men will be with four of ours. Our men are being forced to do it and are unarmed. Horse will keep them in line when Freigard's men might no' be able to."

"No' when we have anything to do about it."

Her aunt smiled. "I'm ready to do whatever we must to take down the brigands." She glanced at Accalia. "Are you happy with the white wolf?"

"Very. We are very much in love, and I adore his three sons."

"Sons?" Davina sounded surprised.

"Aye. They are only five summers old. That is another reason I want to return to camp. We can help protect them should Freigard's men come across the camp."

"I'm happy for you. When Erik stole you away, I was afraid that Dunbar was right in saying your da shouldna marry you off to him. But when Freigard arrived at the castle, I realized Dunbar had a darker purpose in mind." Davina let out her breath. "I approve of Erik. Even his actions of coming to our aid immediately proves he's a good leader of a pack, and you and he will be perfect to lead it."

"He is. If anyone can right the wrongs against our people, he and Alasdair and their men will win this battle." Accalia prayed it would be true.

When they came to the tunnel exit, Accalia hated to have to leave her clothes and weapons behind, but as two women on foot, they couldn't safely travel that far. She began to remove her weapons and then her clothes. Her aunt removed her clothes, and they both turned into their wolves. They exited the tunnel and tore off into the night, the woods dark and deep.

Here, Accalia thought they would be arriving at the castle,

welcomed with open arms and enjoying a feast and merriment. She couldn't believe what had befallen them instead.

She and her aunt loped for a while, then walked several miles. Only when her aunt seemed to slow down did Accalia nudge her to lie down and they would sleep for a while.

She hoped that Erik and the others would be successful, they would all be safe, and only the villains would die by the sword.

BEFORE ERIK and the others began to search for Freigard's men, Baldur shifted and said, "Many of their men are in the barracks, taking turns sleeping and pulling guard duty. But I must warn you that five of Dunbar's friends are allies in his treachery and plan to have higher positions in the pack once I am eliminated. One of them went with the men headed for Whitehaven with a couple of Freigard's men as well."

Erik suddenly wondered if his mate would go after those men. He suspected that she might. Now he wished he'd sent a couple of men with her. Then again, she was protecting her aunt and probably wouldn't want to risk her safety so maybe she wouldn't.

"Most of my pack is in the great hall at night, while guards watch them."

"What about Freigard?" Erik asked Baldur.

"All I know is he watches everyone, his men serving guard duty, my people, just everyone. No one I could speak secretly with knows where he sleeps. He must at some time or another."

"Is there a chamber below?"

"Maids' quarters, but the maids are all herded into the great hall with everyone else, I was told."

"So he could be sleeping in there."

"Aye."

"What about the men who side with your brother?" Erik asked.

"They stay with everyone else in the great hall. I dinna believe Freigard entirely trusts them. As far as he's concerned, they're Dunbar's men and loyal to him. They helped him to allow Freigard and his men entry into the castle grounds, but he still doesna trust them, knowing they only want power."

"If we could take out Freigard first, that would be the best way to manage this. But instead, we may have to take out his guards where we can, hopefully without alerting anyone," Erik said.

"Aye. We go to the kitchen first. I've heard that some congregate in there, filling their faces with ale and whatever they can find to eat. Mayhap we can take care of a few that way and reduce their numbers," Baldur said.

Erik smiled. "Lead the way." He admired Baldur. He had a good head on his shoulders, was a tactician at heart, decisive, and ready to face any danger head-on.

Baldur shifted into his wolf and then headed down some back-stairs until they reached a hallway and heard some men talking and laughing in a room not far away. Erik could smell mead, ale, bread, and poultry.

They crept down the stairs after Baldur, his nephew wanting to go with him, but Erik held him back so they could protect him.

Erik made out the voices of four different men. Erik motioned to eight men to follow him while the others stayed in reserve.

They moved silently toward the kitchen and heard a couple of men talking down in the cellar where the ovens for baking bread were located, Erik assumed. He sent three of the men down the stairs.

He and the others rushed into the kitchen where the four men were stuffing their faces with chunks of boar and cheese and slurping up ale. All of them were armed and Baldur suddenly joined Erik and nodded, telling him they were Freigard's men. The brigands didn't even know what hit them.

Erik took on one of the men, cutting him down before he could react. The other men with Erik acted as quickly to eliminate the threats, stabbing them in the hearts, and the men slid to the floor where they took their last breaths.

Then the three men who had gone into the cellar came running back up, indicating they had killed the two men below the stairs. Erik directed the men to haul Freigard's men from the kitchen into the cellar.

Baldur shifted. "There's a secret tunnel in the cellar." He shifted and ran down the stairs with the ones moving the bodies to show them the hidden entrance.

Hiding all the bodies was a good plan so no one would be the wiser. The castle was eighty feet tall and encompassed nearly ten acres. It would take a while for Freigard or his men to determine people were missing—until they learned Dunbar, Baldur, the guard, Accalia's aunt, and her younger cousin were gone. Hopefully, no one would discover it until Erik and the other men with him took care of the majority of Freigard's men.

Once Baldur and their other men joined them, they waited a few minutes, listening to learn where they might go next to take out a few more of Freigard's men without alerting anyone else. They knew they only had a short time left before a guard came to relieve the other at Baldur's chamber and discovered the guard and the clan chief were missing.

More than anything, Erik hoped that Accalia and her aunt would be safe at the camp soon.

Baldur shifted. "Freigard's men will be manning the wall walk. If we can slip up through the eastern and northern towers, we could take out the three on the east and north wall walks. Then we can move across the wall walk along the west side, remove the three there, and then on the south side and terminate the other three.

"Some are guarding the great hall. Some guard the stables to guarantee no one steals a horse and leaves. I suspect my fighting men are locked in the dungeon."

"We'll take out the men on the wall walks first," Erik agreed. If they did, they couldn't shout a warning if a friend showed up. But they still had the problem with the guard's relief at Baldur's chamber.

Baldur shifted and led them to the north tower first. Alasdair and some of his men went up that way. Then Baldur escorted Erik and his men to the east tower, ready to do battle—silently, quickly, and without alerting the enemy. At least that was the plan.

ACCALIA WANTED to get her aunt to the camp where she would be safer and inform the men guarding them that they had trouble. That Freigard had sent some men to Whitehaven. Before Freigard's men got too far away and could cause problems for Erik's pack, she wanted to eliminate them. She didn't know if her aunt could manage a battle with the brigands.

They had traveled for a long time, smelling the scents of the men—men that Accalia recognized—four of them having been loyal to her da, and the one, Horse, Dunbar's friend. The other two men were unknown to her and had to be Freigard's men. They only had to get rid of three of the men, and hopefully, once they began to fight them, her people would help them eliminate the brigands.

She and her aunt were getting closer to the men heading for Whitehaven, their scents growing stronger. She and Davina continued running until they heard the men close by. Peering out from the woods, she saw the men stop to give their horses a break. This was the time to act. She glanced at her aunt. She inclined her head to her.

Who should they go after first? And would the men who had been loyal to her da help them? She noticed none of them were armed. She assumed that was because Freigard feared they would turn on their guard. Only Horse and Freigard's men were wearing swords and *sgian dubhs*.

Horse crouched down on the creek bed, filling his flask.

Freigard's men were drinking ale while keeping an eye on their four hostages, the horses all tied to trees nearby.

If she could take down one of the guards or Horse, her da's men might be able to grab their weapons and help her. She didn't expect much assistance from her aunt—though she was a good-sized wolf, but she was Accalia's da's age. Yet, her aunt surprised her when she tore after Horse, who was alone, leaning over the creek and now splashing water on his face. Her aunt bit into his neck and pushed his head into the water.

He thrashed around and Accalia rushed to help her aunt. By the time Accalia pounced on him, he was no longer moving.

Accalia whipped around and raced toward one of Freigard's men before he saw her and could react. They only had the two men to eliminate, but they still could lose the battle.

Before she attacked him, two of her da's people saw her, their eyes widening in recognition. They would know her as a wolf anywhere and she had to have shocked them to the core when they saw her coming to fight their guards.

The guard she was going after was sitting on a stone, drinking from a flask of ale when she leaped and tore into his neck. She wanted to be quiet about it, as quiet as her aunt had been when she took down Horse—no growling, no barking, no noise at all. But Accalia had never playfought with a wolf where she did it silently.

Growling was a natural part of wolf behavior. She didn't growl as vigorously or loudly as she would when playfighting, but she was not as quiet as her aunt. She so admired Davina.

Cursing at her, the other guard ran in her direction, his sword drawn. She shook the dead man, making sure he was truly deceased. Before the other guard reached her, she knew she had to run off or be killed. But then, as if the men loyal to her da had woken up from the nightmare they were living, they raced to grab the sword and the *sgian dubh* off the dead guard and ran after the remaining guard.

He turned to fight the man holding the sword, another holding the guard's *sgian dubh*. When he did, Accalia leaped forward and bit Freigard's man in the back of his calf.

He screamed out in pain and felt to his knees. She wanted to ensure he couldn't injure any of her people. Between the man wielding the sword from the dead guard, and the other man with the dead guard's *sgian dubh*, they quickly dispatched him with a stab to his shoulder and heart.

"Lady Accalia," the man with the sword said, bending down on his knee in reverence.

The other men joined him, showing their reverence to her and her aunt. She shifted. One of the men took his cloak and wrapped it around her.

"My mate, Erik, has taken men to the castle and freed my da and cousin. Baldur killed my uncle, the traitor. Davina and I learned you were headed to Whitehaven with a guard force and came to your aid."

"We need to return to the castle then," one of the men said, removing the belt from one of the guards, fastening it around his waist, and then sheathing the sword.

Two of the other men went to retrieve Horse's weapons and the other guard's.

"What has become of you must remain a secret. Off to the west is a camp where you can reinforce the guard. Then I'll take some of the men who came with Erik and Alasdair to help Erik with his mission."

Accalia's aunt shook her head.

"I must. If I dinna and those men die, all will be lost," Accalia said.

"Aye, we will do as you bid," the man said.

"Good. If anyone comes looking for your party, I suggest we dump these brigands in a bog no' far from here." Accalia shifted and the man took his cloak back. She was the only one who knew where the camp was and had to lead them to it.

Then the men put the three dead men on their horses and followed her to where the peat bog was. They left the villains in the bog and took their horses.

She led them to the campsite after that. As soon as they arrived, everyone looked shocked to see her, another she-wolf, and four men on horseback arrive in camp. The men told them what their mission had been before Accalia and Davina had come to their aid, while the boys hugged Accalia's neck, and tears of joy filled her eyes.

She licked their faces and then she and her aunt went into their tent. She gave her aunt some clothes to wear, and once her aunt had shifted and they were both dressed, they left the tent.

Accalia explained what had happened, though the men they had freed had been talking about the situation while the ladies dressed. They didn't know what Erik and the others had done. She described how they had been forced to go with the other men as a ruse to infiltrate Whitehaven and learn what was going on with her and Erik and when she would be returning home.

"We wanted to go with Accalia back to Hillshire Castle and help Erik, Alasdair, and Baldur battle against Freigard's and Dunbar's men," one of the men said, "but she has the right of it. If we return, they'll believe we killed the guards and Horse. And we would be put to death. Our families would be an example to anyone who might rise against Freigard."

"'Twas our own Accalia and her aunt who had taken out two of the men, and helped us with the third," another of the men said, sounding like he deeply admired them for it. Probably because they hadn't done anything to deal with the matter before that.

But she understood that because they hadn't been armed and were being watched.

The boys looked on at her in awe. Bessetta smiled at her. Isobel inclined her head, telling her she had done well.

Accalia hugged her aunt, proud of how she had handled the situation herself.

"I want to return with you," her aunt said.

"These boys are now my sons. You are their great aunt. I need you to be here for them. You've proven what an excellent warrior you can be," Accalia said. "I need to take more men back with me to the keep though. Who will come with me?"

They still had to have a force here to protect the boys and the other women if any brigands showed up, but if Erik, Alasdair, and her da died because they didn't have enough men to overwhelm Freigard's forces, all would be lost.

"We will help to guard the women and lads," one of her people said.

"We'll send a dozen men, a mix of Erik's and Alasdair's," Finlay said, Hans agreeing.

She knew they would want to help their brothers, not sit back at the camp, waiting for word. She also knew Alasdair and Erik would be furious with them if something had happened to the boys and Isobel and Bessetta because their brothers hadn't remained there to ensure their safety.

"Then let's go. We will do as before. We'll ride, then a couple of men will return with the horses, while the rest of us will make it to the tunnel system," she said.

"Be safe, Accalia," her aunt said, hugging her.

The boys hugged Accalia soundly, tears filling their eyes. Then Bessetta and Isobel embraced her and wished her well.

Davina said, "You keep them all safe, and we will do the same here."

"Aye." Determined to do everything to make that happen,

Accalia mounted her horse, armed again, and headed out with the dozen men.

"Do you trust the men you freed?" one of the men with her asked.

"Aye. But if they cause trouble, Finlay and Hans will take care of them. They will have them watched, not leaving anything to chance."

Then they rode in silence. All she could do was pray that their people were victorious, maybe even that Freigard was already dead, and her people had helped Erik and Alasdair to take the castle back.

After riding for an hour, she repeated what she'd done before. Two men returned to the camp with their horses, the others moving through the woods as humans, all but two who ran with her as wolves to further protect her.

She hoped they could return in time to help and that they wouldn't discover her mate, and the others had fallen at the hands of Freigard and his men.

22

E rik and his party went after Freigard's men guarding the wall walk to take them down before anyone could alert Freigard and the rest of his cohorts. They crept up on the first man leaning against the wall, looking out at the forest. The other two guards were out of sight. Erik cut into the man's throat before he could react. The problem was Freigard's men were gray wolves, so they could hear as well as Erik and their men.

The guard dropped to the stone floor dead, his brown eyes lifeless. Erik and another of the men with him lifted the dead guard over the wall and dropped him to the ground below. That's when Erik saw Accalia as a wolf, leading some of Alasdair's men and his own into the woods to the tunnels. Another dozen. They could sure use them. He was glad she was still unharmed.

Though he hadn't expected her to return to her da's castle and would have preferred her to stay out of danger, he was relieved by the extra help. Their men wouldn't have known where the tunnels were without her escorting them there.

As soon as the guard fell to the earth, she glanced at the wall, and so did the men with her, but they continued moving to the tunnel's hidden entrance. It was good that they were taking down the guards on the wall walk, or one of them might have seen Accalia and her party.

Erik knew they had only enough time to take care of the last two men on this part of the wall, and then some of them would have to intercept the guard who would replace the one guarding Baldur's bedchamber.

Two men had bypassed Erik while he and the other man had thrown the guard over the wall, and he heard a thud up ahead. When they caught up to them, they found they had tossed the second one to the ground, forty feet below. The third guard came into view, his eyes widening, and jaw dropping. Logan shot him with an arrow in the chest before he could call out a warning.

He crumpled to the wall walk floor. They disposed of him, lifting him over the protective stone wall and dropping him.

"Accalia has brought another dozen of our men," Erik told the ones with him. "I need one man to go with me to take down the replacement guard at Baldur's bedchamber. The rest of you help the others eliminate the remaining guards on the wall walk."

Then he took one of the men with him and they headed back down the stairs, slipping behind walls, ensuring they weren't seen, then reached the tower where they could make their way to Baldur's bedchamber. They needed to hide the bodies they had thrown over the walls to the ground below also.

They reached Baldur's floor but heard voices and paused. He hadn't counted on two people being there.

"What are you doing here?" the black-haired guard asked.

"That haughty white wolf chief turned me down. Now, if your chief would ally with my da, I will wed Freigard," Accalia said.

When Erik heard Accalia's words, he nearly had a heart attack.

"But how did you...you were no' here before. Freigard would have said something to us about it. You are armed. How come you are carrying a sword?" Freigard's man asked.

"I always carry one on me. You never know when you'll find danger in our troubled times."

"None of you were to be armed."

"I dinna recall your name," Accalia said as Erik moved toward the guard at his back, to get close enough to kill him.

"Who...who is that?" the guard asked, hearing Erik advancing on him.

"Him? Oh, no one of consequence." Accalia's voice was calm and reassuring.

"He's...he's armed." The guard pulled out his sword.

Erik didn't wait for Accalia to say another word. He had to silence the guard before he alerted anyone else that they had breached the castle. Close enough now, he rushed forth and the man with Erik hurried after him. Just as Erik reached the guard, the man swung his sword at Erik. He hit the guard's sword so hard and sent it flying. Erik didn't hesitate and stabbed him in the heart.

The other men who had come with Accalia left Baldur's chamber.

"Glad to see you reinforced our numbers. Carry the guard into the tunnel," Erik told a couple of the men. Then he and the others moved into Accalia's chamber and shut the door. "Is everyone all right at the camp?"

"Aye," one of his men said. "Accalia and her aunt took down the men accompanying some of hers to Whitehaven. Her men are helping guard the camp, though Finlay and Hans are having them watched in case they are no' on the right side. Accalia brought us here to back you up."

Erik's admiration for Accalia had no bounds. "We've been eliminating Freigard's men little by little. We dinna have enough people to make a full assault on theirs yet."

"Unless we can arm my people. No' the civilians so much as the men at arms," Accalia said.

"We would need to eliminate the guards at the barracks and the stables. Baldur believes your fighting men might be in the dungeon." He prayed to every god there was that Freigard hadn't killed them all.

"He will be housing his men in the barracks, I suspect," Accalia said. "I think you're right about da's soldiers."

"Can you show us where it is?" Erik asked.

Her cousin joined them, dressed and armed. "I'll show you where it is."

"Did Freigard kill your soldiers?" Erik asked Cameron.

"They are well-trained. Freigard hoped to convince them to bend their knee to him. If they didna, they would be killed. But he was waiting until Accalia was his," Cameron said.

"All right."

"I'll stay in my da's chamber in case anyone comes to check on him since he doesna have a guard any longer," Accalia said.

Erik looked at two men who had traveled with her this time, and they inclined their heads to him. He pulled Accalia into his arms and kissed her, then placed his forehead against hers. "Be safe, my love."

"Aye, and you too." Accalia glanced at the others. "All of you."

Then she and the two men headed off to her da's chamber, and Erik and the others followed her cousin to the cells in the dungeon.

As Erik and the others moved down into the dungeon, he saw lanterns hanging on the walls damp with groundwater, the stone green with moss and glistening in the lamplight. The stone steps were narrow and uneven as they made their way down to the grate locking Baldur's men in. No one was guarding the men. They did not need to since everyone was guarded above stairs—so Freigard thought.

"We need to arm the men if they can fight," Erik said, not sure how long the men had been incarcerated or the ill-treatment they had received—the lack of food and drink—down here.

"I can take you to the armory after this, but it will no' doubt be heavily guarded to ensure none of the pack members break in and arm themselves," Cameron said.

"Where did you get your sword?" Erik asked.

Cameron smiled. "I had a secret place to hide mine under the bed. They never found it. My *sgian dubh* also."

"We need to get rid of the bodies we dumped off the wall walk, but we must gather their weapons also. We couldna carry their weapons with us while we were unsure if we would be engaged in more fighting. We have Dunbar's and the two guards' weapons that we can use. Do you know where the key is to the cells?" Erik asked the boy.

"Aye." Cameron pushed a stone on the wall, and it receded. Inside, the keys hung on an iron hook. "So many guards kept losing the keys that Uncle Baldur had this made to hide them from view."

"Ingenious."

Cameron knew which key to use on the outer door. Once he unlocked it, he went inside. The men incarcerated there were so quiet Erik was afraid they had all died.

As they walked into the dungeon, he could see them moving silently to the cell bars, holding onto them, peering out at them.

Relieved to see them alive, Erik said, "I'm Accalia's mate, Erik Norwulf, and we've come to free you. We need every able-bodied man to help fight Freigard's."

"I'm Tormod, in charge of the fighting men. Dunbar is in on the takeover."

"Baldur killed him." Erik was glad to deliver some good tidings to the men.

"Baldur lives?" Tormod asked.

"Aye. We know about the five who worked with Dunbar. One of them is dead," Erik said, as the boy opened each of the cells. "We are gathering weapons for anyone who can use them to help us with the scourge within your castle walls. But we still need to do this discreetly to ensure Freigard and his men dinna murder innocents."

"He already has," Tormod said.

Erik assumed that Freigard had. Anyone who had spoken out against him would have been felled by a sword, either by his hand or one of his ruthless men's. "Then we need to ensure he canna do any more harm."

"Where is Baldur?" Tormod asked.

"He is leading a group of men from Alasdair's pack and mine to take out Freigard's guards on the wall walk," Erik said.

"How many men have ye?"

"Twenty-five originally, but another dozen have joined us."

"There are forty of us, and all of us will fight," Tormod said.

Erik slapped him on the back. "We will need all the manpower we can get. We threw a dozen guards from the wall walk outside the castle. We'll need to hide the bodies in the woods for now, but whoever moves them can gather their weapons and use them. See Accalia in her da's chamber and she'll show you the way to leave the castle in secret to take care of the matter. Then return here and we'll make our plans."

He needed them armed before they could take on Freigard's forces. He wished he knew where the devil himself was staying right now.

"Aye," several men said, and in short order, Tormod led several of the incarcerated men out of the dungeon and up the stairs to where Accalia would be.

"I'll go with them so she knows the men are on her da's side and no' on Dunbar's," her cousin said and left with them.

"We can get knives from the kitchen," one of her da's men said.

"Aye, we took care of the brigands in there and the ones down below where the ovens for baking are. Their bodies are in the cellar's secret tunnel," Erik said.

The men they had released all smiled. "You have been busy," one of the men said.

"Aye. We have much more work to do. Return here and we'll go as a force to the barracks."

A dozen of their men went to the kitchen and the cellar to arm themselves.

Then Erik and the remaining men with him waited until Alasdair and his men joined him in the dungeon and learned the plan.

"We saw Baldur's men haul off the dead guards' bodies into the woods while we were up on the wall walk. Baldur identified them as his men who had been imprisoned, so I figured you were down here releasing them from the dungeon," Alasdair said.

"Aye. We needed to hide the bodies and gather their weaponry," Erik said.

Alasdair glanced at the other men who had been prisoners. "It appears we need a few more weapons."

"Others are grabbing knives from the kitchen and the other men we'd left in the cellar," Erik said.

Alasdair nodded. Then they heard people moving about upstairs and one of Baldur's men went up to peek inside. He hurried back down to them. "Guards are taking some men and women who prepare the meals into the kitchen."

Erik hoped the men gathering knives in the kitchen wouldn't get caught. He and Alasdair had the same notion at the same time, and they raced up the stairs, several more men, armed or not, following them into battle.

He only wanted the armed men to help him eliminate the guards and protect the cooks, but everyone was so eager to assist he understood how they felt. Some undoubtedly had families and were concerned about them too.

Erik and Alasdair burst into the kitchen, the other men who had gone to arm themselves nowhere to be seen. He heard someone in the cellar then.

Erik and Alasdair began to fight two of the guards, the cooks and servers hurrying to get out of the way, some going into a side room for safety. More of Baldur's men poured into the room and dispensed with the five other guards. Erik killed the man he was fighting, and Alasdair finished off the one he'd been battling. Now they had even more weapons.

The men came up from the cellar, armed this time, but took the other guards' bodies downstairs to hide them. Once Baldur's, Alasdair's, and Erik's men gathered, they hurried to the barracks. There were no guards on the outside, probably because nobody thought anyone would dare to break into the barracks where a bunch of hostile armed men would be.

Freigard's men would be sleeping to pull the nighttime guard duty.

As soon as the doors banged open, Erik, Alasdair, and the rest of the men with them charged inside. The men on the bunks leaped out of bed in various states of undress, grabbing weapons and fighting to the death. This was why Erik and the others practiced fighting so much between their people and other clans to keep in shape and to be able to battle their enemy.

The man Erik was battling was heavily muscled and taller, but Erik wasn't letting that stop him from eliminating the brute. Still, every swing he made in the crowded barracks—a central hall with beds on either side and chests at the food of each of the beds—Freigard's man blocked them and swung twice as hard in retaliation.

Erik felt a body at his heels and fell backward but regained his balance before the brigand cut him in two. Erik jumped out of the way and landed on his feet on a mattress stuffed with hay. He struck at the guard again.

Suddenly, Logan knocked into the guard from behind him as Logan targeted another man. When he did, the guard Erik had been fighting turned to attack Logan—as if offended by his jostling him.

To protect his brother, Erik attacked the guard with vengeance, striking at him over and over again, not letting up. The guard couldn't strike back, just countering Erik's moves, blocking Erik's sword until he fell on the mattress. Erik attacked him in the chest with his sword, killing him.

Sweat pouring off his brow, Erik turned to see where his brother was. He was catching his breath and uninjured. Swords were still clanking in the barracks, a few were fighting, some were wounded, and most of the villains were dead.

"Where's Freigard?" Erik asked a dying brigand.

He shook his head. He didn't know. Erik asked a few more people, but everyone gave the same answer. They didn't know.

"What about Dunbar's men?"

"In the great hall," one of the men said before expiring on the floor.

"How many of you are there?" Erik asked one of the wounded brigands. His eyes were glazed over, and he didn't answer. Erik suspected they had decimated Freigard's forces at least, and Erik probably had enough men on their own that they could eliminate the rest of Freigard's men.

Erik, Alasdair, and their group of twenty men made their way to the great hall. When they reached their destination, the five guards there looked horrified to see so many men they had to face in battle. They didn't stand a chance the combined forces engaged in a fierce fight against the guards, keeping Baldur's pack members imprisoned inside. Within minutes, the guards were slumped on the floor, dead.

Erik and Alasdair opened the doors to the great hall and peered in to see women, children, and older men huddled against one side of the great hall away from the doors.

"We're here to free you," Erik said. "Members of Alasdair's pack, mine, and your own, freed from the dungeon, are here to help us take down Freigard's men. Does anyone know where Freigard is?"

"Nay, we've been held here as prisoners the whole time. Cook and her servants were supposed to bring a meal to all of us, but—" an elderly man said.

"The guards in charge of them have been dispatched and the meal is being prepared," Erik said.

"What of Lady Accalia?" a redheaded woman asked.

Erik smiled a little. "She is my mate." And he hoped they could celebrate their union here, once they got rid of the vermin in their castle.

"I'm her best friend, Niamh. I'm so happy for you both."

"Dunbar?" a younger woman asked.

"Dead." Erik heard an audible sigh of relief.

"And the others who backed him in this revolt?" another man asked.

"One is dead. We dinna know where Freigard or Dunbar's other men have gone if they are no' here with you," Erik said. "We need to clear the rest of the castle. We'll leave some of the men here to guard you." Luckily after the fight in the barracks, they had enough weapons to go around.

Logan and Rory joined them. "The barracks are clear," Logan said.

"I want you to be in charge of the men protecting those in the great hall," Erik said.

Several volunteered to protect those there.

"The rest of you, we need to go in groups of five to seven fighters, search the whole castle to look for any of Freigard's men, Freigard himself, and Dunbar's men," Erik said. "We should have at least one of Baldur's men with each group who can identify Dunbar's men if they encounter them."

"Where are you going to?" Alasdair asked Erik.

"To check on Accalia and make sure they are all right."

"I'll help clear the castle of the vermin," Alasdair said. "We need to bring the rest of our people here." He sounded anxious to move the pack members they had at camp and bring them to the castle.

"Aye." Erik didn't blame him. He felt the same way. "We will as soon as it's safe here for them."

All the groups searched different areas while Erik and four other men returned to Baldur's bedchamber. When they arrived there, he knocked. "'Tis me."

Accalia threw open the door and hugged Erik soundly. He and the other men went into the room and shut the door. "We are still trying to locate any of Freigard's men, the rest of Dunbar's men, and Freigard himself. But we've taken down most of his men."

"I'm so glad," Accalia said.

"Alasdair wants to move the rest of our people here from the camp, but we need to ensure it's safe for them first," Erik said. "Did any more guards try to take the other ones' places while you've been here?"

"Nay, though we were prepared if they had."

Rory joined them. "We've had Baldur's men search everywhere along with ours and Alasdair's, but they know all the hiding places best. They searched the bodies and didn't find the other four men who were friends of Dunbar, or Freigard. Also, some of his men closest to him and his advisor weren't found. Freigard's men who were guarding the armory are gone."

"Is Baldur and everyone accounted for? Our people? Alasdair's? Baldur's?" Erik asked.

"Baldur is and has taken charge of accounting for his people. Alasdair has another man doing the same. Alasdair intends to ride to the camp and have them pack up and come here. I've been taking care of our people. Three of your men were injured, four of Alasdair's. None were killed. Baldur lost six people and two were injured. They're all being taken care of."

"Good. Stay with Accalia and the rest of our people while I go with Alasdair to bring those from the camp here. I'll take ten of our men."

"Alasdair is taking five."

"That should be enough."

"I'm going with you," Accalia said.

Erik wanted to object. He wanted her to stay within the castle walls if Freigard and whatever force had left tried to attack them. But he knew she wanted to see the boys. "Aye." He could deny her nothing.

Then Baldur arrived at his bedchamber. "The meal is being served. Our people havena eaten anything for two days. Freigard must have left the castle sometime during all the fighting, the coward he is. And those who threw in with Dunbar? The same thing. Alasdair wants to bring the women and children here. I'll send ten men to ensure they get here safely."

"Aye, they will be welcome," Erik said.

"Knowing Freigard, he will go home and lick his wounds and try to come to grips with all the men he lost and then recruit more but that will take time, and they would have to be trained." Baldur gave Accalia a hug. "Are you happy with this arrangement with Erik?"

"I am. We love each other."

"Good. Because after he and Alasdair helped us to overthrow Freigard's men, I would have insisted you stay with him." Baldur smiled as if he was jesting. Then he turned contemplative again. "And I have been apprised of your fighting the enemy and helping Erik and Alasdair to gain entrance into the castle with their men. Without your help, they might no' have ever made it. So I praise you for your cunning and courage."

"Thank you, Da. Will you send men after Freigard?" she asked, as she, Erik, and the others headed down the stairs with her da.

"He willna have much of a force, but we need to secure the castle and see to the wounded."

"We are going after the ones at camp, including Erik's sons." Accalia glanced up at Erik. "Mine as well."

"Now? Before you eat?"

"Aye. Once things have settled down and we have a moment, Erik will sign an alliance with you, and we hope you will celebrate our joining."

"Aye, and the help you have all been while freeing our people from Freigard and his men. We will make it happen."

Erik, Accalia, Alasdair, and the others going with them, mounted borrowed horses and left the outer bailey to go to the camp. They didn't want to delay any longer, and Erik worried that Freigard might still have enough of a force to overtake the camp if he didn't return straight home and ran into them instead.

Riding the whole way, it took them an hour to reach the camp, and they saw that a battle had gone on there too. Blood was on the ground, but no people, no horses, and no bodies.

Sick with dread, Erik and Accalia rushed to the tent where Bessetta, Isobel, and the boys had stayed, but they weren't there. Three tents had been slashed and had collapsed. Horses' hoof prints were all over the campsite, making it appear that a battle on horseback had occurred there.

Erik's blood ran cold with worry and Accalia looked on the verge of tears. Alasdair likewise looked distraught, as they began following a blood trail.

23

Trying to keep tears at bay and with her heart in her throat, Accalia smelled Freigard's scent and announced that Freigard and Dunbar's men, whom she would know anywhere, had all been here. But there was no one there at all. No bodies, nothing. She assumed Freigard's men had taken their party hostage. She had to keep her head and not fall apart now.

One of her da's men yelled from someplace off in the distance, "I found bodies!"

Her heart sank and she prayed it was none of their people's bodies and that the boys, lasses, and other men in their party were all right. They all rode that way, but she smelled the scents of their people heading in the direction she had taken the others in pursuit of the hidden passageway at her castle.

When they arrived at the bog, she saw maybe fifteen men who were dead—all Freigard's men she assumed, because they weren't any of theirs. But they still hadn't located Dunbar's men or Freigard.

"I believe our people smelled our scent trail that leads to the secret passageway," she said, praying it was so, her heart beating hard, and she started riding in that direction.

Everyone switched direction and followed her, Erik and Alasdair closing the gap and joining her.

"I smell them—Davina, Isobel, Bessetta, the boys, your brothers, and the rest of our men. They are riding horses this way." Accalia hoped they had made it to the castle safely.

Riding the horses took them to the castle much quicker, and they saw Finlay, Rory, and the rest of them on foot now, their horses tied to trees nearby while they searched for the hidden entrance into the castle. Hearing them approaching horseback, the others turned to look, some drawing swords. They cheered to see Alasdair, Erik, and Accalia arrive with reinforcements.

Alasdair leaped from his saddle and hugged Isobel and his sister as soon as he was close. Likewise, Erik was out of his saddle and pulling Accalia from hers before she could dismount, the two of them running to grab the boys.

Tears of joy were shed all around. Accalia managed to pull away from the boys only long enough to give Bessetta, Isobel, and Davina hugs.

"We smelled that Dunbar's and Freigard's men fought with you," Accalia said, wiping tears of relief from her eyes.

"Aye," Isobel said. "Twenty men suddenly rode toward our camp. We were prepared if Freigard was chased from Hillshire Castle and ran into our camp. Rory, Finlay, and the others fought the brigands. The others didna stand a chance against our combined forces of your da's men, ours, and yours."

"We saw no sign of Freigard or Dunbar's four men in the bog where you left the other dead men," Accalia said.

"They must have gotten away," Isobel said.

Bessetta patted Isobel on the shoulder. "Despite her carrying twins, she was shooting arrows at the lot of them and managed to take down five of Freigard's men. I was ready with my sword but never managed to do anything. The boys wore their wolf coats, and I made them stay low the whole time."

"We were no' scared," Thorfinn said, as they rode around to the castle's main entrance, no longer needing to use the secret entrance.

"We sure were," Johnne said.

"Aye," Hendrie agreed.

Accalia smiled. "I was scared. You are smart to fear danger. It helps you to succeed against all odds."

"I was too," her aunt said.

"But she was a wolf and biting the bad men," Johnne said, sounding proud of her.

Accalia smiled at her aunt. "She makes an excellent wolf warrior."

When they reached the gates, the guards opened them. Stable hands took care of the horses, and everyone went inside the castle, smelling the venison and honeyed mead, but no music was playing. Those eating were in a somber mood until they arrived and then cheers went up all over the great hall.

They were welcomed with much fanfare, musicians began playing the lyre, cithara, and tympanum and sang songs of heroism and romance.

Food and ale were passed around with Erik vowing, "We will help to hunt some wild boar for our next meal."

Which would be on the morrow as late as it was.

"Aye, that will be welcome," Baldur said.

"I wish to welcome Erik Norwulf into our family, and to congratulate him and Accalia for mating and marrying. We'll have another wedding ceremony here after the meal. And," Baldur said to Erik, "we'll sign that alliance. I also welcome Alasdair, his mate, Isobel, and their pack members, who are already our allies. I offer a special greeting to Erik's sons, whom I intend to spoil as my grandsons."

The boys smiled.

"We have both your packs to thank for coming to our aid in our time of crisis, and we're beholden to you," Baldur said. "What of Freigard, though?"

"He has escaped, we fear," Erik said, "though once he is dead, someone will take his place. Mayhap someone who would wish an alliance with all of us and no' to fight us. We can only hope."

"After decimating their number of warriors, they may no' have a choice," Alasdair said.

After the meal, it was time to perform another simple wedding ceremony. But everyone washed up first.

This time, Accalia wore the blue gown her people had made for her and had been left behind when Erik stole her away to Whitehaven. Niamh was all aflutter, so excited for her to marry Erik.

"I'm so happy for you," Niamh said, and Accalia and she hugged.

"I'm so glad you were safe."

"You too after all the fighting you were involved in. I know you've had training, but I never thought of you being pushed into actually fighting grown men, soldiers. But I want to ask if you'll take me with you when you return to Whitehaven," Niamh said.

Accalia smiled. "Oh, aye, I would love for you to. I planned to ask you later about it, when we had more time to talk."

"Aye! Thank you!" Niamh hugged Accalia.

Then Niamh, Isobel, Bessetta, and Davina wore their best gowns and they helped Accalia to dress in her gown. Davina gave her a gold pendant that her mate had given her years earlier.

"'Oh, 'Tis beautiful, Auntie."

"I wanted you to have it on your wedding day." Her aunt pulled the pendant over her head.

"How frightened were the boys when all the fighting occurred at the camp?" Accalia asked. Though they had appeared happy during the meal, she worried they wouldn't forget the traumatic experience soon.

"Very. I will stay with them this eve," Bessetta said. "But that may no' be enough."

"I bit two of them, but then they got away," Davina said.

"I'm glad that you injured them," Accalia said.

Accalia would have loved to be with her husband in her bedchamber alone after all that had happened, but she wanted to ensure the boys felt safe and secure at all costs.

"They were scared but did what we told them to do to keep them safe," Isobel said.

"Isobel was amazing. When we return home, I'll be working on my archery skills again," Bessetta said.

"Aye, me too." Then Accalia sighed, but she was more than perturbed about it. "I canna believe that Freigard and Dunbar's men got away."

"I saw Freigard once," Isobel said. "But then I had another target and I didna see him after that."

"I saw men fighting. I didna know Freigard or his men. I didna know all of Baldur's men, certainly no' which ones owed allegiance to his brother, Dunbar." Bessetta arranged a crown of flowers on Accalia's head and smiled, changing the subject. "Are you ready to marry your husband again?"

"Aye, I sure am."

"I'm sorry I missed out on that one," Niamh said.

"I wished you had been there too. Certainly safe from Freigard and his takeover." Accalia hoped Niamh would feel settled with a whole new pack and wouldn't get homesick.

Then they left Accalia's bedchamber and went downstairs to the great hall where everyone was gathered.

Erik waited for his wife to be brought to him, and he vowed that he would keep her forever as his wife. She said she would do the same thing as far as taking him for her husband from now until the end.

Then he kissed her in front of the three gathered packs.

Everyone was cheering. They held their hands out to the boys, who ran to join them, and they all hugged each other as a family.

More dancing and celebration followed. Accalia wanted to sit with Erik and relax after all that happened in the last couple of days. She wanted to make sure the boys were all right. They appeared to be, dancing with some of Baldur's pack members, included in all the fun. They needed that.

"About the alliance with your da, I signed the agreement with him while you were bathing and changing into your beautiful gown. Even though he knows I would be there for him if he needs me, he wanted to have the agreement in writing as soon as possible."

"Aye."

"What do you think about the boys this evening?"

She smiled at Erik, glad he was concerned about them like she was. "I was looking forward to us sleeping together alone, but if the boys are scared after what they went through, I'm fine with them staying with us."

"I thought we could see if they would be all right with staying with others to make them feel safe," Erik said.

"Aye. I'm all for that also. Whatever works to set them at ease."

"I agree."

She realized when they left here to return to Whitehaven, her *real* home now, she would be alone with the boys in a tent, Bessetta and Isobel going home with Alasdair and the others of their pack. She would miss them.

She saw her da join them in dancing. She was proud of him for dealing with his brother the way he had. Their people were satisfied with how things had turned out—except that Freigard, some of his men, and some of Dunbar's friends had escaped.

The celebration continued late into the night, but then everyone said their goodnights. The boys were asleep at one of the tables. Isobel and Alasdair would stay in Dunbar's chamber.

Baldur's nephew would be with him, freeing up his chamber for the boys and Bessetta.

"I'll make sure they're fine," Bessetta said, hugging Accalia. "But if I dinna manage—"

"We might have late-night guests," Accalia finished for her.

"Aye."

Davina said, "Bessetta, if you need me to help with my grand-nephews, let me know."

"Aye," Bessetta said.

"Thanks, Auntie," Accalia said.

Erik smiled. "If they need us, we'll handle it. But keep them for a while."

Bessetta blushed and chuckled. "Aye."

"Night," Isobel and Alasdair said.

"Night, see you in the morning," Erik said.

They ascended the stairs to the bedchamber.

Erik and Accalia watched as Logan, Finlay, and Rory each carried one of the lads up to the bedchamber, Bessetta following them, and then went inside with them.

"Mayhap they'll sleep," Erik said.

Accalia took his hand and walked with him to her bedchamber. "We can hope for the best."

"Aye."

They reached her bedchamber, and she was glad no one had used it while she'd been away. She still couldn't believe her uncle had been in on the despicable act of treason.

When Erik shut her chamber door, he joined her by the bed, leaned over, and kissed the top of her head.

"You are so beautiful."

"You are so braw."

And then he began removing her weapons first and she did the same with him. Their wolfish scents calling to each other, they clawed at each other's clothes, yanking off her gown, their socks, boots, his long shirt, and her léine.

They soon were naked, and he lifted her onto the bed, hugging her warmly. "I love you, lass."

"I love you, you big old white wolf," she said, kissing him.

She had never envisioned making love to her mate in her bed, his muscles naked, powerful, and sexy. Reclining in her bed with a virulent male when she'd slept in this very same bed since childhood felt naughty. But Erik was her mate, and this was how it was supposed to be, sharing her bed and the intimacy as mated wolves.

His gentle yet insistent touches, his whispered words of love and desire, and his lips moving against hers in a feathery touch matched her own as she told him how much she loved him and treasured the way he was so tender.

As they lay intertwined in each other's arms, kissing and licking each other's lips, she couldn't help but feel relieved they were here and safe—for the moment. And she could be with the man she adored like this.

She traced her fingers lightly over his bare chest, taking in every curve and muscle. He amused her by flexing his muscles under her fingertips. His blue eyes filled with adoration as he gazed at her, and she couldn't help but smile. Warmth spread through her body, both from the physical pleasure of kissing and touching him and the emotional connection she had with her mate. She felt superb.

The moonlight filtered through the arrow slat of a window, casting a sliver of light across their naked bodies.

Then their kisses grew more urgent, pressuring each other for more. They rubbed their naked bodies against each other, his staff full and eager to penetrate her tight sheath.

He caressed her breasts, making her nipples extend and the sensation was gloriously sensitive to his touch. She moaned, glad the stone walls were so thick that no one would hear them making love. He nipped at her neck, nuzzling her with his lips, then moved lower to latch his sensuous mouth onto one of her nipples and sucked. She nearly fell apart at the exquisite sensation.

He slid his hand down to her dewy curls and began stroking her gently between her legs at first, but as she writhed to his touch, the feeling rising in her like a wave about to crest, he pressed harder, faster. She felt the crest coming and then the pleasure hit hard, and she cried out with joy.

He quickly moved over her, readied himself, and drove his staff between her legs as if he couldn't last if he didn't right then. He thrust deep inside her and she wrapped her legs around him, accepting the length and volume of him, enjoying the ultimate, physical connection between them.

He continued to rock into her, kissing her cheeks, and her jaw, as she kissed his, loving his whiskery face. He was so virile; she couldn't have been prouder to be his mate.

Then he slowed down, eased almost out of her, and dove in again. He began to hurry the process, and she felt his muscles tense right before he sent her falling over the edge of the waterfall and he groaned with release, filling her with his seed.

For a moment, they lay in silence, basking in the afterglow of their lovemaking, still clinging to one another. She loved this just as much.

Then he rolled onto his back and pulled her with him. Kissing the top of her head, he held her in his arms. She felt the warmth of his body against hers and smelled his musky scent, male and wolfish, a constant reminder of their beautiful relationship.

"You are the best thing that ever happened to me," he said.

"As you are for me." She snuggled her head against his chest.

She was so glad they were together for the night in her private chamber, that they had celebrated their wedding with her people, and that they had vanquished Freigard. Though she worried that while he was still alive, he would be a threat.

ERIK AND ACCALIA spent a week celebrating their wedding at her da's castle and then it was time to return home to Whitehaven. Accalia was sad to leave her da alone, but she knew his men would be loyal to him, and one of them would be his new advisor. Her da hugged her longer than he ever had, and when she looked up at him, she saw tears in his eyes.

She sighed. "I'm happy with Erik, you know."

"Aye. All this week, I could see that you are both happy with one another." Her da glanced at Erik as he readied everyone for their journey. "And you have fine young lads to raise as your own, though I hope you and Erik will have more bairns."

"We want you to be your grandsons since they dinna have grandparents."

"I'm happy to be that for them. Davina has played with the lads all week long. She will miss them too. Dinna be a stranger."

"You either," she scolded. "You, Davina, and my cousin are welcome to visit. We'll all be glad for it."

"Aye. We will."

Then they said their final goodbyes, Erik promising Baldur he would take care of Accalia.

"Us too," Thorfinn said, his head held high.

"Aye, us too," Hendrie and Johnne both said.

"But who will protect you?" she asked.

"You and Da," Thorfinn said, and they all smiled.

She said goodbye to her pack members that she'd grown up with, vowing to return, and then she, Erik, the boys, their clan members, her good friend Niamh, and Isobel and Alasdair and their clan members rode out together.

After a few hours on their journey, they came to a glen where they had to split up and go their separate ways.

They dismounted from their horses to hug each other goodbye. Bessetta and Isobel hugged the boys.

"But you'll come back to see us?" Thorfinn asked.

"Aye. I want to watch you in sword fighting and using the bow," Isobell said.

"Will you sleep with us?" Hendrie asked Bessetta.

Bessetta laughed. "Of course."

"We'll come see you when you have the babies," Accalia said to Isobell, hugging her. "And, Bessetta, I look forward to seeing you again."

"Aye, same here." Bessetta embraced her warmly.

Alisdair and his brothers swung the boys around and set them on the ground. "Be good lads," Alisdair said.

"We will. Our mother makes sure of it," Thorfinn said, smiling at her.

Erik and his brothers hugged Alisdair and his brothers.

"Until we meet again and show who is the best at archery," Erik said.

"And archery," Alisdair said.

Then they remounted their horses, waved goodbye to each other, and headed on their way home.

Niamh rode up next to Accalia. "I'm so excited about going to Whitehaven." She glanced over at Logan who was riding a distance from them, watching for trouble.

"You dinna choose to come with us because you are interested in a male wolf, are you?" Accalia was so amused.

Niamh blushed. "Of course, no'. I wanted to be with you. We're practically sisters. And"—she brushed a loose curl of hair out of her eyes—"I may end up with a mate. Who knows?"

Accalia laughed. "You will." She was looking forward to returning to her new home. She hadn't realized how much having Erik and his sons in her life had impacted her. But White-haven was home for her now. The pack members were her family.

And she was glad for that. Having Niamh join her made it even better.

The boys had the same difficulty as they had on the previous journey. They grew tired, especially after taking a break and eating, halfway through the day. Once they started riding again, they would grow sleepy, and some men would take them on their saddles, to ensure they didn't fall from their mounts.

At gloaming, they stopped, set up their tents, and readied themselves for bed. The boys were exhausted. They settled down on their furs and soon fell asleep without a word.

Niamh slipped into the tent to sleep with them. Accalia was glad she still had female companionship on the journey.

Erik circled his arm around Accalia and pulled her close. They kissed each other deeply and hugged, the warmth of his body welcoming in the chilly night air. She wanted him to sleep in the tent with her, but he would keep an eye on the tent. She understood why. He felt he could guard them better while watching over their camp as they slept.

But even though they couldn't share a tent, just having him close by was enough for her. She loved feeling him wrapped around her at night, knowing he was always there to protect and care for her.

They didn't believe Freigard was still intent on causing trouble for them this soon after his last defeat, not when he had lost so many men during the conflict at her da's castle and again at the campsite. She thought Erik and their pack would be safe enough. They didn't have Alasdair and his men now to help protect them, but they had thirty men of their own.

She kissed his cheek. "I canna wait until we're home again."

"You sound like the lads."

She poked him in the chest. "You know what I mean."

He chuckled. "I do. I was thinking the very same thing."

"You had better be."

He slipped his hand up to her breast and caressed it through her gown. "Aye, believe me, I think of naught also."

She tilted her chin up to kiss him and moaned when he got her all worked up. Thankfully, the wolves guarding the camp were not paying any attention to them. At least she hoped not.

Then she wrapped her arms around his neck and rubbed her body against his. "You are ready for me, I can see."

"Always."

"A day and a half and we will be home."

"And retire to bed midday."

She smiled. "Everyone will have a chuckle over that."

"They will understand." He sighed. "Get your sleep. It willna be long before we are traveling again."

"Aye, I will see you in the morn."

Then they kissed again, and she retired to the tent. The boys were sound asleep. Niamh smiled at her and whispered, "You are so lucky." She waved her arm at the sleeping boys. She was on one side of them, taking a protective position while Accalia lay down on the other side of the lads. "And of course the Great White Wolf Chief? He is better than I imagined."

Accalia smiled. "He's mine."

Niamh laughed softly. "Aye. I'm more interested in a bachelor wolf, and you have a lot of them in the pack."

"We do. You'll find someone." Accalia realized that Niamh wanted something that she had, and she would do everything to help her find the right mate.

As she drifted off to sleep, the only sounds were the rustling of leaves and the lads' steady breathing. But in the middle of the night, she felt them snuggling up to her, waking her, and she smiled, hugging them, and keeping them warm.

She thought about Erik and again wished they were together in bed at home, enjoying each other as mated wolves—safe from any possible harm.

WHEN ACCALIA and the boys hadn't emerged from the tent by the time they were ready to break their fast, take down the camp, and start traveling again, Erik peeked into the tent to see them all snuggled together, fast asleep. He loved her. She was so good for his boys, and of course, so good for him.

"Time to rise and eat and get on our way," he said, hating to disturb them. They looked so comfortable. But he knew that the sooner they got on their way, the sooner they would stop for the night again, and the last day would be a short day to travel. Unless they left too late in the morning.

"Och," Accalia said, trying to unbury herself from the sleeping boys. "Up, we must get up."

Niamh sighed. "This is the part I dinna think too much about."

Accalia chuckled.

The boys groaned, rubbing their eyes, yawning, and stretching. Then they all rose and began getting dressed. Accalia and Niamh helped the boys dress, and then they all left the tent.

Several of the men were already eating and as soon as Niamh, Accalia, the boys, and Erik sat down to share bread and porridge, other men were taking the tents down and packing up the camp.

By the time they had eaten, they were ready to begin their journey again.

Until now, the days had been sunny and warm, but today the skies were gray and rainy. They wore their wool cloaks to protect themselves from the constant rain. The day of travel felt much longer. When they stopped for the night, Erik was glad to get Accalia, Niamh, and the boys inside the dry tent. He even joined them to eat while the rain poured down.

"I hope the weather will clear up tomorrow," Accalia said.

"Me too. I dinna think I will ever feel dry again," Niamh said. "I appreciate that we have the tent though."

"We still traveled a full day despite it, and tomorrow we'll have only half a day to ride," Erik said.

"Good."

Thorfinn shook his head. "I felt like I was swimming in the loch all day."

"Me too," Hendrie said, Johnne agreeing. "But no fish to catch."

They all laughed.

"Well, on the morrow, we'll be at the castle, where it will be nice and warm and dry," Accalia said.

Erik kissed Accalia, removed his clothes, and then shifted into his wolf. He would guard as a wolf, the rain not bothering him since his outer guard hairs would keep his soft downy undercoat dry and warm.

Everyone was doing their best on the stormy night—lightning flashing all over, lighting up the forest, thunder crashing overhead, strong winds blowing through their camp—to ensure that Freigard and his men didn't attack them. They could assault them at any time, but Erik figured if Freigard could gather enough men, what better time to attack, than when they were still traveling, half of the men sleeping, while the other half guarded on a wild, stormy night?

The storm was making it difficult to hear anyone approaching the camp and the winds and rain were wreaking havoc with smelling anyone's scents. They were all on high alert.

24

T he boys soon snuggled with Accalia, maybe because they were cold and scared of the storm. Thunder hit right overhead, and Accalia jumped despite trying to be a calming influence on the boys. The rain hammered the tent as if trying to pound its way inside. She hoped it would stay outside.

Accalia glanced at Niamh, but she was sound asleep. Accalia swore she could sleep through a castle siege.

Accalia must have fallen asleep and began dreaming of running as a wolf with Erik, then returning to their chamber and making love, until the storm was too much. The wind whipped the tent about, disturbing her sleep, though the boys were sleeping cuddled up to her, so she didn't want to wake them. Then something sounded like it was ripping through the tent.

Ripping? The wind had torn the tent? She opened her eyes to see a sword slicing through the tent—not the wind ripping it apart like she had thought—and rainwater dripping in through the opening. Her heart beat like crazy as she heard fighting in the camp, both close by and farther away.

Swords slashed at swords. Steel struck steel. And Erik growled like an angry wolf as he tore into someone next to the tent, the bodies thudding against it, shaking it.

Trying to keep the panic from her voice, she said to the boys, "Remove your clothes and shift. We're under attack."

Stirring a wee bit, the boys barely moved.

Accalia shook them. "There's a battle in camp. Shift into your wolves and keep low. Niamh, wake!"

"Och, nay!" Niamh yanked off her woolen cloak.

The boys opened their eyes and looked at Accalia, seemingly not understanding her, but then they heard the fighting. They hurried to remove their clothes and shifted while she finished undressing and turned into her wolf. Whoever had sliced his sword through the tent had stopped, the sword withdrawn. She suspected Erik had taken the enemy down.

"Wolves, aye," Niamh said, quickly removing her clothing and shifting.

The boys stayed with her until the tent collapsed. Accalia, Niamh, and the boys struggled to get out from under it. Accalia shifted and found the opening. Jerking it open, she helped the boys and Niamh out of the tent, shifted again, and left the tent. She was scared to death for the boys and Niamh.

Now she, Niamh, and the boys were out in the pouring rain. Lightning still flashed across the sky and in streaks striking the ground off in the distance. Thunder sounded moments afterward. The boys jumped a little. A wolf's chewed-up body lay next to the tent.

Accalia glanced around at the men in combat—heads, arms, and legs bloodied, their swords slicing at each other, sweat pouring down their faces. Every man fought as viciously as he could to be the victor. As a wolf, Erik grabbed a warrior's leg with his hefty bite and pulled the man off his horse. He tore into him before he could cut him with his sword, Eric's fur coat already wearing blood. She prayed it wasn't his blood, but one of the rogues he'd been fighting.

Then she saw Freigard battling Erik's brother Finlay, trying to cut him in two. Finlay was bleeding from a head wound. She had to reach him and help him against the devil himself. Erik still fought the man he had pulled from his horse and tore into his throat with his wicked wolf's teeth.

Once the man fell to the ground dead, Erik tried to reach Freigard, but other men kept rushing in to fight him. The only way to stop these men from coming after Accalia, threatening the boys, Erik, and his kin, was to eliminate Freigard.

She knew that he wasn't going to give up in his pursuit to have her or kill her. And she had to do everything she could to help Erik and his men in the fight to stop the villains.

She meant to stay with the boys. She meant to protect them with all the strength she had. And to protect her good friend Niamh.

Freigard attacked Finlay and he fell back, unable to fight Freigard off. She feared the monster would kill Erik's brother.

Erik couldn't reach him with all the men fighting in front of him. As a determined, growly wolf, Accalia leaped past several fighting men, dodging swords, and targeted Freigard.

She realized she had left the boys alone with Niamh. But her action was wolf instinctive. Everyone else was so busy, they didn't see her dashing around the attacking men. Freigard was concentrating on Finlay and likewise didn't see her approach.

Then Finlay stumbled. She soon reached Freigard and leaped at him, slamming her large wolf paws against his chest, and knocking him off his feet. The boys suddenly were there, growling and trying to bite Freigard. She feared for the boys' safety. Niamh was there with them, snapping her vicious teeth at another of Freigard's men as he tried to cut Accalia.

Freigard tried to regain his footing, and the boys bit his legs. They grabbed hold and yanked his legs, growling viciously as if they were playing tug-of-war. Accalia went for Freigard's left arm, his right still yielding his sword. She couldn't reach his sword arm because Finlay had been targeting him on that side and had fallen, so he was in her way.

Niamh was still growling and biting a soldier behind Accalia, and she wanted to help her but had to concentrate on Freigard.

Suddenly, Erik was there. Accalia didn't know how he could have navigated through all the battling men except that he had the greatest incentive in the world—save his sons, his brother, and his mate from the devil wolf.

She had never seen Erik so viciously tear into anything or anyone. But his resolve was welcome as he went first for Freigard's sword arm, crushing the bones. Freigard cried out in agony. And then Erik grabbed Freigard's throat, bit down, and ended his life. Freigard wouldn't ever go after Accalia or his sons again. He wouldn't threaten Erik or any of his kin any further.

Immediately, Accalia turned to help Niamh, and they tore at the prone man's neck, ending him.

She saw Finlay on his feet again and he struck down one of Dunbar's men. She witnessed another of Dunbar's men dead nearby. Then the last men under Freigard's command began breaking off from the fight and scattering, trying to get away as fast as they could. They realized their leader had fallen and this was no longer their fight.

Erik's men began to pursue them, but Erik howled to tell them they were done. They needed to regroup, to ensure their people were taken care of if anyone had suffered injuries, and she suspected Erik would want a shelter set back up for her and the boys to stay in until morning.

In the aftermath of the violence, she surveyed the carnage and injuries suffered by her fellow pack members and those of Freigard's men. The boys huddled up to her and she licked their faces. Niamh joined them and they all licked and nuzzled her. Erik was standing next to them in protective mode.

As Accalia scanned the faces of her pack, she could see the fear and pain etched on their features. She knew she needed to be strong for them, providing comfort and reassurance amid chaos and loss. She wanted to help Erik and bandage the injured but comfort the boys too. With more gentle nudges and comforting licks, she reassured the boys that they were safe now, that Freigard was dead and wouldn't hurt anyone anymore.

She couldn't help but feel a surge of pride in her pack, in their resilience and strength. They had faced and overcome so much, and she knew they would continue to do so in the face of any obstacles that came their way.

And she was so glad her friend Niamh had come out of the whole fight without being injured. She knew Niamh could play-fight as a wolf, she'd played with her often over the years, but she proved she had what it took to be a warrior wolf in a real fight.

She didn't think they would have any more trouble with Freigard's people now that he was dead. Someone else would take over and she was certain they would think twice about causing Erik and her pack more difficulty.

Logan and a couple of other men patched up the tent she, Niamh, and the lads had been using while Erik saw the injured men, including his brother Finlay.

"I know you want to help us with the wounded men," Logan told Accalia, "but Erik wants you at Niamh to stay with the boys."

Inside the tent, Accalia and Niamh shifted and dressed, hugging the boys still wearing their wolf coats. They were all wet. "You can wear your wolf coats to stay warm," Accalia said to the boys. "Are you all right?"

They nodded and once she lay down, they hurried to snuggle against her, helping to warm her, though they were a little damp. So was the tent and her clothes now. Niamh joined them.

Erik entered the tent, shifted, and Accalia hurried to stand to hug her returning hero. They kissed and hugged, and then he hugged his boys in their wolf coats. "Thanks for saving my brother. And to you, Niamh, for protecting Accalia and the boys' backs."

"We were all there for each other, the way it should be," Niamh said.

"Exactly. I knew you were having a difficult time reaching Freigard, Erik." Accalia hoped he wasn't mad at her for leaving the boys to fight Freigard, which led them into the fight.

"I was. You gave me time to reach Freigard." Erik motioned to the bed of furs they'd made so that Accalia would lay there on the other side of their sons while Niamh was on the opposite side. Accalia lay back down.

Then Erik climbed under the fur covers with Accalia to her surprise.

"Will his men regroup and attack us again?" She didn't believe they would have any reason to do so. Freigard had been obsessed with having her and eliminating Erik.

"They're leaderless now. Someone will take over their pack, but unless they want revenge, I doubt they'll fight us any further." He kissed her cold cheek, his mouth warm on her skin as he pulled her into his arms.

"What about our injured? Your brother Finlay?"

"Minor sword wounds, but they'll heal because we're wolves. Eight were injured, and they've been taken care of. Finlay will be fine. He'll show off his wound to the lasses to prove his prowess in battle."

Accalia managed a small smile. "And Freigard's men?"

"They're all dead, except for the ones who fled." He pulled her tighter against himself as if he had to reassure himself that she was fine.

She raised her brows and kissed him. "You are no' going to guard us?"

"Aye, I am. Right from here."

The boys woofed, appearing to be pleased that they were all

together. She was glad for it too. She smiled, relieved, as she watched the boys turn around a few times, scratching the bedding, and then settling down for the night. They had finally found a haven from the storm raging for hours. The wind had died down and the rain had slowed to a gentle shower, the pitter-patter against the tent's roof lulling them into a peaceful slumber.

As Accalia lay there, listening to the soothing sounds of nature, she couldn't help but feel grateful for the company of the boys and her mate and that even her best friend was with them. The boys' tails wagged, and they kicked their feet in sleep.

Now she didn't need to dream about Erik because he tucked her in his arms for the rest of the night, but she still couldn't wait to reach the safety of the castle, surrounded by thick walls that would protect them all.

ERIK COULDN'T BELIEVE his mate and boys had joined the battle to take down Freigard. He'd nearly died to see it when they had. And then Niamh was out fighting, putting self at risk. He couldn't fault Accalia for going after him, knowing she was trying to protect Finlay and eliminate the threat to Erik and the boys. But he was surprised that his lads had run to help her.

He was glad Niamh had the wolf-fighting skills to protect Accalia. She was a welcome member of the pack.

When they woke the next morning, the rain had stopped, and they hurried to dress and break their fast. Then they mounted their horses after that and rode off in the direction of Whitehaven Castle. He smiled at Accalia. "You are a true leader when it comes to battle."

Accalia smiled at him. "Now, if you told Isobel that, I could see that."

"Everyone is talking about it. They're glad you're also their pack leader. Finlay, Logan, and me, most of all."

"Thank you. I know I should have stayed with the boys." She sounded like she felt guilty about leaving them behind during the battle. She glanced over her shoulder at the boys, riding behind them on their horses. "When I saw you trying to reach Freigard who was fighting Finlay and getting the best of him, I reacted instinctively as a wolf."

"You did what was right. Getting rid of Freigard ended the battle completely. It was an important learning experience for the boys. They proved their courage to fight for family—you and Finlay. I was proud of them. They were so small that no one noticed them running after you while everyone was fighting."

She sighed, appearing relieved he was proud of her.

"They were safer no matter where they were if they stuck by you. If they'd stayed by the collapsed tent, they could have been killed as easily. You, Niamh, and the boys did the right thing," he continued.

"Thank you for saying so. I felt bad about it when I tore off to fight Freigard. I was so worried when the boys began tearing into him. He looked shocked to see a pack of wolves, three of them were pups, fighting him. But that meant I had to ensure he didn't hurt the boys."

Thorfinn spoke, "Our mother needed our help and like she said it was instinctive to attack our enemy, we felt the same about going to her aid and Uncle Finlay's."

"And we learned from Great Aunt Davina all about biting the bad guys to distract them," Johnne said.

Erik glanced over his shoulder and smiled at his lads. "I am proud of you."

They smiled back at him. He was glad that they had gone to Accalia's aid. He was sure they had made a difference in taking

Freigard down by biting him with their sharp little teeth and distracting him.

He was also relieved it wasn't raining on the return to White-haven. They had sunny skies, a few clouds, and a light breeze, perfect for the ride home. The boys were holding up, though because of the fight in the middle of the night, he figured they would start drifting off to sleep. But they only had half a day to ride so they could make it to the castle without falling asleep on their horses.

Still, when they were getting close to the castle, the boys drifted off to sleep on their saddles. Finlay, Logan, and Erik each took a boy onto their horses for that last little bit of the journey.

Then they reached the castle. Everyone came out to greet them, including the wolfhounds that licked everyone, especially the boys. Even Beathag was there, but she was unsmiling. If she'd had any hope of mating Erik, it was gone.

Everyone welcomed Niamh, and quite a few of Erik's bachelor wolves eyed her with intrigue. Though some of his men that accompanied them had been also, talking low, smiling at her, hoping to catch her eye. Erik wouldn't be surprised if she found her mate among them.

Those who had traveled with Erik were telling those who had remained behind about the battles they'd been involved in. The wounded were carried into the barracks and their healer cared for the injured men.

Cook hurried to have the meal prepared for the returning pack members. Then everyone, including the wounded, came to sit in the great hall to eat.

Everyone was still talking about their wild and dangerous adventures.

Accalia leaned over to speak with Erik and said, "So where are *your* escape tunnels?"

Erik smiled at her. "I need to show you where they are if we ever need to get you and the boys out of the castle. Their nannies know where they are, but I need to take you and the boys through them to ensure you know how to get to them and out. And how to get inside—since you were instrumental in taking us secretly into your da's castle, giving us a fighting chance to take down Freigard's men."

She smiled, kissed him, and then stole his bread.

He chuckled. "I love you."

"I so love you. And when we retire for the night—no rain, no fighting—"

"No lads in our bed..."

She smiled. "Aye, we'll prove to each other how much we love each other."

"Certes, always."

EPILOGUE

"I want to see Isobel now," Accalia said to Erik. Several months had passed since they had seen them. She wanted to see Isobel when her babies were born, to be there for her. And she wanted to visit Bessetta again also.

Niamh was just as eager to go and planned to help her watch the lads on their travels. She had great fun with them, and admirers galore. Beathag wasn't happy to see another woman catch the bachelor wolves' eyes.

"You want to tell her you're with child now too," Erik said.

She smiled up at him. "Aye. They will be close in age when ours are born. Besides, I want to know what she has."

"But she might no' have them right away. Or she might have had them already," he warned her.

"Aye. So if that's the case, we willna have to wait." She smiled, then frowned. "You dinna have to come with me."

"Oh, I do. I wouldna think of you leaving without me."

"What about our sons?" She wanted to take them with them but knew how tired they would get on that long journey.

"We will leave it up to them. They can go with us or stay here with Logan or Finlay."

"That sounds good." Better than either she or Erik deciding this.

Erik ran his hand over Accalia's growing belly. "This is another reason you want to go now."

"Aye." She was afraid when she was too far along, she wouldn't be able to travel all that well.

"We can take you in a wagon."

She gave him a get-real look. Prisoners, wounded, or the infirm rode in a wagon.

He smiled. "All right. We leave on the morrow."

"Really?" She was surprised he would agree so readily to leave.

"Aye. I've already made the preparations. I knew you wanted to go soon. You've told everyone, including me, enough times already."

He'd paid attention! She smiled. "I love you."

"I know."

The boys ran to join them, and Thorfinn said, "We saw men getting ready for a journey on the morrow. Where are we going?"

"I guess we have our answer." Accalia hugged the boys. They were excited about her having babies that would be their brothers or sisters. The midwife wasn't sure how many she would have, but at least two.

The lads knew they would be boys, but no one knew.

Two days later, they arrived at Isobel and Alasdair's castle where she was in labor. Erik couldn't believe that she would be. It was as if Accalia had known that Isobel would be.

Accalia joined her in her bedchamber where Bessetta, the midwife, and several other women were helping with the delivery. Erik and his boys kept Alasdair occupied, though he continued to return to Isobel's and his bedchamber to check on her. Erik would do the same thing when Accalia was having their babies.

One of the maids ran into the great hall where Alasdair was waiting with an ale in hand with Erik, his lads, and their brothers.

"The first bairn is here—a male," the woman said.

Alasdair handed his tankard to Erik, but Erik handed their drinks off to one of the men celebrating with them and hurried after him.

Once they arrived at the chamber, Erik could hear a wolf woof. Isobel was having her babies as a wolf. He peeked in and saw that they had a second pup.

"Another male," the midwife said.

"Two sons," Alasdair said, looking a little faint.

Erik patted his back. Bessetta and Accalia were smiling at them. The pups were nursing.

The midwife said, "She's having triplets." And then the final pup was born. A little girl.

Alasdair held the female pup, smiling down at her, then placed her on her momma so she could nurse too. He leaned down and hugged and kissed Isobel. "I love you."

She woofed at him.

Erik hoped things worked out as well for him and Accalia when their babies came.

For a week, they stayed at the castle, Accalia helping out. Isobel was so glad that Accalia was having bairns too and promised to join her when the time came. Though her babies would be so young, Accalia said she didn't expect her to.

BUT WHEN THAT DAY CAME, Bessetta and Isobel were there for her, Alasdair making sure he could support Erik as he was anxious while Accalia was having their babies. Etta and Niamh were on hand as well.

Isobel had a nursemaid with her to help with her triplets. Even Accalia's da and aunt were there. Everyone was waiting to learn what happened, including Erik's sons, now six summers, and Erik's and Alasdair's brothers.

Then the news came, though Erik was outside their bedchamber the whole time. The boys were right there with him. So were Erik's brothers and Accalia's da. The wolfhounds were also, eager to go to Accalia and check on her.

The midwife came out and smiled at Erik, handing him a male wolf pup. He showed the pup to the boys who smiled at him, carried him to Accalia, and let him nurse. Then he kissed her, but she was panting heavily, and he figured the next baby was coming. The baby was a little female. Just like he was with his new baby son, Erik was thrilled.

Thorfinn, Johnne, and Hendrie looked at the wolf pups nursing and Thorfinn said, "But it's going to be forever before they can play with us."

Erik laughed and Accalia smiled at them and gave a little woof. The boys hugged her around her neck. Baldur and Davina did as well.

Finlay said, "Do you want me to announce the arrival of your son and daughter?"

"And another son," the midwife said, as she delivered the last pup.

"I knew you could do it," Baldur said, sounding like a proud grandpa.

"Three little dears," Davina said, smiling.

Erik smiled, glad he had taken Accalia home with him and that he'd made enough right decisions to win her love.

Erik was eager to show off his new son and daughters to the rest of the pack, but Accalia gave him a wolf's growly look, telling him they stayed with her for now. He smiled and kissed her furry head, then ushered the boys out of the chamber.

"I'll be down to announce our new arrivals," Erik said to Alasdair, their brothers, and her da, "in a moment."

Then his brothers and Baldur smiled at Accalia, congratulated her, and left the bedchamber. Isobel and Alasdair did as well and took their leave. Niamh, Bessetta, Etta, and Davina stayed with Erik as Accalia shifted, and so did their pups, now sleeping but in human form.

Etta, Bessetta, and Davina swaddled the bairns. Davina cuddled the little girl and said, "She looks like you when you were born, Accalia."

Accalia smiled.

ERIK GAVE Accalia a warm embrace and kissed her lips. "I love you. You are amazing."

"You are pretty amazing yourself and I love you with all my heart." She was tired, but also relieved the babies were all well. She still couldn't believe they had three more children to call their own.

"I will eat with you while the whole pack and our friends celebrate," he said, taking hold of her hand and kissing it.

She smiled. "You need to be down there bragging about our bairns. While they are asleep, take them down to the great hall and show them off, but the ladies will help you with them."

Bessetta said, "We will bring you food and sit with you."

Accalia nodded. She was hungry but she'd be nursing the babies again soon, and she needed to sleep.

Then everyone left, carefully carrying the babies down the stairs to the great hall. The wolfhounds were eager to see the babies, but no one cheered or said anything she could hear. Then she slept. She woke to the smell of wild boar and honeyed mead. Cook smiled as she set the feast on the table.

"Congratulations, my lady," Cook said as Bessetta, Etta, and the midwife returned with the bairns.

They set them in a cradle together, and servants brought more food for the ladies.

"If you need anything else, send someone to ask for it and we'll bring it to you." Then Cook and the servants left the bedchamber.

"I didna hear anyone cheering about the news of the bairns," Accalia said.

"Upon threat of going to the dungeon," Bessetta said. "Erik made sure no one shouted a word and woke the wee bairns. Your da even held one of the babies up like a proud grandfather."

Accalia smiled, but her smile brightened when she saw Erik return to the bedchamber with his meal. "Everyone is so busy celebrating the wee bairns' births, they dinna even notice I was gone."

"Sure they do and they know what a remarkable da you are. And a husband to me."

"As you are the only one for me."

Then they heard running footfalls toward the room and wondered what the matter was.

Thorfinn said, "Hendrie, quit running into me or I'll drop my food."

"Shhh, we have to be quiet, or da will put us in the dungeon," Johnne said.

"He might anyway for going to our mother's bedchamber to eat with her," Hendrie said.

Then the boys entered the room, their meals in hand and they saw Erik sitting beside the bed, Bessetta, Etta, Niamh, and Davina eating at a table and their mouths gaped.

"Come, eat with us, but keep your voices low," Erik said. "The bairns are still sleeping."

The boys hurried over to the bed and sat at the foot of it, not exactly what Accalia had expected. When Erik looked at her to see if she was all right with it, she smiled. She adored her family.

"'Tis good to have the whole family together for this special occasion, dinna you think?" she asked Erik.

"Aye," the boys all said, then looked at the bassinet to ensure they hadn't awakened their new brother and sisters.

"Aye," Erik said, "as it should always be."

The End

WANT MORE of the Highland Wolves of Old? Check out Wolf Heir.

ACKNOWLEDGMENTS

Thanks so much to Darla Taylor and Donna Fournier for all your help catching my mistakes! I can't thank you enough. And to Lor Melvin, who helps me with ideas when I get stumped! We have this cosmic meeting of the minds.

ABOUT THE AUTHOR

USA Today bestselling and award-winning author **Terry Spear** has written over a hundred paranormal romance novels, young adult, and medieval Highland historical romances. Her first werewolf romance, *Heart of the Wolf,* was named a 2008 *Publishers Weekly's* Best Book of the Year, and her subsequent titles have garnered high praise and hit the *USA Today* bestseller list. A retired officer of the U.S. Army Reserves, Terry lives in Spring, Texas, where she is working on her next werewolf romance, shapeshifting jaguars, cougar shifters, vampires, hot Highlanders, and having fun with her young adult novels, helping with her granddaughter and grandson and raising two havanese.

For more information, please visit her website at: http://www.terryspear.com

Blog: https://terryspearbooks.blog/

Follow her for new releases and book deals: www.bookbub.com/authors/terry-spear

Twitter: @TerrySpear.

Facebook: http://www.facebook.com/terry.spear

ALSO BY TERRY SPEAR

Adult Titles

Romantic Suspense: Deadly Fortunes, In the Dead of the Night, Relative Danger, Bound by Danger

***

The Highlanders Series: His Wild Highland Lass (novella), Vexing the Highlander (novella), Winning the Highlander's Heart, The Accidental Highland Hero, Highland Rake, Taming the Wild Highlander, The Highlander, Her Highland Hero, The Viking's Highland Lass, My Highlander

Other historical romances: Lady Caroline & the Egotistical Earl, A Ghost of a Chance at Love

***

Heart of the Wolf Series: Heart of the Wolf, Destiny of the Wolf, To Tempt the Wolf, Legend of the White Wolf, Seduced by the Wolf, Wolf Fever, Heart of the Highland Wolf, Dreaming of the Wolf, A SEAL in Wolf's Clothing, A Howl for a Highlander, A Highland Werewolf Wedding, A SEAL Wolf Christmas, Silence of the Wolf, Hero of a Highland Wolf, A Highland Wolf Christmas; SEAL Wolf Hunting; A Silver Wolf Christmas, SEAL Wolf in Too Deep, Alpha Wolf Need Not Apply, Between a Wolf and a Hard Place, SEAL Wolf Undercover, Dreaming of a White Wolf Christmas, Flight of the White Wolf, All's Fair in Love and Wolf, A Billionaire Wolf for Christmas, SEAL Wolf Surrender, Silver Town Wolf: Home for the Holidays, Night of the Billionaire Wolf, You Had Me at Wolf, Joy to the Wolves, The Wolf Wore Plaid, Jingle Bell Wolf, The Best of Both Wolves, While the Wolf's Away, Christmas Wolf Surprise, Wolf Takes the Lead, Wolf on the Wild Side, Her Wolf for the Holidays, A Good Wolf is

Hard to Find (2024), Dreaming of a Highland Wolf (2024), Wolf Bound, Mated for Christmas (2024) , The Wolf of My Eye

SEAL Wolves: To Tempt the Wolf, A SEAL in Wolf's Clothing, A SEAL Wolf Christmas; SEAL Wolf Hunting, A SEAL Wolf in Too Deep, SEAL Wolf Undercover, SEAL Wolf Surrender

Silver Town Wolves: Destiny of the Wolf, Wolf Fever, Dreaming of the Wolf, Silence of the Wolf; A Silver Wolf Christmas, Between a Wolf and a Hard Place, Home for the Holidays, Jingle Bell Wolf

Wolff Family Lodge Wolves: You Had Me at Wolf, Wolf on the Wild Side, A Good Wolf is Hard to Find

Highland Wolves: Heart of the Highland Wolf, A Howl for a Highlander, A Highland Werewolf Wedding, Hero of a Highland Wolf, A Highland Wolf Christmas, The Wolf Wore Plaid, Her Wolf for the Holidays, Dreaming of a Highland Wolf, The Wolf of My Eye

Billionaire Wolf Series: A Billionaire in Wolf's Clothing, A Billionaire Wolf for Christmas, Night of the Billionaire Wolf, Wolf Takes the Lead

White Wolf Series: Legend of the White Wolf, Dreaming of a White Wolf Christmas, Flight of the White Wolf, While the Wolf's Away, Mated for Christmas

Red Wolf Series: Seduced by the Wolf, Joy to the Wolves, The Best of Both Wolves, Christmas Wolf Surprise

Greystoke Wolf Pack: Wolf Bound

Wolf Novellas: Day of the Wolf, Seal Wolf Pursuit, Wolf to the Rescue, Night of the Wolf, United Shifter Force

***

Heart of the Jaguar Series: Savage Hunger, Jaguar Fever, Jaguar Hunt, Jaguar Pride, A Very Jaguar Christmas, You Had Me at Jaguar, The Witch and the Jaguar, Dawn of the Jaguar

***

Heart of the Cougar Series: Cougar's Mate, Call of the Cougar, Taming the Wild Cougar, Covert Cougar Christmas, a novella, Double Cougar Trouble, Cougar Undercover, Cougar Magic, Cougar Halloween Mischief, Falling for the Cougar, Cougar Christmas Calamity, Catch the Cougar (Halloween Novella), You Had Me at Cougar, Saving the White Cougar, Big Cat Magic

***

White Bear Series: Loving the White Bear, Claiming the White Bear, Bear of a Halloween

Grizzly Bear Series: Bear in Mind

***

Wolves of Old: Wolf Pack, Wolf Alliance, Wolf Heir

Heart of the Huntress Series: Killing the Bloodlust, Deadly Liaisons, Huntress for Hire, Forbidden Love, Deadly Liaisons, Vampire Redemption, Primal Desire, Huntress Unleashed

Vampire Novellas: The Siren's Lure, Vampiric Calling, Seducing the Huntress

***

Comedy Romance: Exchanging Grooms, Marriage, Las Vegas Style

***

Science Fiction: Galaxy Warrior

Young Adult Titles

The World of Fae:

The Dark Fae

The Deadly Fae

The Winged Fae

The Ancient Fae

Dragon Fae

Hawk Fae

Phantom Fae

Golden Fae

Falcon Fae

Woodland Fae

Angel Fae

***

The World of Elf:

The Shadow Elf

The Darkland Elf

Warrior Elf

***

Blood Moon Series:

Kiss of the Vampire

Bite of the Vampire

Night of the Vampire

The Vampire Chronicles Series:

The Vampire in My Dreams

Demon Guardian Series:

The Trouble with Demons

Demon Trouble, Too

Demon Hunter

Non-Series for Now:

Ghostly Liaisons

The Beast Within

Courtly Masquerade

Deidre's Secret

The Magic of Inherian:

The Scepter of Salvation

The Mage of Monrovia

Emerald Isle of Mists